THAT'S LOVELY

THAT'S LOVELY

TONI McBRIDE

atmosphere press

© 2025 Toni McBride

Published by Atmosphere Press

Cover design by Kevin Stone

No part of this book may be reproduced without permission from the author except in brief quotations and in reviews. This is a work of fiction, and any resemblance to real places, persons, or events is entirely coincidental.

Atmospherepress.com

To my dear friends, who have helped me grow as a writer—thank you for your honest feedback; your insights have been invaluable.

To my family, thank you for believing in me, encouraging my dreams, and for your unwavering love and support.

To my husband, you've been my cheerleader, my comfort, and my inspiration. I'm so grateful for you and for the magic you've brought into my life.

And to all the readers, thank you for picking up this book and sharing in this journey with me. Your support means the world.

Contents

Part I: Before
... 1 ...

Part II: Falling
... 31 ...

Part III: Going All In
... 163 ...

Part IV: The Set Up
... 303 ...

Part V: I Got You Back
... 347 ...

Part VI: After
... 441 ...

PART I
BEFORE

INTRODUCTION
THE WAY IT IS

No New Friends

I find it quite difficult to meet new people and not have the expectation that they will eventually do something to show their true colors and disappoint.

From what I have experienced, people can't help but take advantage of others when the opportunity arises. Usually, it's when it's least expected. When it's *safe*. When everyone is comfortable. No, I don't look for people to do something bad; they show that all on their own and that is exactly why I prefer to keep my eyes wide open.

I don't have the need for new friends and, because of this, some would argue that I am mean, but that doesn't bother me. I have had the same close group of people in my life for a very long time now. I trust them completely. My brother, Jonathan, and his best friend, Gabriel, are both my business partners now. And there is my best girlfriend, Elizabeth. The four of us have been through just about everything together. With close friends like this, honestly, it's hard to let other people into my life.

CHAPTER 1
THE BIG BUSINESS IDEA

I didn't know what to do with myself career wise when I decided to go to college. All I knew was that I wanted to continue my education after I completed high school. I made it through pretty far too, and ended with two masters. I considered going further, but I didn't know what for though. I was kinda stuck. It was just at the right time because I am very thankful for the career that chose me.

My brother, Gabe, and I own a pretty successful nightclub in the city. After college, we were still figuring out what we wanted to be as grownups when we went into business together. We work very well with each other considering the fact that we're 'family.' I love it and I am very proud of what we've been able to build. The way we came about, however, was a little disrespectful to say the least. My brother is not the best 'asker' of things...

"Listen, Sammy. Gabe and I have this business idea that we want you to be a part of. We're opening a club, and since you're always out running the streets at night anyway, we figured you could use your club rat experiences to help our place be a success."

Yep. That asshole is my brother. I really want to smack

him after that comment.

"Sam, don't listen to him," Gabe chimes in.

Jonathan is surprised at Gabe's interjection. "What?" he says, looking between us. "Wait, you took that wrong? I meant what I said in a good way. You've got a good mind for stuff like that, and we *need* you as a partner anyway," trying to redeem himself, but it doesn't really work. I can't do anything but look at him and shake my head; I'm beginning to believe that he doesn't even know he has an asshole personality problem.

"Sam, what he wants to say is this," Gabe explains. "I came across this building at work. It's in the perfect location, already with a liquor license, and it needs very little work to bring it to where it could be something great. Even better, it's at a price that can't be passed up. The owner is very eager to sell. I have a good chunk saved from my real estate commissions. Your brother has his share from your dad's inheritance and, well, we need you too, as an investor and a partner."

I should change Gabe's name to Switzerland; he's always trying to be Mr. Neutral. Although I'm really annoyed at my brother, I like what they're saying. My interest is piqued by the thought of us having our own club. My stupid brother is right, I do like to go out dancing. I hate it when he's right like that. "Yeah, Sammy, we need your money from Dad," Jonathan confesses.

And there it is.

"He's an ass, Sam, you know that, but what do you say? Does the idea sound interesting to you? Do you think that you would want to go see the spot we're talking about at least? I mean, before you just say no. Let me take you to see it first, alright?" says Gabe as he starts to show me some pictures from the file he has in his hands.

CHAPTER 2

A GOOD IDEA IS A GOOD IDEA, BUT WHAT THE HELL?

I know I can get in my own way when it comes to my brother. He drives me mad oftentimes and the only thing I can think of here is the way he approached me about possibly doing a club together.

I can't help thinking on repeat, is this really how my brother comes to me with a business deal? Even though Jonathan can be a complete asshole, I really, really do like the *'owning our own club'* idea.

I know exactly where that building is, and it *is* a great place for a club. Damn it. Should I actually consider this? This could be a really good situation on the cheap, and it already has the liquor license, too. I hope I don't regret this but, damn, I'm already hooked on the idea.

I'm in, and it doesn't even seem to matter that I'm gonna be stuck with these two knuckleheads through it all. I know we can make this thing work despite them. I can already feel the wheels turning.

I'm getting excited thinking about the possibilities, but I have to keep my cool. If we pull this off like I know we can, we will get paid for doing what we like to do and I'm so keen for it.

Okay get it together Samantha.

I'm definitely in. But I really need to play this casually, so I'm not treated like the little, little sister on this.

Here goes nothing.

"Alright, I'll do it with you, *but* proper. I want a business plan completed, contracts written up on exactly what our partnership will entail, who will be responsible for what, and so on," I say as grown up as possible.

"I knew that those college degrees of yours would come in handy for something Sammy but, damn, don't go thinking you can boss us around just because we asked you to be a part of this. You're still my little sis, don't forget."

Sigh. And there he goes again with that asshole personality.

This is where I have to show them that I really mean business.

"Shut it, Jonathan. Do you want me in or not? Because you better get this: if I'm in, we need to do this right, especially if we want any kind of success. Are you interested in that?"

I turn to Gabe and say, "So, I think I will be working with you mainly on the business end of things, right? Let the asshole there handle the schmoozing, marketing, and promotion crap since he's so *charming*," I say as I turn to give Jonathan a look. He doesn't say anything; he just makes a face at me.

I look between the both of them as I say, "But both of you let me know one thing right now: Am I going to be taken seriously as a partner?" I wait a second. I get no response, so I continue. "Like I said, if I'm in, I'm in all of it; you can't use my money and then treat me like a little kid in this and shut me out. Will my opinions count, and will I be included to help make the big decisions? Because if not, you really need to let me know *right now*."

I direct this last part to my brother, "And don't lie to me, Jonathan, just because you need my share of Dad's money, because I will be pissed."

"Sam, it's not like that. We really need you to help make this work, seriously," Gabe adds.

I look at Jonathan again and he nods his head in agreement.

"Okay then, remember you said that 'cause you know that I certainly will." I give them each one more of my *I'm serious* looks.

"Let's get to work then, before someone else snatches up our club," I say, walking out towards Gabe's car.

CHAPTER 3
SOMETHING ALWAYS HAPPENS

Don't Mess With Her

It's been a lot of hard work, getting that building to where we wanted it. And I mean it really took some work, but I think we have things down to a pretty good system and we can start to see our vision really come together now.

I am thankful. And I'm finally able to feel like we actually know what we're doing, so I decided to take my night off and enjoy myself.

There are so many great parts to the city we live in. Each little pocket neighborhood has so much to offer, but even with a long overdo night out, I want to stay close to home. So we chose a place near where I live.

It's always busy toward the end of the week on this trendy little street in my neighborhood. It's the place to be if you enjoy good food.

Tonight is Thursday. I'm usually off from working at the nightclub this evening and the girls and I have made plans to meet up for dinner. I'm looking forward to it. *The plan is:*

- *Run errands for the club early in the day: use my brother Jonathan's truck.*
- *Drop everything off to the club: to be sorted later.*
- *Go home to get girlied up and then walk over to meet the girls for dinner and drinks.*

The reality is:

- *Nothing ever goes as planned and I am always running behind schedule...*

Why the hell is that?

What time is it? Oh no! Am I really running that far behind schedule? I can't wait to meet up with the girls, but I need more time to get myself together before our night out. I don't want to show up looking like this much of a mess, except it looks like I have no other choice but to drive Jonathan's truck over, instead of going home like I originally planned.

Worst case scenario, if I drink a little too much I could always walk home after dinner and then come back for the truck in the morning. I may feel like drinking the roughness from the day away after the afternoon I've had. I'm frazzled. Today was a bad day. A few drinks with the girls are just what I need tonight.

Looking in the rear-view mirror, I think to myself that I suppose I look decent enough, even though I feel like such a bum. I really want to change, but I'm so late. What I'm wearing will just have to do.

Now, where to park?

"Are you leaving?" I say more to myself as I see a couple getting into their car near me.

This spot is perfect, right in front of the restaurant. I can see Lizzie and a couple of the other girls have already arrived and are seated near the front window.

This couple is moving like molasses.

"Yes, yes, I am still waiting for your spot. I am so glad you finally remembered me sitting here," I mouth as the driver acts surprised to see me still here in his side view mirror.

Wait, he's not...I can't believe it. Where is this car turning? He can't make a U-turn like that. He's gonna make me hit him if I pull forward.

A little yellow sports car comes thumping up the road from the other direction and as soon as the couple pulls out of MY parking spot, that little car recklessly makes a U-turn in front of me, cutting me off, taking the empty space I was waiting for. I barely avoid hitting him.

"WHAT THE HELL?!"

"Yo! I was waiting for this spot," I say as I jump out of the truck. "Why did you think you could just swing a 'U' and take this space? I know you saw me waiting for it. MOVE YOUR CAR!!"

The driver takes his time to casually get out of his

car. He looks at me and shakes his head pitifully, mocking a frown before saying, "You shouldn't frown your *pretty little* face like that, sweetness. You don't want to get yourself all wrinkly too early now, do you?" He points down the road and continues. "Just go ahead and find another spot 'cause I'm not moving, babe." He then proceeds to walk to the bar across the street next to the restaurant with his two buddies. I'm so shocked by this that all I can do is watch them go, laughing at me as they walk inside.

It takes me a minute, but I snap out of it finally, finding myself really fighting the urge to jump into Jonathan's truck and run over this guy's ugly little tricked-out car like it's Monster Truck Sunday.

I'm super-heated. Then I notice Lizzie standing in the window. Watching.

Of course she is.

She has accused me of overreacting to things in the past, but I know I cannot let this one go. That asshole needs to be taught a *pretty little* lesson.

I wave and smile at Lizzie; I give her an *I'm alright* gesture to reassure her that nothing's going to happen. *No worries*, I shrug. I get into Jonathan's truck, take a deep breath, and drive home.

Why home? I go to freshen up and to change. I take this little bit of time not to cool down, but to give Lizzie peace of mind. She will know that I went home when she sees that I have changed instead of thinking that I spent this time starting some kind of trouble with those jerks.

I make it home and freshen up in record time.

I want my payback, I say to myself as I head out the door. I decide to go ahead and walk back to the restaurant even though I am already late, and I have a nice plan all sorted to get my revenge on that dude before I even leave my driveway.

As I walk back towards the restaurant, I can't help but think about how sad Lizzie looked while I was waiting for that spot. She recently broke up with her longtime boyfriend, Brian, because he just took a job that he 'couldn't pass up' in another city. He didn't ask her to go with him but I'm not really sure she would have if he did. She's so independent. But I think the fact that he never asked is what's making this breakup extra hard for her. I know she was in love with him and thought he was in love with her, too. She kept saying that she just didn't understand why he never asked if she wanted to go.

I don't know if there is anything I can do to help that sadness go away.

Walking back, I keep hoping to myself that the little ugly car is still there when I arrive. *Fabulous, it is*, and I feel an evil grin appear on my face.

I stay hidden as I check to see if more of our friends have arrived, distracting Lizzie from watching for me, and they have. Good. I go to work.

I brought a tire gauge with me from my brother's truck to help me release air from the asshole's tires. I wouldn't want to mess up my nails in this process; I think that would piss me off even more — I just got my manicure.

I go to the driver's rear tire and check to see if the tree across the road on the sidewalk blocks Lizzie's view and it does. Perfect.

I ease down carefully next to the tire and release as much air as possible. As cars and people go by, no one seems to notice me and that's just what I want.

I move to the passenger rear tire then the passenger front, again releasing as much air as I can from each. I stand back to look at my handy work. The car leans back to the right a little, and that puts that evil little smile on my face one more time. I can't wait to see that asshole find his car like this.

But looking at my handy work, I can't help but think, *it still needs something more*. I dig out the perfume spritzer and little notepad — the one with the extra-girly paisley design, of course — that I have in my bag and give it a couple of sprays of perfume then write, "You shouldn't frown your ugly little face like that, sweetness. You can't afford any wrinkles at all, you fucking asshole." I seal the note with a kiss and leave a lovely lipstick imprint. I walk to the driver's door as if I am waiting to cross the street. Reaching behind me, I quickly stick the note in the jam of the driver side window, then cross the street and go into the restaurant.

I sit down next to Lizzie, facing the window, which is perfect because I get to watch the boys come out to the car and see their reactions.

A couple of hours have gone by when I finally spot them crossing the street. They seem to be having a great time with themselves; I can only imagine how much they've annoyed everyone else around them, though.

One of the passengers goes towards the back of the car, notices the driver's side flat and calls out to the driver. The driver, at his door, sees and grabs the note. He gives it a smell, thinking it's a pickup, no doubt, because I see a smile on his face as he turns. Strutting, he then goes to have a look at the flat. After a quick moment, he goes and opens the trunk. The other passenger, in the meantime, goes around the front of the car and notices the other two flat tires. Scratching his head, he then calls out to the driver and all three guys end up on the passenger side, looking at the other tires. The driver then decides to read the note he pulled off his car. His facial expression is priceless and is all I need to be okay with losing that spot like that.

I go back to enjoying my girls' night out when flashing lights catch all of our attention. The police are there taking the driver's statement. I see the police officer shaking his head *no*. I imagine that he is telling the driver that there is nothing that can be done. No visual damage so not considered vandalism, just no air in the tires.

A flatbed tow truck shows up and I can't help but giggle to myself a bit. Why did I do that? As soon as that giggle comes out, Lizzie jerks her head in my direction and gives me a look of horror. There's nothing she can say; what's done is done. I just give her that *I'm alright* gesture again and go back to my dinner as if nothing ever happened and I think to myself, *today wasn't so bad after all*. But I already know, this is another thing I won't be able to live down.

CHAPTER 4

TROUBLE? WHO'S TROUBLE?

Of course, Lizzy told the boys about my little girls' night out shenanigans and now I'm at her place getting an intervention from them and am being told how much I need to tone down all of my get-back-at-people bullshit. Adding that I'm way too old for the nonsense that I do when I have been bothered by someone.

Blah blah blah blah.

I guess I should feel bad about what I did, but I don't. Those guys were jerks and needed to learn that their behavior was not okay. It's not like I go around looking to start trouble; it's just that I have no problem ending trouble when it finds me. Besides, they should know better than to try to get me to change my ways. I am well aware that I can be petty sometimes, and they already know that I have zero issues with who I am. So what, really, is the point of all of this?

"Okay, guys, I get it. You're not happy. I'm too old. I need to stop. Did I miss anything?" I say as I get up and walk towards the door.

Lizzy stands up, too, and says out of frustration, "One day you're really going to get yourself into big trouble. You're going to come across someone who is going to want to get you back for getting back at them. And then what, Sammy?"

I have no words for that, so we just stand there looking at each other for a moment.

"You are really going to meet your match and that scares the shit out of me, and I don't know why it doesn't scare you at all." She shakes her head at me in disappointment and heads towards the kitchen. The fellas stay quiet, so I just say, "Okay, really guys, I'm sorry." I grab my things and head out. No one says anything else before I leave.

All the way home, I have a conversation with myself trying to reckon with what they've tried to say.

What are they so upset about? I don't get it. It's not like I'm the one starting messes. I don't do anything further than give back a taste of what they give to me. But why would they be okay with just letting people mistreat them? That is what I really don't get. And besides, it's not like it's every day that I have a problem with someone. I mean, seriously.

CHAPTER 5
SHOW 'EM WHAT YOU GOT

All Grow'd Up

The service industry is a tight little community in this area. The owners of restaurants, bars, lounges, and clubs all get together about once a month, taking turns hosting socials for each other. I like the idea of supporting each other this way and so we join in shortly after the club opens. My brother and Gabe make tons of new friends straight away.

Me? I tend to keep to myself more. I like to people-watch before I decide how social I want to be. Usually at these events, after the proper hellos, I park myself at a small corner table or at the far end of the bar and just enjoy the night out.

During one event in particular, sitting at the bar, I became friendly with the bartender. After my second drink or so, she approached me to warn me about the man who was watching me from the other side of the bar. I had seen him before but paid him no mind. I was not interested in any way. He was *so* not my type. I assumed the position of 'ignore him and he will go away.' I guess he didn't see it that way.

She told me that she knew of him from dating a friend of a friend. She said that he was a brute and if he was interested, he wouldn't take no for an answer very well; that I should be very careful. She seemed really afraid of him.

Because of this warning, I took a closer look at him. He wore leather biker-ish pants, heavy black studded boots, a grey T-shirt and a dark jean jacket; he was so, so, so not my type. His hair was longer than it needed to be, and he was unshaven. He towered over everyone standing next to him and he used this to his advantage. He put on airs like he was a rough and tough guy, but I was not feeling intimidated by him. After I gave him the quick once-over, I went on about my night, not giving him another thought.

I mingled a little but ended up back at my post, sitting at the bar. After a minute, the bartender came over with a drink — bright blue and full of fruit, something that I would never consider trying on my own. She told me the giant biker dude had this drink sent over for me. Him doing that seemed to really worry her, based on the look she gave me. I took in her expression carefully, declined the drink, and got up from the bar. I didn't acknowledge him as he tried to get my attention from the other end when I walked away.

As the night moved on, I decided to get a bite to eat. I walked over to the carving station, grabbed a plate, and placed my food request. The chef told me that he needed to make a quick run to the kitchen for more of what I asked for and that he'd be right back. I got cornered from behind by the big dude just as the chef left and he grabbed me hard, on my arm, near my right wrist. He caught me off guard by touching me, so I gave a little jump. I think he mistook this as fear and gave me a devious grin. *Give me a break*, I thought to myself, and I couldn't help but roll my eyes at him. I calmly told him to let me go. He didn't, of course. I had expected as much, but what I didn't expect was that he would squeeze harder.

Feeling uncomfortable from the slight pain his grip was causing, I placed my plate down, leaned on the table with my other hand for support, and I told him again to let me go. Even though he was starting to hurt me, I refused to give him the satisfaction of telling him so. He ignored my second request to let go and was really beginning to annoy me.

I decided to turn towards him more directly as best I could, to face him — to look him in the eye, if you would — to let him know that I was not afraid of him. He squeezed again as he told me how he didn't like the idea of being turned down at the bar with the drink he sent me, making sure to include how rude he thought I was to walk away like I had, yadda, yadda, yadda. I stopped listening to him at that point. His voice was a bit gruff and his breath was stale. I don't respond to what he says, still staring him down. I felt myself starting to get really pissed at his refusal to let me go.

Okay, he was actually really hurting me. I was afraid that if he kept it up, he would have ended up breaking my arm; his grip was that tight.

I realized that not only did I have to make him let go of my arm, but I needed to send the message for him to really leave me alone. That I was not at all interested.

As I figured things out, I gave a quick look around. I saw behind him that the bartender was watching us from her post. No one else seemed to have noticed, though. I looked down at the carving table and the chef's knife sitting near my plate caught my eye. I told the big dude very quietly that it was his last warning; that he had better let me go at that moment or he would leave me no choice but to *make* him let me go. To that, he just laughed and tightened his grip one last time, and I was certain my arm was about to snap.

Tired of this little game, in one motion I grabbed the knife, flipped it blade side up, and hacked him on the arm that was gripping me with the dull side of the knife as hard as I could.

Mr. Giant Biker Dude yelled out as he let go and fell back to the floor. He thought I was going to cut him, I guess. Maybe I should have. I saw a red mark growing on his arm. I took a step forward and stood over him with the knife still in my hand, trying to look as psycho as I possibly could. He was yelling at me, calling me a crazy bitch and other names that meant nothing to me. He was looking around asking for someone to get me, the crazy girl, out of there before I really hurt somebody, but no one seemed to move.

He started this nonsense, no need to be crying out now, I thought to myself as I looked down at him. Then

I noticed that he seemed to be getting his nerve back. He began threatening, saying what he would do to me, that I shouldn't have done what I did, so I leaned down closer to him with the knife still in my hand, still all psycho killer like. I told him in my best crazy girl whisper, so no one else could hear, that was his only warning; if he ever touched me again, I would be sure to cut all of his shit OFF. That was a guarantee. That shuts him up instantly.

As I stood up. I looked up at the bartender, gave her a slight smile, and winked. I put the knife on the cutting board and noticed the chef standing there looking a bit horrified. I had guessed that he heard my little threat, too. Oh well. I ignored his look, turned around, grabbed my things, and headed for the door.

That's when I realized that he was right, that biker dude; I really was crazy. Yep, crazy-crazy. I felt every eye on me as I left, and I knew at that moment that I would never hear the end of this from Jonathan or Gabe.

I didn't make eye contact with anyone on my way out.

This is so not what I wanted, but I didn't know what else I could have done to stop myself from really getting hurt by that guy.

I remembered my last thought as I left was that Lizzie was right with what she said before; I really *do* need to tone all of this down. I'm getting way too old for shit like this.

By reputation now, I am forever more seen as that crazy-crazy psycho chick by everyone in the industry because of that biker dude and his bully antics. I had a wraparound multi-colored bruise on my arm for a few weeks after that night. It wasn't pretty.

It took a lot of insisting from me to convince Jonathan and Gabe not to try and go after that guy. One, I didn't want to get them involved with any of my troubles and, two, I wasn't 100% certain that they wouldn't get their asses handed to them. Nobody wants to play nursemaid to two guys who get beat up trying to defend your honor.

Because of that night, I decided to stay under the radar and let the boys be the faces of the club moving forward.

CHAPTER 6

SAMMY, SAM, SAMANTHA

'Crazy lady' reputation aside, I am known by three names: Sammy, for people who have known me for a long time; Sam, for those who feel acquainted with me but aren't really 'in the inner circle;' and Samantha for those who do not know me personally or who I do not wish to know me. I do prefer Samantha and don't understand why people feel the need to nickname me. I've always been very particular about whom I allow to use anything other than my given name.

In life, I am very happy. I like who I've grown into. I live a great life by most standards. I am a single, young, successful woman. I am my own boss, I own my own home, and I have taken advantage of the opportunities that have presented themselves to me. All of these things have helped me become the confident woman I am. I couldn't want for more. At least that's what I thought before...

CHAPTER 7
THE GIG IS WORKING JUST FINE

It was such a great decision to get this club together. I actually really love what I do. My brother will always be my big-head brother but, for the most part, he doesn't treat me like a little, *little* sister. Gabe is cool to work with, too. I call him Shadow sometimes because he always seems to be right wherever my brother is. I see him 'secretly' sneaking those looks Jonathan used to accuse him of, but I just ignore them as usual.

The looks definitely don't bother me now that we are a little more grown-up. He has become such a player with the ladies, taking a different girl home just about every week. The club is his feeding ground. I tell him all of the time that behaving like this is going to catch up with him, but he just laughs and says I should take my own advice. Whatever that means, because I go home alone. He, however, is never without a new chick, it seems.

Jonathan, Lizzie, and I come to refer to all the girls he dates as *Birdy* because we just can't keep up with all of their names. Besides, Birdy keeps it more impersonal. We've learned not to get too attached to anyone he's 'dating' because he doesn't keep them around for long.

Lizzie is still heartbroken. Even though Brian took that job out of state and didn't ask her to come with, I know they talk to each other all the time. That just seems to make the heartbreak that much worse for her. You know, having access to him without actually having him with her. She started to think about the idea of moving to follow him but changed her mind, reasoning that since he never asked her to, so she shouldn't chase him. She is now throwing herself into her work instead. We hardly see her anymore. Although we still talk over the phone a lot, it's not the same. I miss her.

Jonathan has been in and out of the same relationship with the same person for years now. Lydia is great. I don't know why they do this to each other. They break up for a bit, then they end up right back together. I don't understand it. Maybe the make-ups are well worth the break-ups. Who knows? She doesn't come around as much anymore either, but I think they were made for each other. I can't wait for them to realize this once and for all so they can stop this back-and-forth nonsense. Lydia seems to be the only one who can really keep Jonathan in line. He needs her.

Me? I've had boyfriends here and there. No one that has really swept me off my feet, though. My brother tells me that I'm too independent for my own good. What the hell does he know? The problem for me is that I really fell for my first love in college, but he didn't feel the same and it truly hurt me when we broke up. I don't know what I expected from him, though. I never grew up thinking about getting married like other girls do, but I never really imagined myself with anyone else either. I was crushed, to say the least.

No doubt that damaged me. Because of that little experience with amor, I am such a skeptic about love now: I don't even know if I believe in love for myself or not. I always have it in the back of my mind that something will break my trust sooner than later when I do decide to date someone.

All I know is that it's just easier to be by yourself sometimes. I don't think there is anyone out there that's a match for me anyway. Perhaps my expectations *are* too high, but I'm not willing to settle for someone who will mistreat me.

No worries, though; Jonathan and Gabe usually scare off most guys who show any interest in me by playing the Mr. Protector roles, so I'm good. There's absolutely nothing to worry about when it comes to the subject of me having a real relationship.

Love lives aside, one reason I credit for our club's success is how good Jonathan is at promoting; he keeps things interesting. This was a shock to me when we started. I don't know why. Looking back, he was always so popular in school with those crazy things he came up with for us to do. Never a dull moment with him around, that was for sure.

We all have our roles to play. As far as sibling business-ships go, we're golden.

Gabe and I run everything else beyond the marketing

and promos. Gabe's in charge of the bouncers, liquor, and all things bar-related, which includes the cocktail waitresses, so, of course, he's happy with that gig.

I get to choose the look of the club, the gear for the employees, and I deal with everything else staff-related.

We each take turns managing each night. We are all at the club on Fridays and Saturdays, naturally, those being the biggest and busiest nights. My brother and Gabe do Thursday's Ladies' Night. And man, I am so glad I opted out of that night, with some of the stories I hear. Talk about craziness.

I work with Gabe on Sundays, which is Old-School Night — my favorite. Not like Motown old-school but old-school hip-hop, which is cool, because I get to see the old heads come out.

Mondays, the club is closed except for private parties. I work Tuesdays, the slowest night, on my own and my brother works Wednesdays solo. That gives us each four days on/three days off every week. I like my schedule. Gabe works the four busiest nights in a row (Thursday to Sunday) so he has the best time-off schedule, having his three days off together (Monday, Tuesday, and Wednesday) but he really earns it.

Unless we have a special promo or private party, I pretty much have all morning and afternoon to do what I'd like, too, so it really doesn't seem like we work that much if you add up the time actually on and working.

I have to say, besides having a decent schedule and getting to be on the club scene nightly with the music and dancing — which I love — we are doing really well financially, too. Better than we planned.

I am always worried, though, that these days will be short-lived, so I make sure we all stick to the salaries we've contracted for ourselves in the business plan. This is just in case we get rainy days that won't leave us. Although it's been four years and we seem to still be going strong, I've seen most clubs burn out in two. So, I am worried that we may really be on borrowed time. That the fun could end at any moment without warning.

PART II
FALLING

CHAPTER 8
THIS IS HOW WE'RE INTRODUCED?

The employees gather every Friday before their regular start time for the weekly goings-on meetings. It's coming up on summer, and I'm looking forward to the summer crowd. Everyone appears a little more carefree and I love that. Winter seems to be for worriers.

The staff is here getting the details for the upcoming events and specials. Besides the seasonal changes, Jonathan has some contests and promotions that he advertised on our social media sites. The last time I checked, there was a lot of buzz about the things coming up. That makes me happy.

My brother announced to me two days ago that the club is going to be going through a great transformation. Using exaggerated hand gestures and all. He can be a little over the top with his ideas, I swear. He is such a dude. When I asked what the hell that means, he just said, "No worries, Sis...trust me; you will be thanking me in the end." This does not put me at ease. He better not try to bring on any new surprises — like those ugly hula girl lamps he tried once for that luau-themed promo — or he's done for.

Right, the weekly meeting.

I'm in the middle of saying, "Alright, there are two things left on my agenda. First, don't forget the employee summer party coming up. This year's theme is 'country barbecue hoedown.' Dress for the theme. We'll have contests, of course. Be sure to bring your appetites. Finally, the summer campaign starts tomorrow."

As I tell the employees this, I see this handsome guy walk in and give a quick look around, like he's looking for someone.

My attention goes back to the meeting. "Remember, that means your gear is going to change."

When I look up again, he's watching me and I feel a bit embarrassed, but I don't know why, so all I can think to do is to just quickly look away. When I look back, Jonathan is walking up to him and is greeting him like they're old friends, but I don't remember ever seeing him before. They go into the office.

I continue. "We're going to all white on Saturdays only; the rest of the week's gear stays the same until further notice. Any questions for me? No? Okay then, the floor is open for any suggestions or concerns. Does anyone have anything?"

Things continue with input from a few of the staff members. We believe that everyone's contribution is important and this, too, may be one of the reasons why we are still going strong. We have great staff.

I follow the comments pretty closely until my brother and that handsome guy distract me again when they begin to walk around the club. *Well, hello again, Mr. Good Bar*, I think to myself while watching him. I get to have a good look at him without him noticing while he's focused on whatever Jonathan is telling him. Looking him up and down, he's dressed in brown-belted, dark wash *Levi* jeans, a white button-down shirt, a navy plaid blazer-style jacket, and great brown New York street-chic shoes. Besides being handsome, he's looking very cool.

I get distracted too easily by men sometimes I tell myself. I lose track of what's going on in the meeting because of this guy. I wonder who he is and why he's with Jonathan. I know I've never seen him before. I would have remembered him because he's that good looking. I do like watching him and the way he moves.

Hold on. Why does it look like he's getting a formal tour of the place? Why are they in the booth? This snaps me out of my man candy trance. I start to put it together. Wait a minute. Wait a minute. Wait. A. Minute! Is he hiring a new freakin' DJ?

Damn it! He's doing it again; he's doing things without us. Where the hell is Gabe? I look around and see Gabe approaching. Good, here he comes, right on cue. Maybe he'll get answers about all of this. I have to focus. I have to finish with the meeting so I can find out what's really going on with Jonathan and the stranger.

"Alright people, I will post the meeting notes in the employee lounge. The promo will continue to be placed on all of our social sites so our customers will be in the know. That's it for everyone but bar folks; you need to go over the new drink specials with Gabe."

What's up with Gabe? He just walked over here like

nothing new was going on. Why didn't he ask 'what's up with that guy with Jonathan?' when he first came over? He walked near enough to see them. I know he did.

I guess I have to keep an eye on Jonathan by myself. Where did they go now? Crap. Do I hear Jonathan sorting out the play schedule? Great, it's a done deal then. He *did* hire that dude as our friggin' DJ. That makes the new guy an ass automatically in my mind, I don't care how cute he is. He's going directly to the top of my shit list. He can thank Jonathan for that one.

Oh hell, here they come.

Jonathan starts talking before I can say anything. "These are my partners. You may remember my mate Gabriel, but everyone calls him Gabe. Gabe, you remember Drew?"

"Hey, Gabe man, nice to meet you again, yeah. I do remember you. I look forward to working here," says the new guy, with an English accent, no less.

Wait, what? They've *all* met before? I can't believe my ears. That's why Gabe didn't ask what was going on — because he already knew. What is this backroom dealings mess? Gabe is now on my shit list too, the traitor. I give him the death stare.

Gabe says, "Yeah, you too. I heard you at the Vegas Nite event. Everything was awesome. I think you can do good things here. I'm looking forward to the hype." He's pretending to ignore me, but I know he sees me looking at him.

Oh, Gabe, you ARE such a shit. I hope you can feel the fire from my stare.

I'm pissed but I'm stunned by all of this too. I find myself speechless and, what's worse, I can't walk away for fear that I may be kept out of another part of this deal by these bozos.

I just can't stop thinking about all the negatives to this new set up; there can be so many problems with this move that this could really change the dynamics of the club. My head is spinning. Why is it that I'm just catching on to the new DJ thing? I usually sense when Jonathan is up to something, but this just slipped right past me. I have to figure things out before it truly turns into a disaster.

I really do have to snap out of it. I need to recover my composure and figure out how to get us out of this DJ deal, because I can't help but freak the fuck out over this. It's too much. First, everyone knows about him but me — *hello*, business partner here. I should have been included in the decision-making for sure. Second, I've never heard him play and he's got the nerve to be English, no less. Stupid Londoner accent and all. The Brits have no sense of rhythm or music, as far as I can tell in the club scene. Hiring him is gonna muck up the flow of the club. I can't even think about what will happen to our Sunday nights. There's no way he can know old-school the way we do old-school. I am so angry with Jonathan right now. Our borrowed time has just met its end, I'm afraid.

"And Andrew this is my sister, Sammy," Jonathan introduces.

"Samantha. My name is Samantha," I respond, looking at Jonathan.

"Excuuuse me, this is my sister Sa. Man. Tha," Jonathan says as he tries to save face.

"Right, hello Samantha, nice to meet you. I look forward to working with you, yeah?" says the Englishman.

"Yeah, I bet," I say, not taking my eyes off Jonathan. I see him and Gabe look at me, a little horrified. But I don't care. I'm not the one trying to impress this dude and, besides, I am totally pissed. They should not be shocked by any way I respond.

"Jonathan, I need to speak with you NOW in the office," I say, and he gives me a stupid look.

"Don't make that face at me. Let's go; I'm not playing," I demand.

I want to kill him. Who does he think he is just throwing this guy in my face like this? I don't care if Jonathan is my friggin' brother. I want to take him in the back office to really kick his ass.

We're barely in the office when I start in on him.

"Jonathan! What are you thinking? Who is this guy, and why are you bringing in a new DJ without talking with me first?" I demand.

"Listen, Sammy, Gabe and I were at this event..." he tries to explain as he closes the office door.

"Yeah. I heard. You guys were at this Vegas Nite promo. So what? That doesn't mean you shouldn't speak to me first!" I say, almost popping a vein.

"But Drew is like no other DJ we've heard. I saw him a while back in London. He's great. He kept the crowd on the floor all night long. He was that damn good. So when I heard that he had just moved here and didn't have a permanent spot yet, I had to track him down for our place. Trust me, his skills are gonna make you go crazy," he continues to explain, ignoring me again. "Besides, you knew Arturo and J.J. were leaving; they both got new gigs. We had to get someone else to replace them and the timing is perfect."

That explanation is not good enough; it leaves me with more damn questions than answers. Is he really trying to replace two guys with this one? Is he a super DJ? And, what's the catch? Why hasn't anyone else given him work if he's supposed to be so damn good?

I can't help but think that something is wrong with him, so I say, "Okay, so answer me this. If he is so damn great, how can *WE* afford to hire him, number one, *AND* why is it that no one else has the brains like *you* to snatch him up?"

"He just moved to the States and hasn't really had the chance to get a true gig yet. I heard him at this lounge, then went to the Vegas Nite event to hear him again. He has done a couple of guest stints here and there and I think he's trying the acting thing, too, but I dunno and I don't care 'cause he already signed the contract and he's officially our DJ whether you like it or not now, so just deal with it."

Whoa. He thinks that will be the end of it, does he? He knows me better than that. I can't believe his reaction towards me on this. He knows he's wrong for not including me. I am about to lose my mind.

"What?! You gave him a contract, too, without talking to me? How long!?"

I'm screaming and I know a vein or two popped that time. I'm so angry I could really just *murder* him right now, I feel so partner betrayed!

"Keep your voice down, Sis. I don't want him to think we don't really want him here; he may try to void the contract and take on another job somewhere else before he even starts," he says, not really answering my question.

"How. LONG. Jonathan?!" I demand again.

"C'mon, can I get some credit? Damn, and why aren't you fussing at Gabe, too? We both brought him in. You should be thanking me, not in here acting like a bitch about this whole thing."

Wow. He is clearly avoiding the question 'cause I know he knows that I don't get affected by being called a bitch by him; he's just stalling. He's trying not to answer my question, mofo.

"HOW LONG?!" I scream louder as I take a step closer to him. I imagine I look like a cartoon whose head is about to rocket off. I am super mad. He takes that stupid little grin he's been wearing off his face and frowns a little before saying, "Shit, Sammy, it's just for a year."

"A YEAR? ARE YOU KIDDING ME? DO YOU KNOW HOW LONG A YEAR IS IN THIS BUSINESS?! I'm going to kill you if this doesn't work out, you ass! And, for the record, I *don't* really want him here. I know nothing about him. You should have clued me in first," I say loud enough for the Englishman to hear if he's still outside the office.

"Sammy, really? Give the guy a chance. Don't go taking shit out on him like you do when you don't get your way," he says quietly.

This catches me off guard. Is he trying to turn the tables on me here? So, I ask, "What the hell is that supposed to mean, Jonathan? You think I'm pissed because I'm not getting my way? You're a dumb ass."

"You know what I mean. Don't go taking shit out on him when you're mad with me. Being all mean and cold when you do talk to him, you know, the way you normally do…" he explains.

"Whatever, Jonathan. If you were so worried about that then you really should've clued me in at the start instead of keeping things a big secret. I don't have any more time to spend on this. I have real work to do for tonight," I say as I start to walk out of the office, still very pissed.

My thoughts are a whirlwind. What the hell? Man, he is so lucky he's my brother or I'd really effin' kill him, the way I feel about this right now.

Damn it. I knew Arturo was leaving, but this is way too fast. *Why isn't Jonathan coming out of the office?* I think as I look behind me. Whatever. I really don't have time for his nonsense. I walk out glaring at the new guy and Gabe.

Why is this guy staring back at me so hard? "Give off already, would you?" I say as I walk past them.

I hear Jonathan finally come out of the office, so I

stop and turn back, asking, "You haven't said, when do you have *him* scheduled to start anyway?" gesturing at the DJ guy.

"Tomorrow," the Englishman answers instead.

I know the look of horror flashes across my face as I realize what tomorrow means. Tomorrow is Saturday. The busiest night of the week + new summer promotion + new English DJ = total disaster.

That's it. It's over. I'm convinced. Might as well hang the "Gone Out of Business" sign up right now.

"Just fantastic!" I yell out as I throw my hands up in the air, looking at the new guy then at Gabe as I start to walk away again. Gabe is looking at me as if I'm really being unreasonable.

No, Gabe, don't give me that look. You know the deal. You know you two were wrong for doing things this way.

"Sammy, why do you have to be so mean? Andrew hasn't done anything to you; it was us, me and Jonathan, not Drew." Gabe starts to follow as I continue to walk.

I can't speak anymore I'm so angry. I need to get it together. I take a few deep breaths, but they don't really work. I give the death stare to everyone as I pass. I can't help but think that Gabe has betrayed me, too. All they had to do was talk to me, tell me about all of this beforehand. Instead, they kept it a big secret and then act like they don't understand why I'm upset. Gabe is still trying to make it seem like I'm the issue. *Give over, you traitor. Stop talking*, I think to myself, *I'm putting you underneath the bottom of the shit list.*

He continues to follow me, so I stop, turn, and say, "Gabe, I don't want to hear it, 'cause you could've talked to me well beforehand. Both of you had plenty of opportunity to include me in all of this; if you did, I wouldn't be reacting this way."

I start to walk away again but decide to say one last thing to prove my point: "You saw him two times, Jonathan says, and neither one of you thought to speak to me about him? That's not okay. Think I'm being mean now? Keep excluding me and there'll really be hell to pay."

"I'm just stating the obvious. He did nothing to you," he says again as he backs away.

I look over at the DJ and he's still staring at me. Stop it. Stop your goddamn staring.

That's not a way to get in good, Englishman; but damn it, he stares hard. I can't get a grip; I really need a distraction. I turn, close my eyes, and quickly count to ten. I refuse to let this ruin my night. I open my eyes again and look for that distraction.

Good, here are a couple of cocktail waitresses from the back room coming to save me.

I try to calm down as I speak. "Hey ladies, did you get the new gear for tomorrow night? I want everything sorted before your shifts, alright?" I ask as coolly as I can.

"I have mine Sammy," says Lisa.

"I have only half of it. I need the top in my size, I didn't see any in the locker room," announces Angela.

"Right, I have more in the office. Come with me and

I'll get it for you. What size?" I have to turn back, going past the DJ again as we walk towards the office.

"Extra small, but if not then small will be okay," responds Angela.

"Hey Sammy, is that the DJ from Vegas Nite? Is he starting here?" asks Lisa as we get closer to the office.

Great, no friggin' escape from this, I see.

"Oh my God! Shut up! That's him? No way! God, he's sooo gorgeous, I'm in love with him already," says Angela.

Shit, that means Angela is a fan, too; everyone knows about him but me, what gives? Why am I so out of the loop on this?

"Yes ladies, that's what I hear; yes and yes. He is the DJ from Vegas Nite and, apparently, he is now working here," I answer with disdain. "Starting tomorrow."

"No way! Seriously? I'm so blasting that on my pages right now. We are going to blow up when the word gets out," Angela says.

Angela is such a kid. Note to self: verify her age on the files again.

So it's worse than I thought: not only does everyone know who this guy is, but they are all excited about him being here. Am I getting that old that I'm out of it like that? So this is what flying under the radar gets me. I think I hate him for real now.

CHAPTER 9

THE ENGLISHMAN

Moving here to the States was a big leap. But it looks like things are going to work out. That guest appearance I sorted out with my mate did what I wanted, and I finally landed a permanent gig at this club that I heard good things about. The dudes I signed with didn't tell their other partner, the sister, though. That's not good. She was so brassed. I think she may really dislike me because of it.

She stood out to me straight away. Her poise and beauty sitting there, watching me when I walked into the club.

I have to figure out how to change her view of me. Maybe if I apologize for the trouble I've caused. I dunno. Maybe that'll work.

She's lovely, though. I couldn't stop staring at her. That seemed to piss her off even more. She is not happy with me, but I like her anyway, I know that already. I can't help it. There's just something about her that I can't get over that has me really attracted to her.

She is the first one to catch my interest since moving here and she doesn't want anything to do with me. Funny how things like that work. No worries, I'm up for the challenge. I'll do the work and use my charm. I've got the feeling that sooner or later, I'm gonna turn her opinion around about me.

CHAPTER 10

WHAT? ME WORRIED? BUT OF COURSE...

Big night tonight. It's the first night of the summer promo and Mr. Vegas Nite starts his contract. Thrills. And I get to have an idea as to what to expect for the season. This is worrying me more than I could have imagined. I gotta get to the club early to make sure everything is set. I've been looking forward to the summer starting for so long. I can't let this new DJ thing take away from that. I will enjoy the evening if it kills me, damn it.

Arriving early today puts me at ease because I can tie up all of the loose ends that have been floating around my mental to-do list.

Oh good, looks like the last of the deliveries for the promo have arrived already. I see the new uniforms for tonight look better on than I thought, nice.

All that's left to worry about now is the DJ thing.

I wonder what start time he worked out with Jonathan, if he has his own setup, if he knows how to really prepare for our type of crowd...sigh, I have a feeling that it's going to be a long night.

Worrying about this is such a disruption. I wish I

could feel confident, like everyone else, about him starting tonight. All of this is driving me really nuts; I need to find another distraction from him and he's not even here yet.

CHAPTER 11

THE ENGLISHMAN

This is it, starting day. I have a bit to do to sort things out before my shift begins and I want to make an impression.

I'm here hours ahead, I know. I hope that's not an issue and someone is here to let me in.

I like the fact that the club has its own small side lot. Parking here makes it easier for me to unload all of my albums and equipment.

As I begin to pull my things from the boot of my car, I hear Samantha outside and it catches me off guard.

"Hey! What are you doing?"

I almost respond until I realize that she hadn't seen me and was walking towards a homeless man who was beginning to make himself very comfortable alongside the front of the club.

"Do you know that I have been looking for you for a couple of weeks now? Why did you just disappear like that? You had me worried sick. Where were you? What happened?" She looks at him as if she's a mother questioning a child. "Seriously. And I want real answers." She rattles off as she walks towards him with takeaway containers in hand.

I'm completely off guard. I thought for certain when she first called out to him that she meant to remove him.

"Well? What do you have to say for yourself?" she asks him.

"Eh, it's no big deal. I just wanted a change of scenery is all. Why are you making a big deal out of nothing?" he replies matter-of-factly.

"A change of scenery? Yeah, right, what really happened? Did you get sick? Was someone bothering you?" She questions him again as she sits next to him and hands him the containers, waiting for a proper answer. "I really want to know."

He ignores her for a moment and puts his focus on the food before he begins his explanation. I watch them for a minute longer. They seem like they're pretty good mates.

I realize that she is now posted in a spot where she can see me directly and I don't want to risk her catching me spying, so I go back to the task of setting up for the night and take my things inside the club.

CHAPTER 12

THE NEW MAN BEGINS

Wait, *he's* here now, that's just friggin' fantastic. How did I not see the DJ arrive? I had forgotten all about worrying about him for a moment and seeing him now is making me super nervous for tonight all over again.

Staring again. He stares hard and he looks straight through me. I wonder what the hell he could be thinking about when he looks at me like that.

Shit. Here he comes. Great. What would he possibly want to come over here for? Cheesy little grin. Looking like trouble. Is he trying to start something with me already?

He's dressed cleverly tonight, though; DJ gear, I guess. He's wearing a casual black suit with a dark grey Bob Marley tee that says *'the good thing about music is that when it hits you, you feel no pain'*, a belt with the Jamaican colors on the sides, and grey and black Saucony sneakers with a little bit of green neon. He coordinates well, I see. I love the tee. Hell, if it wasn't for my brother's antics I might have liked him because of that T-shirt alone. Ha, like him? That's so not happening tonight.

"Hello, Samantha. I'm afraid we didn't get a good

start at things. I apologize if I was sprung on you unexpectedly, yeah? It was not my intent to stir any trouble with you lot. I've heard good things about your club and I look forward to being a part of that. I just wanted to let you know I love music, I love DJing, and I hope that translates into good business for you," he says like we're having an ordinary everyday conversation.

This little speech of his does nothing to change how I feel, so I say, "Right, Andrew, thank you for your apology. However, it was not necessary." I then try to walk away but he continues.

"I think you're wrong. It is necessary. I know it upset you that I was hired without your input, so, can we please start that introduction bit again? Let's see... Hello, I'm Andrew. I am your new employee. I begin tonight, if that's alright," he says as he puts on a sexy little smile, then he steps closer and reaches for my hand. I'm caught off guard by his forwardness, by the way he smells, and then by his touch as he grabs my hand.

I can't tell if he is making fun of me or not. I'm preoccupied by my thoughts and when he shakes my hand it's as if electricity begins to flow straight through me. I start to feel warm and notice my breathing is a little off. He's got me flustered.

I finally snap out of my trance and say, "I don't have time for this. You're not a regular employee; you're contracted. There is a difference. I also don't think that you're funny in the least, by the way. Just do what my brother and Gabe hired you to do." I try to pull my hand away, but he holds on. I look him in the eye. Damn, he's handsome, and I think he looks hurt by my response. I feel a little bad, but I can't allow him to get to me so easily.

Feeling bad or not, nothing has changed. I still don't like the way he was hired and that means I have no love for him. He is going to have to really prove himself to me first, before I can even start to change my mind about him.

He says, "Seriously, I'm not trying to be funny. I just wanted to show you the respect of being one of my employers, nothing more. No games. I'm not trying to play with you."

"Whatever, I have work to do. Cheers!" I say pulling my hand away and off I go. I feel his stare on me as I walk away.

I'm just not sure what to think of the Englishman after that little dance of his just now. What is he really trying to pull? Was he playing with me or not? Very suspicious, that one. I can't help but notice the effect he just had on me so effortlessly, though. I was truly weak in the knees when he held onto my hand. Damn it, I can't be attracted to him. That would be the worst. I really don't have the time to deal with any of that right now. I just can't.

I can't stop myself from looking back at him to see if I can tell if he was messing with me or not. He's still watching me. Why? Why in the hell is he still watching me? I don't get it. Now I'm really confused. And I'm so not in the mood for any of his little games, either.

I hide out until the night starts, to avoid more speeches like that from the Englishman.

The night is finally beginning. The club is open and the staff looks great.

The first song I hear the Englishman play is a version of Butterflies. It's normally sung by Michael Jackson, but this is a female funky version instead. Nice, but an odd choice to begin with on a Saturday night.

...All you gotta do is just walk away and pass me by, Don't acknowledge my smile, yeah, when I try to say hello to you, yeah...

S-C-R-A-T-C-H

There it is. He cuts into his beats and the dance floor gets busy right away.

CHAPTER 13

THE SUMMER IS STARTING OFF NICELY

The night is going great. The crowd is nice. I know some of that has to do with the Englishman being here. Jonathan promoted the hell out of him coming in tonight on the socials today. I have to admit, he is a great DJ. Better had been or there would've been big trouble up in this place.

Am I being paranoid? It feels as if he's been looking at me all night. I know that can't be, because he has not missed a beat with the music. I don't think I will ever admit this out loud, but he *is* going to be great for us if he plays like this every time.

There's another one of my favorite songs. I can't keep on that dance floor all night, there is work to be done. We are really busy. Damn, I can admit to *myself* when I'm wrong…he's really, really good.

"Hey, Sammy. So, what do you think of Drew so far? Is he winning you over with his set?" asks Gabe. "I saw you out there on the floor a couple of times tonight."

"Gabe, I'm not in the mood to play with you tonight."

I respond this way because I know he's starting some shit.

"What? I just asked a question," he laughs.

"Oh, is that all? Really, Gabe, you forget I *know* you. You're coming to tell me I told you so and I'm not falling for it."

"Nooo, that's not it, Sammy. But, umm, I did tell you so," he says, laughing harder now.

"Yeah, you have jokes, I see. Don't you have some managing to do somewhere?" I say, trying to seem extra agitated.

"I knew you'd see the light sooner than later. He's gonna be great. Bring us up to the next level," he says.

"Yeah, yeah, yeah, Gabe, leave me alone already would you please?" I ask.

"He's good and you know it. I knew you'd come around is all. Laters." And he walks away.

Damn it. I am not gonna hear the end of this, I know. I'll give them one night of gloating and then it's a wrap. I can't let those fuckers get too cocky, then they'll be making all kinds of decisions without me. Can't have any more of that, that's for certain.

CHAPTER 14

CELEBRATE THE START OF THE NEW SEASON

This is my favorite part of the night. The club is closed. Most of the staff has finished up and have headed on their way.

Only a couple of us are at the bar celebrating the evening. Me, my brother, and Gabe are having a drink as we finally get to relax. I don't ever really realize how much work goes into getting ready for the summer season until that first night is over and it seems like I can actually breathe again.

Damn, I thought that Englishman had packed up and left already. What is he doing still here? Of course my brother is calling him over for a toast.

He would.

"Hey, Drew, come on over and join us. Your first night at Club Essex was a huge success! C'mon, man, let's have a drink to it," Jonathan calls out as he plays bartender.

"Alright, I can do one drink," says the Englishman as he looks in my direction.

"Don't be afraid, my sister won't bite you," Jonathan says, not missing anything.

"My brother is not a funny man, do not laugh or humor him in any way," I say as coldly as I can, looking at Jonathan. Yes, I am being *that* bitch.

Thinking that makes me smile to myself.

"No, Samantha. I won't laugh at you, no worries," responds the DJ.

Good boy Englishman, you've learned already, but I still look to see if he's playing with me again.

Wait a minute. Did he just wink at me? What the? I need to give him the ol' evil eye, I see. Put him back in his place; he's getting a little too comfortable too soon.

Jonathan clears his throat and I turn to see him giving me a look. Well, if I am going to be forced to play nice here, I need another drink. I move my glass towards Jonathan for a refill.

The Englishman approaches, staring at me the whole way over. Damn it, he is some kind of handsome. Why is it that it seems that he is extra handsome to me now after he grabbed my hand? I mean, yes, I did think he was really attractive when I first saw him, but I must not have given him a proper thought because I was pissed. But I can't help but notice now that he's really *really* put together well. I actually get another good look at him as he comes over and, damn, is he fine.

I catch myself in his spell again. I shake my head a little to break out of it.

Okay, handsome or not, he's still on the top of that list. I can't fall for his looks. I have to remind myself that I don't like him in any way as I look away.

Shit, it's not working. I catch that I'm staring back at

him again. I need another distraction from him. Where the hell is my refill?

Jonathan gets Andrew a drink and the fellas begin to yuck it up a bit.

"What a great beginning to the summer, cheers!" Says Jonathan.

"Cheers!" responds Andrew.

"Here, here," adds Gabe.

So now there's three of them it seems. Great. Well, I guess that's my cue to go home — forget the refill.

"Goodnight, I'm heading out," I say as I gather my things.

"Ohh yo, why so early??" says my brother, with a big smile on his face.

I know it's just Jonathan the asshole starting some trouble now too; he doesn't really care if I stay. He is not fooling anyone.

"Yeah, Sammy, you never leave this early after a good night. What gives?" asks Gabe, the traitor.

Really, are they both trying to put me on the spot? Do they think that I will play nice like that? They know me better than that, but I'll give them this one time. Yes, I will pretend since they are extra happy with themselves tonight and leave them on their own.

"I'm tired is all. Goodnight," I say as I head towards the door.

"Boooooo," my brother yells after me.

I give him the look that says *shut it* then I respond, "Yeah, well, boo on you, too. Goodnight."

I leave, but not before I hear Gabe calling me a big grump.

Oh man, is he going to pay for that later.

CHAPTER 15

THE ENGLISHMAN

I had a good first night. I was really nervous. The fellas liked the job I did, but I still can't get a good read on the sister. I thought maybe after they called me over to have a toast that she would lighten up on me a bit. Didn't happen. She could not get up fast enough when I sat down. I have to say that hurt my feelings a tad. That doesn't mean I like her any less, of course.

I really can't read her. The way she looks back at me. I am so used to ladies basically falling at my feet and she acts as if she'd rather I would just disappear.

I know she liked the job I did tonight, even if she didn't say anything. I saw her on the dance floor the better part of the night. That was the only response I needed to see from her. I think maybe I'll try to use the music to reach her.

CHAPTER 16

E DAY II (ENGLISHMAN DAY II)

Sunday nights happen to be one of my favorite nights at the club. The crowd is so different from the rest of the week. Shit! That's right. I hope that Englishman knows what music to play tonight. I can't even imagine what old-school songs he knows, growing up in England.

I need to make sure we sort that music out as soon as he arrives. I guess I will go in now to try and meet with him to get a playlist together. Where is my bag?

Yes, it's way earlier than my normal time again, but I'm worried about getting started tonight. I run into Ms. Louise and it's such a nice surprise. She is the owner of the cleaning company we use for the club. She's good people. She is in the business of giving a second chance to those folks who have made bad decisions in their lives. Her company gives jobs to people who have been incarcerated for lesser offenses. This is the main reason we chose her company. It makes us feel as if we are a part of helping, too. My only concern initially was the type of business we have and if it would be an issue with all of the alcohol around. When I asked about the liquor, Ms. Louise simply said, with the most stern face, it would only be a problem if I decided to drink it all, then she would have to call an intervention for me, that I would leave her absolutely no choice, she'd have to do it. I never laughed so hard. I was ready to have a serious conversation and she caught me so off guard with her response; I loved it. We became friends instantly.

The club looks good. I was a little worried about that after leaving so early last night. I wasn't sure if my brother and his shadow, Gabe, would be up to the task of closing up properly. I'm happy they did though — one less thing to worry about tonight.

I find myself smiling when I see the Englishman arrive; telling myself I am pleased he's here, but only for the reason of going over the music for tonight. Yep, here early like I was hoping he'd be; we definitely need to sort out that playlist.

CHAPTER 17

OH NO!

Just as I am about to go and speak with the DJ, I notice one of our cocktail waitresses walking in looking a bit of a mess. I could tell she had been crying and when the other girls see her, they rush right over. They stand around her talking near the bar. I give it a minute, then go to see how serious things are.

I see all of the guys that are at work already are keeping their distance. Too much for them to handle, I suppose. Boys are such big chickens about girls crying.

After a few minutes, I find out that Brittany, our youngest cocktail waitress, had to put her dog down unexpectedly this morning and she's really a mess about it. I get that; he was her little baby. She really loved that dog.

What do you say to someone dealing with this? This is awful, yes, but what do you really say? I'm looking at her as she's talking and crying and all I can think is that there's no way she should be here trying to work tonight. She needs to go home. She needs to deal with this. I don't think coming in to work was the answer. The only thing I can think to say after her explanation is just to tell her to leave.

"Brittany, what are you doing here? Go home. You don't *need* to be here. Really, go home," I tell her.

"I can't, there's no one to cover my shift," she says back, looking at me a little desperately.

"Seriously? That's what you're worried about?" I can't believe it.

"Yeah, Sam, it's Sunday night. There's Lydia's thing going on and I couldn't call out without having my shift covered," she insists.

"Brittany, go home. Go and take care of yourself. You can't work like this. Please, just go…now."

She begins to cry again and looking at her now, all I can think is that she really is a mess.

If she would've said that she needed the distraction, then I wouldn't insist. But her being worried about covering her shift doesn't make any sense to me. I have to send her home, it's the only thing to do.

"Brittany, seriously, go on home. I've got your shift now; I'll be you for tonight. And listen, don't worry about things here, you have a couple of days. Take the time tonight, use the time tomorrow (the club is closed), you already have the time Tuesday 'cause you're scheduled off, and if you need your shift covered for Wednesday, call *me*. I'll come in for you. You really shouldn't be here. It's alright, I'll fill in for you," I try to assure her by giving her a little smile. "No worries."

After I say this, she comes over, hugs me and thanks me, still crying. I look around and everyone is looking at us. I see the DJ in the booth and notice that he's the only one not focused on what's going on over here.

"Brittney?" No response as I begin to pull from the hug. "Are you okay to drive? Should I ask Gabe to take you?" I say, looking around to see if Gabe is near.

"No, I'm okay. I can call my boyfriend. He'll come for me," she says more to herself, pulling out her phone as she walks towards the door. I ask some of the other girls just to make sure she gets picked up okay.

Brittany was scheduled to work a small party tonight, which is actually for Lydia's youngest sister, Mara. Lydia is Jonathan's on-again off-again girlfriend and they are celebrating her sister's twenty-first birthday; so me covering this is a no-brainer. I would probably be with them most of the night anyway, so finding coverage for tonight really wasn't as big of a deal for Brittany to worry about as she thought.

CHAPTER 18

TRY IT AGAIN, SAM

Okay, now that's worked out, I still have to get that playlist sorted for tonight or I won't be able to focus on anything else. Now where is that DJ? Good, he's still in the booth. I'll go over to speak to him now.

"Excuse me, Andrew, can we go over a few things for tonight, please?" I ask.

I think I caught him by surprise. I saw a little jump; I don't think he expected me to say anything to him. I smile to myself at his reaction.

"Right, of course, Samantha. Let me put this gear down and I'll be over straight away," he responds.

"I just want to go over the playlist for tonight," I confess.

"Oh, right. I'll bring my computer over then. Just one moment, yeah?"

He looks worried. Should I be worried, too? I feel myself begin to panic a little as I walk away; now, of course, thinking the worst.

He comes over wearing that sexy little smile of his and it distracts me for a second but then I catch myself and snap out of it.

He says, as he comes to where I've sat down, "Is

everything alright there? I saw that you sent one of your girls home."

I'm the one who's caught off guard now. I didn't expect to have to answer anything to him, especially when I didn't think he was paying attention, so I just tell him, "Yes, everything will be fine *there*."

He tilts his head and gives me a weird look that I can't read.

"Right, what would you like to go over for tonight then?" he says, getting back on topic.

I look back at him for a moment before I say, matter-of-factly, "Well, I'm just a little concerned whether or not you're aware of the theme for tonight and if you have the right kind of songs to play."

"What do you mean about the right kind of songs? Sundays are old-school hip-hop nights, I was told," he says, looking worried again.

"Yes, they are. But your definition of old-school hip-hop and my definition may not be the same and I want us just to be on the same page before we open tonight, is all," I say to him.

"Oh. Right. I understand. You want to make sure I don't play what then?" he says, clearly now feeling more comfortable with the conversation.

"I don't want you to play jungle house music or the Spice Girls or anything like that. 'Cause if you did, we'd both be in trouble," I say, now annoyed as he laughs.

Wait, is he laughing at *me*, though? I can't tell. I hope he is not taking things as some kind of joke again. I feel myself glare at him.

He notices that I am not amused. "Oh sorry, I don't mean to laugh. It's just that you caught me off guard there with that. I didn't realize you knew about jungle music and I'm not really the Spice Girls type; that was more for my younger sister," he says, still laughing a bit.

"Yeah, okay then, great. Well, what *are* you planning on playing tonight then?" I ask, keeping to the task.

"I was thinking more towards maybe including some Poor Righteous Teachers, Boogie Down Productions, Black Sheep, a little De La Soul, and some Eric B. & Rakim, to name a few. Just to show you the direction I thought you guys meant for your theme. Are those alright then?"

I am pleasantly surprised. "Yes. Good. Those really work, but please don't forget a little Sugar Hill Gang, Afrika Bambaataa and stuff like that, too," I add, trying to sound official.

"Right, no problem. If you think of anything else you'd like me to play, let me know, yeah?" he says. He seems relieved that I approve of the artists for his playlist tonight and, honestly, I'm relieved, too.

"Yep," I say as I start to work on something else, acting as if he's no longer standing there.

He waits a moment, watching me, and then says, "Was that it then? There's nothing else?"

All I say is "Nope." Not even looking up. He stands there another couple of seconds. I feel him watching me, as if he wanted to say something, and then he turns and walks back towards the DJ booth.

Thank the Lord he knows what he is doing tonight. Disaster averted. Where is he now? Good, he did go back into the booth. He sees me looking and just looks back at me with that intense stare of his, looking straight through me. It's all I can do to look away.

Well, if he's not gonna go back about his business of doing his set up, then I'm going into the office to get a freakin' wall between us. He's too much for me right now. I'll just distract myself from thinking of him further and check the feedback on our socials.

The socials took longer than I thought. The Englishman did his trick. A lot of good feedback has been coming in about him and last night. That means hopefully another busy one tonight, too. I need to get a move on then.

Good, I see Gabe is finally back from making last night's deposit. We never do nighttime deposits after closing. That's an additional risk we are not interested in taking. I'm glad he's back, I have to speak with him before we get into our regular opening routines. We need to sort out some of the kinks we had last night with the larger crowds before we begin again tonight, and I need to let him know about Brittany.

Oh, never mind, I see him beginning to set up for Mara's birthday in the V.I.P. section. I guess he must already know about Brittany. I'll speak to him more about it later, when Jonathan comes in for the party; that way I can tell them both at the same time.

I decide to go help him set up, but I call out to him first because I'm excited about the feedback and can't wait to say something about it.

"Hey, Gabe, the socials are on fire about last night!" I yell across the floor.

"What are 'the socials' you use?" the Englishman asks in what sounded like right in my ear. He startled me; I didn't know he was that close.

As he looks at me waiting for a response, my mind goes crazy, thinking, *Where the heck did he come from? Was he over there hiding until I came back out of the office? Was he trying to sneak up on me? Why is he always trying to speak to me? I mean, really, what's his deal?*

I honestly thought I was clear of him until later tonight. I was hoping to ignore him for the rest of the evening.

But I can't ignore him now it seems. Then I notice a glass in his hand; he must have been walking back to the DJ booth from the bar. That makes me feel a little silly about thinking he was waiting for me to come out of the office, so I answer his question.

"We use the regular socials, you know, like IG and Twitter. Oh yeah and Facebook for the old heads. I was looking into what people were saying about last night to get a gauge on what the season is going to be like," I respond as professionally as possible, because that stare down is really starting to win power over me, I feel. It's getting to the point where I don't even want to look back at him directly because I would just stare in a trance at him.

"Right, anything good? What do you expect then?

For the season, I mean," he says as he smiles, and for some reason that agitates me.

Why is he trying so hard to be my friend? Always trying to be nice to me. Can't he take a hint? I can't deal with him trying to win me over; it's really annoying when someone won't let you ignore them.

"Yeah, things look good. You did great last night." Which comes out meaner than I meant, even though I'm a bit annoyed at his niceties; so I try to soften it a bit by saying, "Thanks for the good music."

He is too close and is still looking straight down to my soul. I need to put some space between us again. I say, "Excuse me, I have some things I need to work on before we get started tonight."

Walking away, I say to Gabe, as I see he's just about done with the party set up, "Hey, do you have time to go over a few things with me right now?"

Besides work that still needs to be done, I really need a task to break away from the trance that Englishman seems to be pulling me into every time he's near.

CHAPTER 19

THE ENGLISHMAN

I can't get an understanding as to why she dislikes me so much. Samantha. Hiring process aside. I've tried to start conversations with her, but she really wants nothing to do with me. All business. Short, to the point, and then she's done. Her face when she looks at me half of the time mostly is one just short of disgust. I don't get it really. I don't know if I should try to take the hint and let her be for a bit or not. No promises about that, though. I do really like her in spite of her behavior towards me. I see that she's not really as hard and tough as she tries to portray. She is a good person. I like the way she interacts with others and, from the little I've seen, she's great. I know eventually she *will* soften up with me. I'll just keep showing her that I meant no harm with the way I was hired to help win her over sooner.

CHAPTER 20

BUSY, BUSY, BUSY

"Well, Gabe, I guess you heard what happened to Brittany, the poor thing," I say.

Walking over to me, he says, "Yeah, Angela told me when I got back. She said you'd be covering for her, so I thought I'd help out and get the section ready at least."

I don't know why, but I'm caught off guard. "Thanks man, really, I appreciate that."

He smiles at me, and I decide to give him a tease. "Look at you, being all helpful and what not." He just shakes his head, still smiling and, just like that, he's off the list.

I don't wait for Jonathan to come in. I tell him that Brittany might not be back in until next weekend because of the way the schedule works out. Then I tell him that we need to sort out the queues for outside. The crowd became so large yesterday that they blocked the entire walkway and I know if that happens again, we could get cited by the fire marshal, "So we need to sort that out," I say, trying to busy myself from checking on the Englishman again.

Gabe gets a little bright eyed now as he says, "Oh

yeah, I saw that when we were busy, too, but I didn't know quite how to fix it and thought I'd wait to talk to you about it today to see if we can figure things out together. What do you think? Any ideas?"

"I definitely think we need to place another bouncer at the door and maybe add velvet ropes to help guide the lines if it gets that crowded out there again. We just need to have it all in place beforehand," I say, showing what I meant about the ropes with my hands and arms.

"Great, I think the ropes will work, but I would go with at least two more bouncers — have you seen outside yet?" Gabe says, kinda excited.

"What do you mean outside? Now?"

"Yeah, the line has already started out there for tonight. It's small but still, we've never had a line before opening on a Sunday," he admits.

"What? Are you serious? They're lining up now? We don't open for another 30 minutes," I say, shocked. Well, at least now I know why he got so into helping set up the section tonight.

Where is that Englishman? As I look for him, I wonder if he knows about the line, too? There he is, walking up to the booth with someone. Who the hell is that *now*? Did Jonathan hire another freakin' DJ and not say anything again? Sigh, I'll deal with that later. All I can focus on is wondering if that Englishman can keep the people coming like this on the regular as I look back at the main door, trying to see the people outside waiting.

I turn to look for the DJ again and he's still there, busy in the booth. If he *can* do this type of magic every night, I just may decide to think he's okay. I look up at him again and he is now watching me; great. Looking at him, I find myself a little more curious about him now, wanting to know what his deal really is.

CHAPTER 21

THE ENGLISHMAN

I have to really make a good impression tonight. This old-school night is a little tricky for me since I didn't grow up listening to a lot of these songs, but I have my mate here helping me on this one. He's good on all of this and he wants to learn how to DJ more. A fair trade, I thought. I heard Gabe say there were a few people outside queuing up already and Jonathan will be in tonight celebrating. Right, so the pressure is on. I've got to make sure they don't think last night was just a lucky start; a fluke.

Wait, is she watching for me? She is, but why? I've seen her look for me a couple of times now. What could I have done this time? Right, I can't think on that or I will lose my nerve tonight.

Getting a read on her is difficult to say the least.

CHAPTER 22

OLD-SCHOOL IS REAL COOL

Lydia's sister is having a ball. Jonathan and Gabe are helping cover for Brittany, too. We take turns getting drinks for the other party guests and most people are on the dance floor most of the time anyway, so there's not too much running around. I'm making a real skill out of working and partying at the same time; the music has been great tonight. I'm really happy about that.

The fellas decide that they want to surprise Brittany with a new puppy. This throws me for a loop, but I agree. They say that she always comes in for her paycheck when she has off on Thursdays and since it's my day off too, they asked if I'd be the one to get everything and bring the puppy to her when she comes in that day. I'm happy to do it; she's a good kid and she really loved that damn dog.

That Englishman is doing it again. I cannot stay off of that dance floor tonight. But it's odd. Two things are now catching me off a little. One, whenever I look up at the booth, he's looking back at me. I don't see how he can do that and play his songs at the same time. It's not that he's watching me, but every time I look up at him, he then looks at me. And two, the other guy seems to be assisting him like an understudy — what's going on with that? When do we hire understudies? I need to ask about that later, but right now I've gotta get off of this floor. I need to get myself back to work.

In between a few of the songs, I hear a little Soul II Soul.

...However do you want me?
However do you need me...

and Loose Ends mixed in

What did I do wrong?
It's all a mystery to me...

English artists. Yeah, haha, I get it, Englishman; not the Spice Girls.

The night is going well. I'm getting some great feedback from the old heads. They like the changes for summer and are just as surprised as I am that the Englishman is keeping things flowing the way that he is. I already know that, sooner than later, I'm going to have to fess up and admit out loud that Jonathan and Gabe were right. I'll give it a month or two first, of course. Can't give them that straight away or I'm afraid that I'll never know what's going on moving forward.

Next thing I know, I'm singing along to Freedom by The Sugar Hill Gang & Grandmaster Flash and, damn, that's one of my absolute favorite old head songs. Well, back onto the dance floor for me, as I sing along...

...Young ladies in the place
Feel the highs, feel the bass
If you want to rock 'til the break of dawn somebody say come on...

Yeah, he'll do.

CHAPTER 23

THE ENGLISHMAN

My mate was the help I needed to make sure tonight was a success. The crowd is bigger than I thought with older music like this.

Samantha seems to approve. That's good. She's been on the floor dancing quite a bit again. I noticed she was watching me a little tonight, too; yesterday she acted as if I was invisible. I don't know what that change means. At least she acknowledges that I exist with the looks. That's something.

I'm really trying to watch her dance, but every time I look over at her she's looking at me. I don't get it. I seriously can't get a handle on what she really thinks about me. She went from ignoring me to watching me in just one day. Does she not trust me now? She's starting to drive me a little mad.

"Good night tonight, Drew. I think this is our strongest Old-School Night yet. I can't help but think it's mainly because of you. Everyone wants to come out and see the new DJ spin his magic," says Gabe to Andrew.

"Yeah, thanks Gabe. I appreciate you saying that. To be honest, I was really nervous about tonight. I know it's one of your choice nights and with Jonathan having a bash for his missus, I just wanted things to go really well," admits the Englishman.

"No worries, Drew, you handled it with style, would have never guessed you were nervous."

"Thanks, mate, and thanks again for letting Stix work with me tonight. I wanted to ask, is there any way we could work out him being my stand-in in the booth on a regular?" asks the DJ.

"I don't have an issue figuring that out because I can see how that worked, and we did have two DJs before, but let's make sure we include Sammy in this conversation, if we know what's good for us," says Gabe, laughing, as he makes a gesture towards Samantha.

"Speaking of that, what's the deal? Why does she act as if she dislikes me so much? What have I really done?" asks the Englishman.

"Believe me, Drew, I know she's a tough one, but it's not like that. Seriously, if she did not want you to be here, you really wouldn't be here. I think she is just taking out on you the fact that we didn't add her in on our plans to hire you," confesses Gabe.

"If signing me on is an issue, then I dunno...maybe we should talk about me maybe looking elsewhere. Honestly, this is not some ploy to renegotiate already, I'm just not sure if I feel comfortable with one of you disliking me so much. I mean, I've tried speaking to her and she only really responds when I ask a question, and even then she will just be done with me without notice," says the DJ, choosing his words carefully.

"Listen, Jonathan and I signed you. Don't worry about

upsetting her. She will be alright. She can already see the difference you're making in just these two nights. Trust me, you're good," says Gabe a little more directly.

"I hope so. I like her from what I can see, and she's good to the rest of the crew. I just wish I didn't feel like she rathered I wasn't here," says Andrew.

"I will speak with her about it. You shouldn't come into work feeling like that. I know that's not how she really feels," insists Gabe.

"Right, I'll take your word on it. I'll try not to take her actions towards me personally then," answers the Englishman.

"Good. But maybe we need to get you two to work on a promo for the club to help sort this out in the meantime," says Gabe, a little deviously.

"I don't know what that means exactly, mate, but it makes me a little afraid," says Andrew, laughing as he walks away.

CHAPTER 24
WHAT THE HELL IS THIS?

The night is done and I'm ready to celebrate, but why am I getting a lecture? Gabe's making me lose my 'we had a good night' buzz. This has to have been the biggest crowd we've ever had for Sunday's old-school. I've admitted to myself that I'm going to have to fess up sooner rather than later that it's mainly because of that Englishman, but damn, do I really need this lecture?

Gabe continues in on me. "Sammy, seriously. I spoke with Drew and he said that because of you he is not sure if he should look for another gig or not. You've got to stop giving him the cold shoulder. You know he is a good choice for the club. I know you see that already."

"Gabe, did he really run to you and complain that I was being mean to him?" I say, laughing a little, being a smart ass.

"No, he didn't. He did ask though, if he should look for other employment because of the rift he caused between us by being hired while you weren't included," says Gabe, keeping the serious tone of the conversation.

"God, why are boys so sensitive these days? Where are all the real men who couldn't give two shits about what a girl like me thought?" I ask, refusing to give in.

"Sammy, you need to speak with him and sort this out. I also think you two need to work on a promo together," says Gabe in his *I'm still serious* voice.

"What?" I say, really surprised at the promo suggestion.

"Seriously Sammy, I know you see what he's done so far for the club. And, it's only been two days. Stop messing around because if he leaves, it will be because of the way you've been treating him." Gabe says to me.

"Oh, shut it already, damn. I'll stop hurting his little feelings, the softy, but I don't see why we need to work a promo together though, that's doing way too much," I say, not allowing myself to be bullied tonight.

"That's exactly why you should do it, because *you* think it's not necessary," he says now, truly annoyed with me.

"Gee thanks, Gabe, thanks for your support and, by the way, I think you're a softy, too," I mumble, agitated over this DJ deal thing again.

It's official; my *'we had a good night'* buzz is nowhere to be found.

"Whatever," Gabe says. "I'm calling him and his pal over for an end of the shift toast with us to thank him for another good night. You better not dash out and you better behave or I'm cluing Jonathan in on our little talk."

I can't help but roll my eyes as Gabe calls them over. "Hey Drew, Stix, come have a drink with us."

That Englishman is causing me trouble. Having me

called out on giving him the cold shoulder. Here he comes. Look at him, with that crooked grin on his face. I try to give him a mean look, but that grin catches me. Damn. But fuck him for being such a big baby.

He and his friend seem to be in a really good mood after tonight. Andrew and Stix. What kind of name is Stix anyway? I know I'm going to have to ask. I just won't be able to help myself.

"Hey, thanks for the invite over. It's been an interesting night. I wasn't sure how it was going to turn out, but it was good, yeah?" the Englishman asks me.

"Yeah, Andrew, it was a very good night. Thank you for a good show. The music was great," I say looking at Gabe, trying to show that I can play nice.

"Right, you're welcome. I could not have done well without my mate, though. This is Stix. He knows a lot about music, and he's been helping me with your old-school playlists from earlier."

"Hello. Stix? How are you? Curious name though, Stix. How'd that come about? A nickname I hope," I say, being my good ol' self until the end, and I see the look on Gabe's face. It's almost everything I can do to not laugh out loud at myself.

"Samantha, right? Good meeting you and thanks for tonight. Yeah, Stix is my nickname. I've been called that since I was little. It's because I was so skinny my legs and arms looked like sticks and I guess it just stuck with me," says the DJ's apprentice.

Okay, he's a good sport. I won't take the DJ mess out on him. Looking at him, Stix doesn't seem too bad up close either. He's not stick skinny anymore, that's for sure, the handsome bugger. Where are these beautiful people coming from?

There that Englishman goes staring at me again. I can feel it. I turn to look at him and sure enough, he *is* staring at me. It's so intense. It feels as if his eyes are like x-rays looking straight through to my toes. I don't know what gives with him always looking at me like that.

Says the Englishman as I look in his direction, "Samantha, I would like to speak with you about adding on Stix as my secondary in the booth, if that's alright? Like I said, he knows music, and he wants to learn all about how to be a proper DJ and, truth be told, I could use the help, but I don't know how to work it out with you lot, or if it's alright with you even."

"Who have you spoken to about this already?" I ask, to see what's really going on.

"I just asked Gabe, perhaps about an hour earlier, and he simply said he couldn't say on it without speaking with you first," he admitted.

I look over at Gabe to see what he's thinking, and I get nothing. Great, now I'm on the spot. If I don't allow him to have his buddy hired on I'm being mean old Sam. If I hire him on, that's another salary to pay. Gee thanks, Gabe.

I have to make this work out for everyone somehow on my own, it seems, but please know, Gabe, you're not going to get off that easy.

"Okay, Gabe, so why are *YOU* so quiet all of a sudden? What were your thoughts about this? He asked you earlier, so you've had time to think on it. What says you?" I ask, and Gabe knows that there is no way I'm going to let him wiggle out of this and have me be stuck on my own.

I can see the wheels turning. Slowly Gabe starts to respond. "Well, it does make sense. I agree, Drew, you'll need help in the booth, but the question is the salary and contract conditions, right?" He asks that last part directly to me.

"I can work any nights you need me to work; I'm really committed to doing this," Stix offers.

"Andrew, what were you thinking? I mean, where are you looking for Stix to fill in at?" I ask.

"Honestly, I was hoping that Stix would eventually take on a day or two by himself and I would take, I don't know, say Wednesday as a second day off, have him take Tuesday as his second day off as well as have him help in the booth on all the other days. I think how it could work at first is that maybe in a month I could start having him take on a little more on his own on the slower days, and then he'd eventually build up more time on until he can solo," he says. But when he said that he wanted Wednesday off, he looked directly at me, which I thought was odd. What is he plotting?

"I can do that. All that will work for me," Stix chimes in again, eager.

Wait, he keeps looking at me with an odd look on his face. Is the Englishman scheming his schedule to be like mine? Am I that arrogant to think he's interested in following my schedule? And how does he know my schedule, anyway, after only two days? Or is it that I'm just being paranoid again? Wish I knew what the hell was really going on with him. I know there is something up with him asking to have that day — I'm not that simple — I just don't know what exactly. And, Gabe didn't pick up on that? He's acting as if everything that Englishman says is golden. Either he's slipping or he's got a bigger crush on the Englishman than he does on me.

"I think all of that sounds doable. You guys should have those days off. I don't want you to get burned out by being here almost every day," says Gabe. "What do you say, Sammy? Does that work for you, too?"

I'm not sure if I want the DJ to have the same days off as me, but I feel that I have to end this conversation pronto and get out of here before I say something that gets me into trouble. I just can't shake the feeling that something is being schemed, though.

"Yeah, okay, Gabe, that will work. Whatever you guys work out is fine," I say as I gather my things to go.

"Great, I'll call Jonathan to finalize it so all three of us are on the same page," says Gabe. "Don't leave yet, Sammy. I'll be right back. Have another drink, guys. It was a great night."

And he's gone.

"I'll be back in a minute, too. I want to call my girl and give her the good news," says Stix.

So now it's just the two of us. Gabe is getting very tricky; my brother is finally beginning to rub off on him. He knew just what he needed to say to manipulate me into staying here, drinking it up with Mr. DJ man.

I feel so uncomfortable.

He looks good; it's extremely hard not to look at him, no matter how I try.

"I'll get us another round. Did you want the same thing as before?" he asks.

"Yes, that's fine thank you," I say, telling him what I was drinking, looking the other way.

He stands there for a half second. I feel him looking at me, then he says, "No worries, one refill coming up," and walks off to get our drinks. It seemed as though he was going to say something else again but changed his mind. I make sure not to look over at him while he gets our refills. I try to distract myself by thinking about the conversation Gabe and Jonathan are having.

He seems to sneak up on me again; I didn't notice him walking back, for being lost in my thoughts, I guess. He sets down my drink and asks if I need anything else, but he doesn't sit. I keep forgetting how polite those Euro men are. This one seems like a good guy. He's a good sport, too, at least from what I can tell. He hasn't reacted badly to any of my antics. Maybe I should stop being so hard on him. He will be here for the next year anyway and it looks as if we'll have basically the same schedule now, so maybe I should just give in a little.

I feel him watching me again.

"So, Samantha, did you enjoy any of the songs from tonight that I should be sure to include on a regular basis?" he asks, sounding sincere enough.

"No, nothing comes to mind. Just play a mix of the

types of songs you played tonight. We have a lot of regulars that come every Sunday and I'd hate to give them the same show every week," I respond, turning to look at him as he stands near me.

"Right, that makes sense. I will mix it up then," he says.

"Oh, and I heard you throwing in a little old-school of your own. Loose Ends, was it?"

He laughs. "You got that did you? Good ear. It was just to give you a little idea of what I could have been listening to when I was younger," he offers.

"Yeah, I got it — definitely not the Spice Girls."

He nods, smiling, then he becomes a bit more serious. "Thank you for keeping an open mind with hiring my mate," he says as he steps closer.

I always notice that he smells so incredible and, of course, I recognize that I'm starting to feel attracted to him again, which annoys the hell out of me. I tell myself that I have to stand strong; don't go falling for this dude.

"Sure, I understand the need for help, the way you've been playing the last two nights. Besides, we had two DJs before you started, so it's a no-brainer. I noticed that you use a lot of energy in that booth when you're playing."

His eyes light up as he says, "I love it. Being a DJ is my first love. I have been getting into the acting scene a little. Well, at least back home I got hired for a few parts. I am trying to break in a little here, too. So far I haven't had many bites, but I haven't been in the States that long, so I'm not discouraged yet."

"That's interesting, though I did know that. Jonathan told me Friday. Good luck to you," I say, a little surprised at this sudden burst of share and tell.

"Thanks, I appreciate that. Listen, would you like to go for a coffee sometime before work?" he asks without missing a beat.

"What? A coffee? Why?" I say, surprised and confused at the same time.

"It's just a coffee." He laughs a little. "I thought that since I started here on your bad side that maybe if I were to try to apologize to you again, but outside of the club, then you'd take it more seriously. You wouldn't think it was a joke. What do you think? Coffee?" he says, as he watches for my reply.

Wow, I really was not expecting this. Go for a coffee? Is he serious? I can't tell. But he's standing there, apparently waiting for a response. This dude is sly. I think he's trying to drive me crazy on purpose. *I see now that I really need to keep on my toes around him*, I think to myself as I look at him with the side eye again.

"Alright, Jonathan's on board," Gabe says, returning from the office. "What are you guys doing? Having a staring contest?" He chuckles a little. "It *is* okay to have a conversation with the guy, Sammy," he says, looking at me. "So, Jonathan's good with Stix and the planned schedule. We'll officially add him on as part of the staff tomorrow. He's also on board for the promo you two are gonna do together." He sneaks that in with a smirk.

"What?" I ask. *You've gotta be kidding me. He was serious with the promo anyway?*

"What do you mean? What's your promo? What do I need to do?" asks the Englishman, being the good sport again.

"Well, off of the top of his head, Jonathan thinks that we could do a contest where someone would win being a guest DJ for a night. You know, stay in the booth, help choose the songs, make any announcements, whatever, except actually DJing. You two would be left to work out the details, the dates, and the rules," explains Gabe as he looks between us.

Great. Lesson learned. Just be happy with whatever major decisions they make without me…

"Well, I guess we have to go for a coffee after all, you know, to sort it all out I mean," the Englishman says as he gives me a wink.

"Great idea," says Gabe, pleased with himself.

Yeah, just great. I'll give it a week though before I'll even think about planning anything. With any luck, maybe they'll all forget this little promo set up well before then.

CHAPTER 25
HOW ARE YOU STILL IN HERE?

I had a good night off. I didn't think about that Englishman one bit. Yeah right. I wish that was the case.

It's Tuesday night. Although Stix officially began yesterday, he had an emergency at home today and couldn't come in tonight. *Great way to start your new career*, I think to myself. Both Gabe and Jonathan are off, too. That means I am working alone with the Englishman. I have to try very, very hard to ignore him. I find myself randomly thinking about him, and that is pissing me off more than anyone could imagine. I've got to find a way to nip that in the bud. I don't want to be another one of his groupies. His fan club is big enough, from the little I've seen. He has tons of girls hanging around his booth at night, giving him googly eyes and such. I definately don't want to follow down that path.

He arrives just after me and starts to walk my way but gets sidetracked by the cocktail waitresses. That gives me just enough time to dash into the office, where I close myself away until it's time to open.

The night goes smoothly. Still the slowest night of the week, but there were more people today than what we normally get for a Tuesday night. Good on you again, DJ.

When the night is finally over. I am happy that I made it through the evening without actually running into him. It wasn't easy though. Because of this, I decide not to stay for an evening drink and tell everyone that I plan to close up as soon as everyone is done. I tell this directly to everyone but the DJ. I can't speak to him again.

Towards the end of the shift, I go back and lock myself in the office until the closing tasks are done.

When I think the coast is clear, I come out of the office and check around quickly. It looks like I'm all set to go; everything is cleaned up and it looks like everyone has left. Fantastic. I made it through the evening without having to interact with Mr. DJ.

I close up quickly and head out.

My phone rings as I'm just almost halfway home. Who the hell is calling me this late? I look at the caller ID and see that it's just Gabe. I ignore the call. He is just checking on whether or not I was nice to the Englishman, no doubt. He calls again. I still don't answer, so he sends me an animated text telling me to answer my flipping phone when he calls. He tries a third time and I indulge.

"What, Gabe? What could you possibly want to talk about so badly *now* that you won't be able to talk about tomorrow afternoon? And no, before you ask, I was not mean to your little man crush," I say before Gabe can get a word in.

"Really, Sam? You don't think you were mean to

Drew at all tonight? That's your story?" he says, sounding really pissed at me.

"No, Gabe, I really had no interactions with him tonight. How could I have been mean to him? Whatever it is he told you, it's not true," I say in my defense.

"Sam, you fucking locked him in the club. He's there now and *he can't leave*. Because. You. Locked. Up. With. Him. In. Side," he says screaming at me.

Dead silence.

"Yeah, I suggest you get your ass back to the club right now before you say another word." And with that he hangs up on me.

Shit. I locked him in? Really?

I'm never going to be able to convince anyone that I didn't do that on purpose. Damn that 'crazy lady' reputation.

I really don't want to go back but it's clear Gabe is not going to be the one to let him out, and forget Jonathan — he probably didn't even answer his daggone phone before for Gabe. I have no choice. I turn around and head back to the club. Damn, I wish I had decided to drive tonight. It's going to take me a bit to walk back.

When I arrive, I expect the Englishman to be waiting at the door in a little state of panic, dying to get out, pacing back and forth or at the very least waiting to tell me off. But, when I finally get there, I don't see him. He's not waiting at the door at all. He's gotta call out my name to reveal that he's sitting at the opposite end of the bar, looking as relaxed as can be.

"Samantha, I'm here," he says.

That throws me off a little. Okay, that throws me off a lot.

When I walk towards him, I see that he's made himself dinner. He prepared a good-looking plate with ham, baked beans and eggs on toast with a pint of beer on the side. Of course he's having that. *Typical Englishman, using any opportunity to have a pint*, I think to myself.

"I hope you don't mind that I made myself a little supper here, I was starved and expected that I would finish before the time you returned so we could just go," he says a little matter-of-factly, still eating.

I am really stunned. I'm not sure what caught me off guard more; the fact that he put that all together from our little kitchen, or the fact that he was chill enough being locked in that he used it as an advantage to feed himself.

"You made that here? In our kitchen?" I can't help but ask.

"Yeah, yeah," he begins to explain. "The beans are from your barbecue special, the ham is from your Cuban sandwich, you had the bread, the eggs, and beer, so I just put together. Would you like me to make you something, too?" he asks.

"Umm, no. No, thank you. I'm not hungry, but, uh, you take your time. I'll be in the office. Just let me know when you're ready," I say, still surprised at how I found him.

"Yeah, alright, I won't be too long then," he says as his full focus goes back to eating.

When I get into the office I decide to call my girl, Lizzie. I need someone to talk this craziness out.

"What's up, Sammy?" Lizzie answers.

"Hey, Lizzie, are you asleep?" I ask, even though I already know the answer.

"Yes, of course I am, but it's okay. What's up?" she asks again, and I tell her the story of accidentally locking the Englishman in the club and returning to find him eating at the bar as if he owned the joint, and I swear a million times that I didn't do it on purpose, locking him in and such...

Cutting me off, she laughs and says, "Not on purpose, yeah okay, whatever with that. Well, at least he knows how to handle your ass already anyway."

"What is that supposed to mean?" I ask, a little offended.

"You know what that means," she insists.

"No, I don't," I insist back.

"I think you might start to like this guy but you're in denial, and because he's not reacting to any of your shit the way you expect him to, you don't know how to handle it," she says, half laughing at me.

"No, that's not true, I am not liking him. You're wrong," I say a little too loudly as I look up and notice the DJ walking towards the office.

I place my hand half over the phone's mouthpiece and wait to see if he wants to say something.

"Right, Samantha, I'm all set whenever you're ready. I'll be just out here, by the doorway, where you can see me," says the Englishman, very sarcastically with a huge smile.

Lizzie overhears him and really starts to laugh.

"*Now* what's so funny?" I ask.

"I'll be where you can see me. Haha. Oh, I like him, Sammy," she says to me.

"Oh yeah, *haha*. I have to go. Have fun laughing by yourself. Bye," I say defensively.

"Bye, girl, you're only mad now 'cause you know I'm right," she sneaks in before we hang up.

I leave the office embarrassed because I'm not sure how much of that conversation was overheard by the Englishman AND, more importantly, because I know that I still need to apologize for locking him in.

"Ready to go then?" asks the Englishman when he sees me coming out of the office.

"Yeah, I'm all set. Thanks."

With that, he opens and holds the main door for me. He decides to stand next to me as I lock up again, not saying a word, just watching.

As I finish locking the door, I say, "Listen, Andrew, I really didn't mean to lock you in before. It was truly an accident and I'm sorry." I turn to see if he believes me or not.

"No worries, Samantha, I won't take it personally," he says with that crooked smile of his. "I didn't have your number, otherwise I would have called you directly. I can't imagine that you would do something like that on purpose to anyone."

Him saying this makes me feel a little better, but I feel the need to confirm what he says by insisting, "No. No I didn't. I did not do it on purpose."

I can't tell what he thinks about my apology or even if he believes me. So I just turn and start to walk away, but stop and look back at him to get him to stop watching me leave.

He flashes me that smile of his again as we say our goodbyes. I stand there by the door. He walks to his car and takes off in the opposite direction.

CHAPTER 26

THE ENGLISHMAN

What a way to end the evening. Being locked in the club did two things; first, it made me slow down a bit and get some real food into my system and, second, it gave me a way to leverage Samantha into being a bit nicer to me. I can use this to my advantage, although I don't expect the need to moving forward. The way she looked at me tonight when leaving was very different than she had before.

CHAPTER 27

NOW YOU'VE DONE IT

I had the next two days off, which gave me the chance to avoid having to face locking the DJ in the club on Tuesday night. And instead of going in on Thursday to meet up with Brittany like the fellas and I discussed, I decided to let Jonathan be the one to give her the new pup when she came in for her paycheck. Even though I was off, my phone never stopped ringing, so I figured I would be in for it when I returned to work on Friday. I also knew that Gabe would be waiting for me no matter how early I made it in for work. I just tried to get there before the Englishman did so he wouldn't overhear me getting the what-for because of having locked him in. No luck on that one — of course he would be here, too.

"So you really expect me to believe that this was not done on purpose? Really, Sam?" says Gabe, on the attack.

"Honestly, Gabe, I couldn't give a shit if you believe it or not. I know I didn't do it on purpose, and I already apologized to him, so it's been sorted," I respond.

"Wow, Sam, this is an all-time low for you. I know you didn't really like the idea of Jonathan and me hiring Drew without you, but I told you to take it out on us, not him. He has done nothing to you to warrant this. He's a good dude. He's doing everything in his power to show you that, but you refuse to see it. I don't know what to say to you anymore," he says, and walks away.

As I turn and watch him leave, I notice the Englishman watching, so I turn to face him directly and watch him back with a smart-ass look. We do the standoff thing for a few seconds, then he puts on a huge smile and goes back to work. I turn back towards the office and see Gabe glaring at me.

Whatever, Gabe.

Now I feel I have no choice. I have to meet with the Englishman to sort out the promotion idea Gabe and Jonathan cooked up. Guess I'll try to figure out plans for Monday, which we both have off because the club is closed. Hopefully that works for him, too, so I can get all of this 'let's be friends' bullshit over with.

Shaking my head, I go back into the office to start my night.

CHAPTER 28

ASSORTING

The night passes by pretty quickly. I notice Gabe is not having anything to do with me. He's such a baby. I don't understand the need for this little temper tantrum. His man crush must be more serious than I thought.

I notice the Englishman is at the bar getting a soda; this is my chance to see if he's available to meet for Monday. I walk over but lose my cool and go behind the bar, pretending that the bartenders needed my help. I busy myself real fast and regret even walking over. This is so childish. Why am I acting this way?

Just as I decide that it's best if I just cut my losses and walk away, he speaks to me.

"Hello, Samantha. How is your night going?"

"It's good, thank you, and yours?" I answer.

"It's a good one. I was hoping to catch you tonight to see if you wanted to schedule a time to meet up and discuss that contest we're tasked to plan. I have some free time in the morning or early afternoon on Monday. Does that work for you? Did you want to meet then?" he says, beating me to the punch.

I look at him for a moment and say, "It's strange

that you should say that. I was just about to ask you the same."

"Good then, Monday it is," he says with a smile.

We set the place and time and then he returns to the booth.

A few minutes later, Gabe walks up to the bar.

"It's settled, Gabe," I say, trying to end his silent treatment.

"What's settled, Sam?" he says without looking at me.

"The DJ and I have plans to meet Monday to work out the promo you came up with," I say, a little too proud of myself.

"Great, Sam. Good for you. You must be feeling really guilty about the other night then," he says, still without looking at me.

I open my mouth to defend myself, but then he turns and looks at me with a look that tells me he is still disappointed in me, so I decide to not say anything. He looks past me, then walks away.

What a tough crowd, jeesh.

CHAPTER 29

THE ENGLISHMAN

My first opinion of her outside of work is what I thought it would be; beautiful. She does casual well. I have only had the chance to see her in club gear really, and it's nice to see that she doesn't dress like that outside of work.

She's walking and I can't take my eyes off of her.

Legs. She's wearing a little black fashionable short set with sandals and her legs have me captivated to say the least. She's wearing her hair down and her face is natural, which is nice to see, too. She's lovely. I will need to work hard to hold back my intentions today. I can't get ahead of myself. No, today, I need to work on removing that wall she's put up between us because of her partners. I understand it from other staffers that her brother has done things like this before — made large decisions about the club on his own — and it has been disastrous.

She agreed to meet me today at 11:30am and she walked, arriving almost 20 minutes early. Good on you, Samantha. Walking must mean that she lives near here.

I'm glad I thought enough to come when I did to get our table sorted.

She just went straight past me. I wonder if she didn't see me sitting here. She's going into line to place an order. Great! I'm bloody well starved.

Right, so it's my turn to now make a good impression on her. Here goes.

CHAPTER 30

THE COFFEE MAN

It's Monday. The club is closed today so it's really my day off, but here I am walking to meet the Englishman for a *coffee* and to sort out the details for the contest Gabe and my brother came up with. It's not a half bad idea, really. I just don't like the thought of being forced to work with the man they hired without me. Even if I did accidentally leave him locked in the club last week. I don't see what any of this is going to change.

What time is it? Oh good, I'm earlier than agreed. Maybe I can grab a quick lunch before he arrives. Let's see, I'll have a sandwich. That shouldn't take long to make. Luckily, the line is moving and it's my turn to order.

"I'll have the special with a side salad," I request.

"Sounds good. Make that two please. Good morning, Samantha. Nice idea to grab a bite, I'm starved," says the Englishman, startling me again.

Damn. He's gotta stop this; the sneaking up on me thing. I can't take it.

He gives a little laugh at my reaction and then says, "I have us a table over there in the corner by the windows. I hope you don't mind. I saw you arrive and didn't know if you had seen me there."

"No, I didn't see you, sorry. I actually didn't think you would be here already, so I didn't look for you," I respond.

"It's alright. No worries, yeah. It worked out because I really wanted to order a bite, too. Can we have two coffees with that, too, and a large still water?" he adds to our order. "Samantha, was there anything else?" he asks.

"No, nothing, thank you."

"I'll get these. Please, go have a seat. I'll bring everything over," he insists.

Euro man manners, gotta love 'em. Funny, he actually chose my favorite table at my favorite cafe. I guess he's not so bad after all. He looks good in the daylight, too. The handsome bugger. Ooops, he caught me staring. Is he making faces? He is. How silly, still working to make me smile even though I've been nothing but mean to him. Okay, I give. I'll be nice. He seems to be a good enough guy. I'll give him a chance; he's been alright, and I can't believe he hasn't used the whole 'you locked me in the club' thing against me.

I sure would have.

At least he knows how to pick out his clothes; he's got on dark brown Bermuda style shorts, brown leather flip flop-ish sandals, a brown and white woven belt, and he's wearing another Bob Marley tee. A white one this time, that says 'Love *the life you live. Live the life you love.*'

Being casual suits him. He looks really good today.

I like the way he always coordinates himself. It's nice to see a guy take care of how he looks. Oh, unless he has a girlfriend and she chooses his outfits; that would make some kind of sense. Girlfriend. This could be a reason why he never fell for any of the groupies that were hanging about his booth; either that or he's gay. Because that would explain everything, too.

"Here you are, mademoiselle, your sandwich, your salad, and your coffee," he offers, as he takes the food off the tray for me.

"Thank you. Really, this was very nice of you. I didn't intend for you to purchase my lunch today," I say in my defense.

"No worries. My father is Jamaican. If I allowed a lady to pay her own way he would gimme blood fire." He laughs at his own comment and looks at me expectantly. I give him no reaction, so he starts to explain. "That means he would raise hell on me." He laughs again, more to himself this time.

"Yeah, I knew what that meant," I say, again sounding meaner than I intended, so I try to lighten things up again. I ask, nodding towards his shirt, "Jamaican, huh? Is that the reason for the Bob Marley love?"

"Yep." He nods his head a little. "That's one," he says with a smile. He then clears his throat and continues, "Listen, before we get started here, I have a confession to make. I asked you to coffee because we didn't have a fair chance when we met, I know, but I want to try and put that behind us. I was hoping you could take my apology seriously today and then give me a chance to show you that I'm not the bad guy; that I'm not against you."

"Alright, alright, you win. Jeesh. Just stop apologizing to me about this. I'll stop treating you…whatever…for now," I say with a smile at the end. "And really, I guess I'm the only one who should be apologizing again. I can admit that I was behaving badly towards you and, yes, I apologize to you for that. I was just angry with Gabe and Jonathan, I know, but took it out on you. I won't do that anymore. I know you're not against me." As I say this his expression relaxes a bit. "And I really, really did not do that to you on purpose the other night, locking you in, seriously," I add. To this, he laughs.

"Thank you, your apology really means a lot, I accept it," he says sincerely, looking at me, and I see a bit of gentleness in his eyes. "Now, what do we need to do to sort the terms of this contest?" he says, smiling as he takes a bite of sandwich.

What a great smile. Damn, he's got me. I think I'm becoming really attracted to him. No matter how I try to fight against it. I think I may like him just like Lizzie said. I feel so much like a groupie now for sure. Still, I hope there's not any of what I was thinking about him a minute ago, a girlfriend, et cetera. He's a little too perfect for me to think he's taken, even if nothing develops between us. Just the idea of him being available is part of what is attractive about him, I think.

He sees me thinking, so he's first to break this silence between us. "Tell me, how did you three come about owning the club?" he asks.

"Jonathan is my brother, as you know. He and Gabe have been best friends since high school. Gabe was working as a realtor; he was pretty successful for being so young and he was able to set a good savings aside from his commissions. He happened to come across the club property while at work, and it was a deal that couldn't be passed up. Jonathan and I had some money that we inherited when our dad passed, so we all went in together. It's a good fit. We each like the arrangement. It works for us. We get to do something we enjoy and call it work," I say, surprising myself at how easy it was to talk to him. Now that he knows my story, I ask him his. "How about you, why did you leave England?"

"Well, I have always wanted to come to the States. What better time to do it than when you're young and without any real responsibilities. It's just me. The chaps I grew up with, we were never the work-in-someone's-office types, and we did our own things. We were all creative in some aspect, I guess, and we couldn't see ourselves as working stiffs in suits being stuck behind a desk. Didn't want to be boxed in. At least that's how I felt. I did what I was passionate about; I worked with music. I've worked as a DJ as far back as secondary school and I love doing that, but a mate of mine asked me to model in this campaign for him when he started designing clothes, and from that I received these acting gigs. I figured I could come here and try to do the same things. If it didn't work out, I could always just move back home. I didn't want to live my life wondering what could've been if I never gave the States a try."

His response is far more interesting than I imagined. I like that he is a bit of a risk-taker for his dreams. I like that a lot, actually.

"What part of England are you moving from?" I ask, keeping the small talk going.

"East London," he says in between bites.

"I love London. I don't think I could have left to come here though."

"You've been to London? Fantastic, when?"

"A few times. We actually had family there. My mother is from England."

"That's why."

"That's why what?" I ask, confused.

"Well, that explains a lot, actually. Some of the words you and your brother use. I really thought you were poking fun at me being English. Using things that are typically English because you were mocking. You know, having a little laugh at my expense. I'm glad to learn that you weren't," he says, a little relieved.

"No, I wasn't making fun. I didn't even notice that we did that," I respond.

"Right," he says as he smiles at me again.

Damn, that smile.

CHAPTER 31
NOT WHAT WAS EXPECTED

Wow! We spent three hours at coffee, *sorting* out the terms of the contest. Not really. Most of the time together was spent talking about everything else. He's pretty interesting. I enjoyed talking with him. We really found a way to talk about anything except that contest idea of my brother's. Working out the promo took only about 15 minutes; he let me come up with all of the rules and details which was a very gentlemanly thing to do.

CHAPTER 32

THE ENGLISHMAN

Samantha. Finally. I get to break through that hard shell of hers. I really have a crush on her, but I don't want to scare her away. I just got her to begin being nice. We had a great afternoon talking. I didn't want to ruin it by asking her out to dinner already.

Their employee party is this evening at the club. It's too bad that I have other plans scheduled; I would like to see her out of that work mode more.

I appreciate the fact that her mum is from England. That means she knows my culture. That actually made me like her even more, if that was possible. She gets my sense of humor, which is a bonus. She likes to laugh. I never would have guessed that from the way she behaved towards me at first. *She* has a sense of humor, too. I like that she's the happy sort and not mean or serious all of the time. I know now I can win her over with my wit and charm.

CHAPTER 33

IT'S A HOEDOWN

Monday night, back to the club since having lunch with the Englishman — oh, excuse me, having a coffee this morning. We're here tonight for the Bar B Q Hoedown event that's a thank you to our employees. I have to make sure that it's not overly obvious that I don't hate him anymore. This is the only time I can work on it and practice because it's an employee bash and we are supposed to be nice to everybody. Yes, that would include being nice to Mr. DJ too.

I arrive a little later than I had planned because of the long lunch with the Englishman and everything is just about set up for the event. There are checkered table clothes on the tables with the plastic red and yellow squeeze bottles for the ketchup and mustard. A little cheesy, I know, but it adds to the cookout effect. There are a few hay bales around that the fellas insisted on. I admit that I like the added touch, but I hope that they know that I'm not cleaning up any of the straw; that's all on them.

There are a few bigger than normal cacti pinatas in strategic locations filled with small bar items like bottle and can openers, unbreakable shot measurers, quirky drink recipes tied with mini ice trays, plastic shot glasses, plastic mini martini shakers, and plenty of candy; 'cause you can't have a pinata without candy, that would just be wrong.

We also have two drink vendors coming to help promote their summer specials and lots of things for the staff to taste, along with T-shirts and other promo items. Keeping this a little bit about business is a way my brother thinks justifies giving our receipts for this to the tax man. He's such a typical dude with that.

We rented an electric bull and removed half of the tables on one side of the dance floor to make room.

We have door prizes for all kinds of things like longest time on the bull, Mr. Hunkiest Hunk-down, the best Ms. Hoedown Daisy Duke, and whatever else makes us feel clever that we can think of.

Then there's the food — my favorite part, food. The caterers are here and the food smells delicious. I. Can. Not. Wait to dig in. I haven't had real barbecue in such a long time. To do the food honors this year, we chose the soul food barbecue joint from across town. We ordered ribs, pulled pork, beef brisket, baked beans, traditional potato salad, pasta salad, corn on the cob, mac and cheese, coleslaw, fresh rolls, watermelon, peach cobbler, apple pie, yellow cake with chocolate icing, and, of course, veggie burgers, hamburgers, chips, and hot dogs.

I can't take it; everything smells way too good. I need to make myself a little sample plate right now.

CHAPTER 34

ARE WE HAVING FUN YET?

Everything is sorted. The decor is done. The food is ready. There's a playlist connected to the music system for hours of play without anyone needing to man the music. Jonathan, Gabe, and I have the bar set up and will be the bartenders for the night. Yep, everything's a go.

I have my little hoedown outfit on: cut off jean shorts (no daisy dukes, not my style), bandana on my head, plaid button down shirt (buttons open, tied at the waist), and a tank top underneath. I opted not to wear cowboy boots and settled for wedge sandals instead. I think I pulled off the hoedown look, if I do say so myself. Jonathan and Gabe are wearing jeans and plaid shirts, too, so we ended up looking like a matching set, which adds to the fun of it all. Jonathan does a little extra by wearing an oversized cowboy hat as he chews on a piece of straw. He's a nut.

About an hour or so after everyone starts to arrive, I find myself looking for the Englishman. It disappoints me a little each time I look for him and he's nowhere to be found. I was rather hoping he would come tonight since we hit it off so well this afternoon. As the night moved on, though, I gave up on it and figured that he just wasn't coming.

After the bar slowed down a bit, I began to put out ballot boxes for a few of the door prizes. The staff would get to say who they thought was the hunkiest hoedown dude and the sexiest hoedown-est chick, and who was the overall country-est styled of the bunch, to name a few.

"Let them do the choosing and stay out of it," Jonathan says, and I'm definitely in agreement. I don't want any part of deciding who wins.

I announce, "The ballot boxes will only be out for the next hour, so make sure you get your votes in. Ladies, remember Jonathan and Gabe are off limits...I am too, for that matter. The voting is strictly between y'all." I get moans and groans at the *y'all* reference, but I thought I was pretty clever and laughed at myself for a good minute.

I make my rounds, mingling and having fun with everyone, cleaning a bit as I go, and it's really a good night. I like to see everyone happy, having a good time; it's nice to be able to give back a night like this.

I head back behind the bar to give one of the fellas a break. Being silly, I work my way there in my best hoedown, two step, line dance, square dance moves. I'm looking absolutely ridiculous, I know, because I have no clue what I'm doing, and just as I finish making it back to the bar, I hear his laugh.

"Nice moves, and here I thought I was going to miss all of the fun," Andrew says with a big grin on his face.

I freeze with embarrassment and don't know what to say. I knew people were hanging out at the bar, but I didn't see the DJ when he arrived. I am about to die because I think that there's no way I could be more embarrassed, then I hear good ol' Jonathan say, "Man that's nothing. You should've heard her trying to sing earlier back here. I thought a cat was caught in the damn dishwasher."

Everyone around is full of laughter at this but me.

There's nowhere to run. I wish I could just disappear but, instead, all I can think to do is punch Jonathan as hard as I can in his arm.

CHAPTER 35
THAT'S NICE, DEAR

The Englishman gets a plate and stays posted at the bar for the night. He spends most of his time talking and laughing with Jonathan and Gabe, so I was not center stage, showing my new attitude towards him. I do join in their conversation here and there because I don't want to give a bad impression to Andrew after this afternoon. I try not to let on, but I'm really happy he came. I'm so convinced that Gabe can sense my new feelings, I try to keep to myself as much as possible without seeming rude. I feel self-conscious and don't really know what to do with myself. I keep thinking that Jonathan is giving me these weird little looks and I hope that it's me just being paranoid yet again. It's such a hard balance and I'm driving myself nuts.

It's the end of the night and all of the employees have left. Most offered to help clean up (including the Englishman) but we insisted that no one was to lift a finger but us. It was a good night but I'm exhausted, so I ask the fellas for a ride home. Gabe volunteers.

On the way, he said he did so because he wanted to tell me what a good job I did tonight without putting me on the spot with Jonathan.

"What a great job. You missed your calling. You should plan events more," he says as he drives. I say an automatic thank you, but I'm really lost in my thoughts. Then his tone gets a little serious, I notice, as he pulls into my drive. "Listen, Sammy, I know I've been on you to lighten up with Drew a lot and I gotta say, I was proud of you tonight. You did a great job making him feel comfortable and I think he noticed your change towards him, too. He seemed more relaxed when we were talking to him tonight. Thanks. He's a good dude. I know it wasn't easy with the way you feel about everything. I hope you continue with this changed approach towards him."

I look at him to see if he is serious or if he's just mucking around with me. He gives a big smile when I do. Who knew Gabe was such a sucker? I wanted to say, *if you only knew*, but instead I just say, "That's nice of you to notice, dear, thank you," and say my goodbye.

Changed approach, really, Gabe? I *like him* like him, you twit. That's the difference.

CHAPTER 36

EVERYONE WANTS HIM

We're friends now, it would seem, the DJ and me. It's the first real day back to work for the two of us, and it's without being under the watchful eyes of my brother and Gabe. It's only been a few weeks since he was hired but I think that after yesterday afternoon, I'm realizing that I'm really falling for him. This scares me a little because he hasn't even done anything to try and impress me. At least I don't think he has, anyway, and I now know that I'm in for it.

He arrives a bit early for the night and I wonder why he's in already. It's a slow day. He doesn't need that much time to set up, right? That's right, his buddy Stix is off today so he's solo; maybe that's the reason he's in now.

I have to keep myself busy so as not to stare at him all night. Oh good, other staff are arriving, too; that will help distract me until I can find some real work to focus on.

"Hey, Sammy. Anything to go over for tonight?" the cocktail girls ask as they go towards the employee room.

"Hiya, ladies. No, nothing beyond the drink specials

that started this Saturday. We're still going with those," I answer.

"Okay," they respond in unison.

I love those girls. We have great people working here. I'm glad we do more than just a Christmas party and prezzies once a year. Employee bashes every now and then is the least we can do to say thank you for all of the hard work they do.

"Hey, Lisa, there he is, he's in already," Angela says as the girls come back onto the floor to set up for the night.

"Oh yeah, he's always in early, I noticed," Lisa responds.

"I'm gonna do it today," Angela confesses.

"Do what?" Lisa asks, surprised.

"I'm gonna get him to take me home after work tonight," insists Angela.

"What? What makes you think he'll take you home when he has all those other girls trying to get him to take them home, too?" Lisa asks with a little laugh.

"Well, I'm hotter than they are. Besides, I've got an in that they don't; we work together and he's a gentleman, he can't tell me no," Angela says too defensively.

"Girl, you're crazy. He's too fine for all of that. He's not taking you home. And dang girl, you just gonna go straight to your house like that? No dinner, no date, no romance? No wonder you don't have a man. Hell, you give away all the goodies first so they have no reason to come back," Lisa says, walking around to get things set up.

"Oh, shut up! You're supposed to be my friend," Angela yells.

"I am your friend. That's why I'm calling you out," Lisa laughs as she walks into the storage room.

Wait a minute! I can't believe the conversation I just overheard. I've changed my mind. I don't like those girls anymore. Angela is after my man. I think I may have to revisit her work schedule. If she actually gets the Englishman to take her home tonight, I'm gonna cut her hours. Heffa.

CHAPTER 37

FRIENDS LIKE THAT

It's a good crowd tonight. The music is good but I like how he is not giving the same type of show as he does on Saturdays. He's controlling his performances, giving different versions. Very professional. He's giving us just the right amount of dance music without it being the full-blown Saturday night club music show.

I see you, Angela, trying to catch his eye. He better not fall for your tactics or he's straight back on that shit list and for good this time, I can promise.

We are one man down, so I help the bartender tonight. I like helping out behind the bar like this when it's not *too* too busy. I get to interact with the customers more personally that way. Oh man, I love this song, too. I dance behind the bar as I help out.

"Hey Samantha, may I have a cola please?" asks the Englishman, catching me off guard yet again. How the hell does he always find a way to sneak up like that?

"Umm, sure," I say, trying to play off being surprised.

"What's wrong? What did I do?" he asks.

"Nothing, you just caught me off guard. I didn't see you walk up," I say. Guess the play off didn't work.

"Oh, don't worry, the music won't stop because I'm over here. I've lined up a few songs before I left the booth," he assures.

"I get that, DJ, I'm not worried that you don't know how to do your job. You just startled me. I wasn't expecting to hear you at the bar, is all," I say as I pass him his drink. He takes it, touching my hand purposely, and it feels like electricity going through me again, which makes me jump a little and he smiles at me. Not sure what to do next, so I ask, "Did you need anything else?" Of course, always sounding meaner than intended.

Oh great, I'm sounding like a bitch to him again and here comes fresh ass Angela. Perfect timing. It seems that I get to sit through her little pickup.

"Dreeeewwww, I could've gotten your drink for you. Just call me over and I'll get you *anything* you want from now on," Angela insists as she stands directly in front of him, putting her hand on his arm.

"Thanks, Angela." He moves his arm and gestures towards his DJ box. "But I wanted a little break from the booth, yeah. To step out, so coming to the bar for my drink was just what I needed. But thanks again for the offer, I'll keep that in mind for next time," he says courteously.

"Okay, 'cause you know I'm your girl with *whatever* you need," says Angela, trying a little too hard to win him over.

"Yep. Thank you, Angela," he says, nodding his head a bit.

She's smiling hard. She turns and sees me looking at

her, and that smile fades immediately.

"Okay, Drew, just remember to call me next time you want anything, and that I'm your girl," she says before quickly walking away.

She better get back to the customers before I throw a drink on her to cool her hot butt down.

"She's a fresh one, eh?" he says when she walks away.

He's talking to me about Angela? He thinks she's being too fresh? Good on him. But to play off my disapproval towards her hitting on him, I try to act neutral.

"You think she's too forward? I suppose. Maybe she's just trying to be helpful," I say.

"Could be, but I feel there may be another motive behind that kindness there, yeah? Just so you know, I'm not interested," he says, a little serious as he looks directly at me.

"I'm not your nan. You don't have to explain anything to me," I say.

"I know, I know. But I WANTED to explain it to you. I didn't want you to think that I was leading her on. She's a nice girl but she's not my *type*," he says, still looking seriously at me, watching for my reaction, I think, but I'm confused at why he's saying this to me. I'm trying to process it; I didn't realize we became friends like that this fast.

He must see me thinking, because he adds, "Besides, there's someone else I fancy. Angela is definitely not my type." Then he winks at me. "Back to work then. Cheers," he says as he walks back to his post.

"Yeah, cheers," I say, still a little confused as to why he shared that with me.

Then I realize what he said. Damn, he likes somebody else.

CHAPTER 38

THE ENGLISHMAN

Maybe I need to keep my backside in this booth. I did not expect to be hit on at the bar when I went to talk to Samantha. I hope she really sees that I am not interested in the Angela girl in any way. Angela's nice enough, but not in the same league as my girl Samantha there. I couldn't read the look on Samantha's face when I was trying to explain that I liked her instead, not Angela, without being too direct. I hope she understood what I was trying to say.

CHAPTER 39

END OF THE NIGHT

The night is over, and I don't have my brother or Gabe as backup so I can get out of here before he gets done in the booth. I saw he denied Angela her ride home. I could tell by her reaction and the fact that she and Lisa are leaving together. Good. I wonder what he said to her? She looks really deflated.

Very, very good.

Maybe I can have everything sorted for the night so when everyone is done, I can scoot them out, close up quickly, and get out of here. I want to get out quick and avoid listening to him talk more about this girl he likes or whatever she is, now that it seems we really are friends. I will make certain that he's out the door first, though, before I lock up. I learned that lesson.

It's funny he didn't mention anything at lunch about having someone. I keep asking myself, *why is this bothering me so much?* It's not like he was leading me on, but I can't help but feel as if I'm the one he rejected tonight. Ugh! I want to get out of here now. I need to hustle everyone up.

"Okay, guys, how much longer? I want to make it an early night tonight. Chop chop and all that," I say loudly as I talk to no one in particular.

Moans and groans.

So what, as long as they hurry up and finish quickly so we can get out of here. Moans and groans definitely do not bother me.

"Excuse me, Samantha, did you need help closing up? I'm finished and I thought since you said you wanted to make it an early night, I could help out," offers the Englishman.

If he doesn't stop that sneaking up on me, I swear I might just have to karate chop him or something to stop him from doing that to me. Why is he looking at me like he's done something wrong? Lord, this man is so confusing. I don't know what to do about him.

"I don't understand the offer," I say.

"I don't want to just leave you here alone to close up, so I thought I could help you out, that way you could leave early like you wanted, and then I'd be near enough to the door so when you actually locked up, you'd see me," he explains, laughing a little at his own joke.

Haha, funny man, he thinks. I side eye him and decide that I am going to ignore that last part because we really could use his help. "Sure...okay, yes, your help would be great, thanks," I say very professionally.

"Right, what do you need me to do?" he says with a smile.

"Could you help Mike at the bar? We're short one person there today. I know he would appreciate the help, too," I say a little more grateful.

"Yep, got it. No problem," he says as he heads towards the bar.

CHAPTER 40

THE FIRST RIDE

"Great, guys, thanks for getting done so quickly. I really appreciate it. Goodnight, everybody," I say as most everyone heads out and I begin to lock up.

But wait, that DJ is still here, I see. I thought he left a minute ago. Does he want to get locked in again? What the hell could he be doing? Oh, he's gathering his things by the bar. Good, looks as if he's ready to leave now, finally.

"Thanks again for your help with the bar," I say as we head to the door.

"It was nothing," he says.

"It's raining? Damn it," I complain.

"What's wrong with a little rain?" he asks.

"Nothing if you're from England, or a duck, I guess, but I walked tonight and I'm not in the mood to get soaked," I say, a little defensively.

"I'll give you a ride home if you need one," he offers.

Ooh! Angela is gonna be mad at me, I know. But her ride home and my ride home are two very different things. I have no intention of inviting him into my house tonight. I'm not that kind of girl. If he weren't the only other person left, I would get a ride with someone else.

But damn, it's raining hard; Mother Nature is giving me no other choice but to take his offer.

I begin to lock up. "Okay, I accept. Thank you again for being such a gentleman. Your daddy would be proud," I say as we stand in the doorway.

"Hmmf, you have no idea," he says quietly.

"What?" I ask, a little shocked.

"Nothing," he laughs. "Just wait here a sec. I'll pull my car around to the door. Try your best to run in between the raindrops," he says with a big grin.

He has a lot of jokes tonight. But if he takes care of a girl like this and she's just a coworker, I can only imagine those Euro manners in a relationship. *Beep, beep.* Here he is already.

Okay, ready, set go...in between the drops, in between the drops.

I get in and try to be as professional as possible. I feel very awkward sitting next to him and I definitely do not want him to think of me like one of those girls who throw themselves at him. He gets plenty of that.

"Right, where am I going?" he asks.

"I don't live far, just a few blocks over," I announce.

"It's nothing. I'm not rushing to anything else tonight, so no worries. Which way?" he says, still smiling.

I give him quick directions. "Go straight for two blocks, then turn at the light and go up four blocks and make a right. I'm in the middle of that block on the right. You can pull into the drive if there's no spot on the street."

We drive along quietly because I'm not sure what to

say. I guess he's just following my cue.

"Right here, this is me. Thank you."

"No, no, you don't get off that easy. I have to walk you to the door. Daddy said," he says with that crooked grin.

"But it's pouring, you'll get soaked, too," I say.

"I'm English, remember? It's always raining there, so trust me, I'm used to a little water. I won't melt, I promise you. Besides, I have an umbrella here in the car," he counters.

"Okay then, but just to the door. I cannot invite you in," I warn.

"No worries, I'm not looking to come in. But should I beep to let whoever know to open the door for you?" he asks, his sly self.

"No, there's no one to tell. I live alone. That's not why I'm not inviting you in," I say, looking directly at him. Then I think to myself, why did I just tell him that?

"Stop, you don't owe me any explanations, I get it." With that, we sit and stare at each other for a minute because I definitely don't know what to say in response to him. He gives me a smile again and then says, "Come on, the rain has slowed down a bit." He opens his door and heads around to my side with his umbrella.

"Ready?" he asks as he opens my door.

"Thank you for driving me home. I hope it wasn't too far out your way," I say now at my doorway.

"Nope, no problem, not at all. Goodnight, Samantha. I'll see you on Friday," he says as he leans towards me.

He's going in for a kiss? Stay cool, girl. Oh my God,

oh my God. Mmm, he smells so damn good. Why do I always notice that? I close my eyes as he leans in closer. He gets me on the cheek and I'm all weak in the knees. I open my eyes to see him walking back to his car. Damn.

Does he know I'm still watching him, I wonder?

"Goodnight, thanks again," I yell out to him.

Yep, I think I really, really like him. I really hope he doesn't have anyone else.

CHAPTER 41

GET OUT OF MY HEAD, MAN

Two days off to think about those signals that the Englishman is sending me. I can't think straight about anything else. Man, he's hitting me fast and hard. I should've kept giving him the cold shoulder. I'm not trying to fall for him, but I'm starting to lose control.

I need girlfriend advice. I need to call Lizzie.

"Hello?" answers Lizzie.

"Hey Lizzie, it's Sam. Girl, I need to talk. Got time?" I say a little desperately.

"I always have time for my girl. What's up?" she says.

"I think I've fallen for that guy..."

"Wait, what? She cuts me off. "You've fallen for that guy? What guy? Don't tell me, it's that DJ, isn't it?" she says, and I can tell she's smiling.

"I hate it when you know every damn thing," I fuss.

"Wait, I thought you couldn't stand him, though?" she asks rather sarcastically.

"No, that's not true," I say in my defense. "I was just so angry at Jonathan and Gabe that I took it out on him like Gabe said. That's what kept me from feeling anything about him sooner, I guess, 'cause really when I first saw him, I was attracted to him," I say now, more to myself.

"Uh huh. So why the quick change?" she asks, laughing at me.

"Don't laugh." I whine a little then take a deep breath. "But I dunno, I'm not really sure. Honestly, I'm caught as much off guard as you sound," I say.

"So what changed?" she asks again, trying to pull herself together, being a bit more serious.

"It's crazy. Gabe just accused me of being me, said I was being way too mean to the new guy. That the DJ was talking about leaving because of me. Then, sigh, I locked him in the club by accident, as you know. I get that no one believes me, but I didn't do it on purpose, honestly, and I felt really, *really* bad about it, so I went ahead and agreed to a truce."

"Yeah 'by accident,' Samantha, really? How can you seriously still try to sell me that you didn't do that on purpose?" she asks as I notice she used my full name.

"C'mon Lizzie, you know I always tell you the truth. I *truly* did not lock him in on purpose. I was trying to get away from him, not spend extra quiet time alone, seriously."

"And there it is," says Lizzie, but I ignore her.

"Anyway, to top things off, we met at the cafe on our day off to sort out that stupid idea that Gabe and Jonathan came up with of having us work together, you know, forcing me to play nice with him. When we met up to figure things out, I thought it would be quick and simple, ya know. In and out. But, instead, we ended up being there for hours talking about everything but that damn promo. Because of that, things are just different for me. And, dammit Lizzie, he's so funny, he's so handsome, and so damn intriguing. I can't seem to stop thinking about him now. It's really, really bad. What am I going to do?" I ask.

"Okay, so you like him. Does he like you back? Is he being extra friendly? I mean, is he hitting on you? Has he asked you out? Anything like that?" she rattles off.

"No. I'm not sure. He's nice to me and he asked me to meet for coffee before we were teamed up for the promo thing. He explained it was so he could apologize properly for the trouble he caused when he was hired on," I begin.

"Apologize properly? What the hell does that mean?" she asks, interrupting my explanation.

"He tried to apologize one night in the club, about being hired behind my back, but I didn't want to hear it, so I basically just walked away from him," I confess.

"Ouch, you are such a bitch," she says laughing.

"I know," is all I can say.

"And you just walked away from him, huh? A royal bitch," she adds.

"I know, I know, okay? I feel terrible enough now on how I treated him because he's been such a nice guy through all of my mess."

"Does he have a girlfriend?" she asks.

"I don't know. He's giving me weird signals, Lizzie. He was hit on by one of the cocktail waitresses in front of me. He shut her down and then when she left, he felt the need to explain that he was in no way interested in her, that he fancied someone else, then he winked at me and walked away. Do I assume that meant he liked me?" I ask, confused, then add, "I don't want to be that arrogant to think it's all about me."

"Hmm, I don't know girl, but yep, very mixed. I'm not sure what the heck you're supposed to think," she agrees.

"But that's not it."

"Ooh, do tell," Lizzie says, a little too excited.

"He gave me a ride home tonight because it was pouring rain when he found out that I walked in. I told him I didn't live far, that I didn't want to hold him up, but he replied that he had nothing that he had to rush home to. He then insisted on walking me to my door and kissed me on the cheek before he left. He didn't even wait for a reaction from me. He just gave a kiss, turned, went back to his car, and left."

"Wow, did he ask you for your phone number or ask to take you out on a date then or anything?"

"NO! That's what's got me. What am I supposed to think? I'm so confused. I see all kinds of girls hanging around the booth and he doesn't give them the time of day, but he gives me a kiss, yet it's only on the cheek."

"Do you think he's gay then?" she asks.

"Shit, I really hope not."

"Well, does he know you like him now?"

"Oh God, you're killing me. I hope not on that too."

"Girl! Why not?"

"Because. What if I show him I like him and he

already has someone or, worse, he shoots me down like he did Angela? That would be so humiliating. Then I would be stuck working with him for the rest of the year. No way. He's got to be clear about his motives before I let him even think that I could possibly, probably, like him…at some point, eventually."

"Okay, that's it! I'm coming to the club Friday."

"Oh, thank God! I don't think I can face him like this on my own."

"I've got your back. We'll get this mess sorted out, don't you worry, girl."

And with that, all was better with the world.

Thank the Lord for Lizzie. No one knows me better. There's no one I trust more and no one who has my back like her. She'll help me get my act together, because right now, he's truly got me in a whirly mess.

Shit! I just realized Friday is still two days away. What the hell am I gonna do with myself with this on my mind until then?

CHAPTER 42

THANK GOD IT'S FRIDAY

It seemed to have taken Friday F-O-R-E-V-E-R to get here. I need to walk slowly to work today; give myself time to work out what I'm gonna say to the Englishman when I see him after the kiss on the cheek. Maybe it's best for me to stay in the office again until Lizzie arrives. Yeah. That's exactly what I'll do. I'll hide. I can't face him like this on my own.

What time is it? Great, it's only 7:00 pm. I feel like I've been in here for an eternity. I still have over two hours before Lizzie arrives. Do I have enough work to do to stay in this office until then?

Oh no. I hear him speaking with Jonathan about Stix and how he made out last night with Ladies' Night. Good, keep him busy out there, Bro-ham.

Shit, are they coming into the office? Great, just great, I gotta look extra busy so they leave me alone.

"Sammy? What are you doing locked away in here?" asks Jonathan as he opens the office door, looking at me suspiciously.

"C'mon, Jonathan, just leave me alone. I have a lot

to focus on. I don't want to be bothered. Can't you see I'm busy here?" I fuss.

"Just give me a minute Drew. I didn't realize Sam was in here. I'll be by the booth in a moment," says Jonathan, just as the DJ begins to enter the office.

"Alright. Hello, Samantha. How were your days off? Good, yeah?" he says, looking in.

"Yeah, they were days off, thanks," I say without looking up.

"Drew, are you sure about what you asked me earlier? Man, I dunno, it seems like you got your work cut out for you. I gotta tell you, this here is not the one to play with, be warned," says Jonathan, speaking in guy code, laughing a little and shaking his head.

"Yeah man, I'm certain," says the Englishman with a smile, then he winks at me as he turns to walk away.

Jonathan laughs again as he shuts the office door.

I'm so confused. "What the hell are you two talking about?" I demand.

"Nothing, Sis, nothing," says Jonathan sheepishly.

My brother is so weird sometimes. What is he looking for in here anyway? "Get out already," I say.

"Relax, I'm done. You'll get your privacy again," he says, looking at me like I have three heads. "You need to chill out, you know that? What's wrong with you lately?" he asks.

I just shrug my shoulders and look at him.

"Alright then, hope you work all of that out. I'll see ya out there, Sis," he says as he closes the office door.

"Bye," I say, but he's already gone.

CHAPTER 43

FRIDAY NIGHT, PARTY HOPPIN', FEELIN' FINE

Knock, knock. "Excuse me, Sam, there is a woman here asking for you. She has a club card that I don't recognize, and she said her name is Lizzie," announces the new-ish guy.

Yay, Lizzie's here! FINALLY!

"Great, let her in and send her straight to the office, would ya?" I say a little too excited. "But wait," I add. "Do you have the card on you that she showed?"

"Yeah, it's right here. It's not the regular V.I.P. thing, so I wasn't sure if it was legit. I didn't mean to give her a hard time," he says.

"No, that's alright, Arturo. I forgot to tell you about these cards. These are for family and very close friends. If you see one, just let the person in. No need to find one of us, they're familiar enough with the club to know where to go. Also, when they're at the bar, they pay for nothing. You just need to keep track of what the tab would've been," I instruct.

"Alright, Sam, no problem. Thanks. I'll go let her in now," he says as he heads back to the front, leaving the office door open. I am praying that the sneaky

Englishman doesn't swagger himself in before Lizzie does.

"Heeeeey girl, where you at?" shouts Lizzie as she comes into the office.

"It's about time you got here. C'mon, I need a drink. Let's go to the bar," I say as I get up to greet her, grabbing her arm and pulling her on the way out of the office towards the bar.

"Damn, girl, he's got you sprung like that already? Back here hiding in the office," she says, laughing at me.

"Oh, shut it and c'mon," I say as I continue to pull her with me out of the office.

"Oh yes, let's go 'cause I want to see the mofo that's got you acting like this." She's still laughing.

I stop walking. "Oh no. Am I gonna regret asking you to come tonight?" I say, more to myself.

"Hell yeah, I've never seen you act like this over a dude before. He must be something AND I gotta see who it is exactly that has my girl all messed up like this. I gotta see this damn *DJ* for myself."

Why is she so loud? I think to myself. Shaking my head at my thoughts, I say, "Damn. Yep, I am regretting it already."

"Well, you can't hide out in the office all night, chick. I'm ready to get that drink, c'mon let's go," she says, now pulling me.

She's right, of course. I can't hide out in the office like I was doing.

Okay, first things first. I need to know where that Englishman is. I have to get my bearings on him so he doesn't sneak up on me again. Okay, good, he's in the booth, right where he is supposed to be. Good boy. We continue towards the bar.

"Sammy, is that him up there?" Lizzie asks, looking towards the DJ booth.

"Yep, that would be him," I confirm.

"Wow! He is a looker, you weren't kidding. I see why you're already sprung. He wouldn't need to do anything but look at me either. And, by the way, he's looking at you now, you know," she tells me.

"See how hard he stares?" I say without turning to look at him. "What do you think that means?" I ask.

"How the hell should I know? I'm single now, remember? I don't know shit. Is he really that good as a DJ, like they say?"

"Yeah, he really is. At least we'll get to dance all night. We haven't done that together in a while. I'm looking forward to a little fun," I admit.

It's so nice to have Lizzie here tonight. Although we talk on a regular basis, we rarely get to see each other anymore. Life is moving us along on our own paths. I love laughing with her. Did I mention that I miss her?

"Lizzie! What are you doing here, girlfriend? Long time no see," says Gabe.

"What's up, Gabe!" says Lizzie as they walk towards each other.

"It's good to see you, Gabe," she says.

"What? You too much of a big shot to come around anymore? It's been a long time, Lizzie," Gabe teases, referring to Lizzie's job now as a junior partner.

"Funny. But it's good to see you, too. I can't lie about that."

"Well, give me hugs then," he jokingly demands.

"Same old touchy-feely, Gabe, huh?" she says to me.

"Oh please. You know you still crushing on me, girl. I thought I'd just let you have a squeeze for old times' sake. You know, the gentleman that I am," says Gabe, still teasing.

"Gee thanks, such chivalry," Lizzie says back sarcastically.

"So, you staying all night?" asks Gabe.

"Why not? You trying to kick me out already?"

"Not at all. Maybe I'll catch a dance later," he says as he goes back to work.

"Alright, sounds like a plan man," she replies.

I gotta get Lizzie to come around more often. I need her here. There are too many guys that I'm dealing with. I need to be around girl power.

"Hello, ladies, planning a good time this evening?" asks the Englishman, walking towards us.

"Uh, well hello there, handsome. Who might you be?" asks Lizzie as she reaches to shake his hand.

"I am Andrew, the DJ guy here," he says, introducing himself.

"Well hello, Andrew the DJ guy. My name is Lizzie, I'm good pals with girly here," she says, pointing to me, so they both look over at me. Of course Lizzie is giving me the googly eyes, and he's giving me that intense stare of his, looking through my soul again. I have to turn away. I can't take it.

"Very nice to meet you, Lizzie. I can tell you two are quite close. That's nice to see," he says as he steps towards the bar.

"Why thank you, Andrew the DJ guy. It's nice of you to notice. Would you like a drink with us?" Lizzie asks as she walks behind the bar, making herself right at home.

"Certainly, I'll take a cola if that's not too much trouble," he says.

"For you, Andrew the DJ guy, it's no trouble at all," she says, flirting with him. She is so bad. I still can't look in his direction. He's too intense for me to deal with right now. I don't want to give anything away about liking him and I'm afraid that if I look at him, I may start hanging my tongue out goofy-like and drool a little; so I don't dare look at him at all. Lizzie hands us both drinks and offers a toast to the DJ to having a great night.

"Thanks and cheers, ladies," he says as he gives a clink to each of our glasses, then takes a sip. He watches me almost the entire time. I feel his stare on me. Finished, he turns and goes back to the DJ booth without saying another word. That's one of my tricks from before; giving me a little of my own medicine I see. I wonder now if I gave him too much of a cold shoulder. But boy, I can't understand the messages he's sending.

"Well bye then, Andrew the DJ guy. Nice talking to you, too," says the outspoken Lizzie that I know and love. She is so damn bold. She's got her head tilted watching him walk all the way back to the booth, and what gets me is that she has no problem being obvious about it. Me? I'm super embarrassed that he even came over here to speak to us because I know that I am falling for him. I feel flushed and know my face is redder than normal.

She turns to me all excited like. "Oh. My. God. Sammy, he is to die for, for real!"

"Shh! I don't want anyone to overhear you," I say, trying to quiet her up.

"Oh, you're too paranoid and he's definitely into you or he would NOT have made a point to come over here to meet your little girlfriend. Either that or he's just plain nosey," she says with a devious smile.

"You talk too much shit, you know that?" I remind her.

"You go with what you're good at, my friend."

"Whatever," is all I can say back.

"And where is that pain in the ass brother of yours, anyway?" she asks, looking around.

CHAPTER 44

GIRLY POWER

The night's off to a good start; the early crowd is a nice one. We head to the dance floor as soon as we hear *Party* being mixed in with the other songs. The song is years old, but Lizzie and I had adopted it as our very own personal girly anthem. We love to dance to it.

> ...You bad girl and your friend's bad too ooh
> We got the swag sauce, she drippin' swagu, ooh
> You a bad girl and your friend's bad too...

How in the hell did he know about that song? Is it just a weird coincidence? It has to be, there is no way he could've known. Never mind about the other part of the lyrics; I'm not ready to give my love just yet. I look up at him; he's watching, shaking his head to the beat with his headphones skew-whiffed, one ear on and one ear off like he does. Then he begins to point his right arm towards us, again bouncing to the beat. Okay, it's about now that I feel like he's starting to send messages through the songs. I know, I'm not arrogant much, but I think I'm starting to get it.

True to form, Andrew kept us on the dance floor all

night long. Days like this, I can't even call what I do work. I have way too much fun with it. But of course, true to her form, Lizzie tries to leave before cleaning up. She might be afraid that she'll be asked to do what she now calls manual labor and be asked to take out the garbage or to bring up a keg from the basement or something like that. As an excuse for leaving, she says she wakes up too early to hang out like she's still 21 any more. For whatever reason she gives, all I know is that she's leaving me to deal with the Englishman alone.

CHAPTER 45

FUN ALL NIGHT LONG

Instead of leaving like she announced, Lizzie is at the bar flirting with the new bartender, Arturo. As I sneak a peek at the booth, I see Jonathan is in there with the Englishman and Stix, doing God knows what. Looking around some more, I see Gabe is schmoozing some girl in the V.I.P. and I realize that I'm here on my own. What to do, what to do? There is no reason for me to go into the office again; besides, I want to be out here where all the action is.

I am trying hard not to look up at that DJ booth every five seconds, so I really need something to do, another distraction to keep my mind off of him. I can't think of anything, so I'm left to pretend that he's not there as I sit at the bar trying not to hear what's going on with Lizzie and Arturo.

Don't look, don't look. I feel like a little schoolgirl who has a big crush on the older kid at the playground. *Don't look, don't look.* I'm successful at fighting off grabbing looks...for now.

Just in time, as one of my favorite songs begins to play. I feel Gabe grab me by the arm and whisk me onto the dance floor. He must have been on his way to the bar because I thought he was still sitting in the V.I.P. section with his girly. He knows that this is one of my very favorites, though. Good on you, Gabe.

I do enjoy dancing with Gabe. He's a great dancer and we have that perfect dance chemistry thing together. He's like me; we really get into the song and let it take us over when we're on the floor. I like a man who isn't afraid to dance. I could dance all night long with someone like that.

CHAPTER 46

THE ENGLISHMAN

"There they go," points out Jonathan looking at Samantha and Gabe on the dance floor.

They look as if they've been dancing together for a long time. They flow together.

"I didn't realize that they used to be a couple," I say, maybe sounding a little too disappointed.

Jonathan laughs and says, "No way. Sam is not interested in him, never has been. He's been crushing on her since high school. But I think he's over that now. She treats him just like she does me, anyway. They both dance all of the time, so they end up dancing with each other," he explains. "And why not? They look good out there. Besides, I think it helps to get other people out on the floor, too, when they dance like that."

"Yep, they definitely look like they've danced with each other before," I say, thinking out loud. Watching.

"You know, even with being around music like this all of the time, Drew, I don't dance," Jonathan offers.

"No? Why not?" I ask.

"I guess I'm just too cool for it," he says, laughing and making fun of himself. Then he says, "I don't see you dancing either, that I can remember. Just a head bob here and there. You know dancing is a prerequisite of hers."

"Oh, I dance brother, I just haven't had the opportunity," I say, still watching them on the dance floor.

CHAPTER 47
THAT'S A WRAP, RIGHT?

Closing time at last. It looks like everyone is ready to go. I'm tired from all of that dancing earlier and it's been a long day. I am ready to call it a night. It was good to have Lizzie here. She was just the help I needed to sort out those signals from Andrew. I'm going to follow her lead and go with the thought that he could like me, too.

Still, I need a clearer sign to be certain before I make any moves on him, though. I am a lady, after all.

CHAPTER 48
THE NIGHT IS NOT OVER YET

"Hey, Samantha, I was wondering, did you walk to work again today?" asks the Englishman.

"Yeah, I did, why? It's not raining again, is it?" I ask.

"No, no, but I was thinking about it, and I don't really think it's smart for you to walk home at this late hour by yourself. I didn't realize you did that before. I would hate to drive myself home, going about my business, when I know you're out walking about on your own. I plan on having a discussion with your brother and Gabe about allowing you to do this for so long already. It just doesn't sit well with me. So, may I please take you home when you walk into work? It would make me feel much better about you being safe," he asks insistently.

"Um, I think I'll be okay, really. I've been walking home by myself for a while now. I do have a car. If I felt unsafe, I would drive myself," I assure him.

"No. I can't let you do it alone. If you insist on walking home, then you leave me no choice but to follow behind you to be certain that you make it home safely," he says rather firmly, which catches me off guard.

"Really, Andrew, you're making a big deal out of nothing."

"It's not nothing to me. I want you to know that I care about your safety. I'm driving you home tonight and that's the end of it," he says, looking at me as if what he says is final.

"Are you really insisting on driving me home?" I say in disbelief, with a slight laugh.

"Yes. I am. Let me know when you have your things and you're ready to leave." Then he shakes his head at me and walks away.

I am truly dumbfounded over this. Is he really serious about me not walking home alone? What the hell just happened? Is this the sign I was looking for? If he's going to boss me around, I don't think so.

In his car again, being driven home. I think he senses that this ride home thing is bothering me so here we sit, riding in silence, left to our own thoughts.

He remembered so well where I lived. How should I feel about that? Stalker comes to mind.

He gets out of the car as I get out on my own. So, he's walking me to the door again, is he? I don't know what to think. What is he doing?

He does walk me all the way to my door. "Listen, Samantha, I apologize for being so insistent about driving you home. It's just that...well, like I started to say at the club, I care about you, and I want to keep you safe when I can," he confesses.

"I don't understand what's going on here, Andrew. You care about me so I can't walk home?" I ask.

He looks at me for a moment, then says, "I like you. No, that's not true. I *really* like you and, and..." he sighs. "Maybe this will help clear things up a bit."

He steps close to me, moving in for a kiss. Doing so as if it was a routine already. I begin to offer him my cheek, but he takes his hand, places it under my chin and turns my face towards his and really kisses me.

A true kiss this time? I didn't realize how badly I wanted him to do this. To kiss me. It's like something I have been waiting for, for a very long time. I can hardly stand. I need to get a grip on myself. I need to take control here. I tell myself to pull away, to pull away now.

As I manage to pull away, he seems to sense that maybe I am uncomfortable and says, "Right, sorry, I just couldn't find the words to express what I wanted to say about how I was feeling towards you, and I've been wanting to kiss you for a bit now. I just had to take the risk. I'm really glad you didn't slap me because I thought you actually might." He gives a half smile, not looking at me directly.

I have no words. I'm lost in my thoughts. He kissed me, something he's wanted to do. Even though he thought it would get him a slap. He kissed me. It was *me* he was referring to then. The '*someone else he fancies.*' I'm the reason why he had nothing better to go home to the other night when he drove me home? Why he really wanted to explain why he was not attracted to Angela? He likes me, too. He likes *ME*, too.

I still do not say anything.

Watching me, he speaks again. "It's okay, you don't

have to respond. I just wanted to be sure you made it home safely. I will see you tomorrow at the club. Goodnight, Samantha."

"Goodnight." Is all I can manage to say. I'm still a little breathless.

He kisses me again — but on the cheek — then automatically turns, walks to his car, and drives away.

Unbelievable. I'm still in shock and can't seem to think straight. All I can do is watch him as he leaves.

I'm calling Lizzie and I'm waking her ass up for this. She is gonna die.

PART III
GOING ALL IN

CHAPTER 49

AFTERNOON SURPRISE

I could hardly get any sleep last night thinking about the Englishman and that kiss. I wonder if he knows that's what I call him...

I've got to snap out of it. I've got to get ready for work. It's Saturday night and it's sure to be a busy one. I know I look a bit of a mess, but that's from not getting much sleep; my mind wouldn't stop. I'm still really reeling from his kiss.

I feel a great big smile spread across my face as I think about it again.

Wow, he likes me. I can't get over that. I was hoping, but I had no clue he actually feels just like I do about him. I guess I'm glad he was the brave one; brave enough to do something about it, otherwise who knows how long it would have taken for us to recognize how the other felt. Or for me to realize how he felt. I hadn't told him yet that I liked him, too.

Since he's got so many 'fans' hanging around his DJ booth, a girl can't seem too eager.

Off I go and, yes, I am walking to work. I don't care what he said. It's gorgeous out and it'll give me the chance to test how serious he was about me not walking alone afterwards. Maybe it'll get me another kiss.

Going outside, I see Andrew standing at the end of the driveway, leaning against a tree at the curb. Looking great of course, but why is he at my house now?

"Umm, what are you doing out here?" I ask, a little surprised, as I walk slowly towards him down the walkway.

"I'm waiting for you. I would like to walk with you to work," he offers.

"Seriously? How could you know that I would still walk to work? How would you have known when I would be leaving? How long have you been waiting out here?" I ask without giving him a chance to respond.

He gives me a look before he responds. "I only just got here actually, a few minutes ago. I figured you would still walk in anyway, even though I told you how I was worried about you going home alone after work. And besides that, I wanted to speak with you more about last night before we go in. You know, since I don't have your number." He pauses for a moment. I don't say anything, so he continues his explanation. "I drove my car ahead and parked at the club so I could drive you back tonight. Doing that gives me the chance to walk with you so we could talk. You don't mind, do you? No worries, I'm not a stalker, but I'll be sure to get your phone number this time so I can talk to you that way instead if you are worried about me showing up," he says, smiling.

"Yeah, okay. Just as long as you're not a stalker," I say. "But if you really are, can you just tell me now so I know what I'm actually dealing with, please."

This seems to really crack him up.

Why is he laughing? I'm serious. If he's a stalker, I need to know now.

"No, I promise you, I am not a stalker. I really just wanted to talk to you before going into the club, is all. I was serious when I said that I have feelings for you."

"I can see that," I say, gesturing towards him. He laughs again.

"Samantha, seriously, I would like to spend time with you. I want to ask if perhaps we could go on a date, yeah."

I turn real quick and look at him like he has lost his mind. He kissed me, yes, but seriously, why does he like me? Why does he want to go on a date with me? I have given him no reason. Hell, after the way I've acted towards him initially, I'm surprised he's even a little bit nice to me.

He flashes that crooked smile, ignores my look, and keeps explaining. "I know you see the other girls hanging about the booth, trying to charm me, but I want you to know that I'm not interested in any of them. I fancy you." He pauses, thinking for a bit, then he continues. "I can imagine, too, that you're probably thinking that I must be off my rocker because of how we started — the way I was hired, your reaction and all — but there was something about you that attracted me to you from the very beginning. From the moment I first saw you, regardless of how you seemed to feel about me."

I look at him again, taking him in. I didn't realize he liked me right away like that.

His tone changes, lighter now, as he says, "Soo, since you did kiss me back and didn't slap me, I assume you have feelings for me as well." He stops, holds my hand and we end up face to face. "Is that true?" We stand like this as he waits for me to answer.

"Yes, I may have a few feelings for you, too. But honestly, I have been confused by your behavior. I thought you were telling me that you had someone else when you were talking about Angela before," I say.

"Right, but that's not what I meant. I am not seeing anyone; I was trying to tell you then that I liked you, but I worried about being too direct." We stand there looking at each other for another moment. He smiles and continues, "Well, that's sorted now and, like I said, I was hoping that you wouldn't mind if I took you out for the evening, this coming Monday perhaps. That would mean, of course, that we would definitely need to exchange phone numbers before then," he says, still holding onto my hand.

"A date? S-s-sure, okay. I would like that, actually," I say as calmly as possible, even though I'm doing cartwheels inside.

"Great," he says, again with that smile.

He lets my hand go and we start walking again. I'm too giddy to speak right away, but I do confess that I changed my view of him when we had met for coffee; that did the trick, I saw him differently from that point forward and began to like him in spite of my best efforts not to. He got a big kick out of that, laughing pretty hard. I couldn't find the joke in what I told him so he explained that it was about then that he was beginning to worry that he would run out of excuses for me to talk to him before he could get me to stop being so angry with him.

I didn't know our walk would turn into true confessions, but we did have a good little laugh at ourselves.

"One more thing, since we're letting it all out the bag," he says. "Remember when your brother and I were walking into the office while you were there the other time and he asked me if I was sure about something?"

"Oh yeah, I remember that. That was bizarre. What was he talking about?"

"Well, I had asked him if it would be okay if I were to ask you out."

"What? You asked him what?"

"Well, he is your older brother. I asked his permission first. I wasn't sure of the protocol with working for you, but he said he had no concerns. Anyway, I wanted to avoid any further conflicts before I asked you."

"Oookaay. I guess that makes some sense in a weird way. Did you go to Gabe, too?"

"No. I saw no reason. Should I have?" he asks.

"Uh no. I'm glad you didn't. Jonathan was enough."

"Right. Subject change then. Is there any place in particular that you'd like me to take you on Monday?"

"No, no you don't, you don't get off that easy. I'm not telling you what to do. You have to figure that out on your own. I want to see where *YOU* would like to take me."

"Very nice, I like that even better. I accept the assignment," he says with another grin.

"Good, I look forward to what you've got, Mr. Englishman."

He lets out a laugh. "Is that what you call me? Mr. Englishman? Because I've noticed that you rarely call me by my name, I just didn't know what you used to refer to me. I'm just happy to hear it's not wanker or something along that line," he laughs to himself this time.

"I do call you Englishman, you know, without the Mr. in front. Sorry, does that offend you?"

"No actually, I think it's a bit clever, yeah. I don't mind being your Englishman. I am from England after all. Well, here we are. After you, my lady, and no worries for you tonight, I will behave all business-like inside."

"What are you talking about? I'm not worried about you," I say as I go inside the club and he follows.

No, it's not you, Englishman, it's Gabe I'm worried about; wait until he finds out I'm going on a date with the Englishman.

Yikes!

CHAPTER 50

IS THE CAT REALLY OUT?

We begin work as the normal *'I don't have a crush on you and you don't have a crush on me'* folks at first. But then, while I was helping behind the bar and Andrew was getting his own drink, he received a phone call. It must have been great news because as soon as he hung up, he gave the bartender a quick man hug and then he turned around and gave me a looong delayed hug. Like, I forgot where I was and forgot to let go, kinda hug. Lucky for me, I was so caught off guard by this that my hands were still down at my sides. But even still, the fellas were by the bar and I saw Gabe take notice. He stopped what he was doing to comment to my brother. He was so loud I couldn't help but hear what was going on.

"Aye yo. Did you see that? Yo, Jonathan. Did. You. See. That?" Gabe asks.

"See what, man?" says Jonathan, knowing good and well what Gabe was talking about.

"See that long ass hug Drew just laid on Sammy! What the hell is he doing?" he says, a little animated.

"Oh, c'mon, man. I thought you liked the dude," says Jonathan, unphased.

"I do when he's not all hugged up on our girl," Gabe answers back.

"Man, please. She's a grown woman. If she doesn't want to be hugged up on, she can let him know."

"Wait a minute. What do you know that you're not telling me? Because any normal situation, you'd be just as hot as me right now," says Gabe suspiciously.

"Look man, I knew you'd act like this, so that's why I didn't say anything."

"What? You didn't say anything about what?" demands Gabe.

"He's a good dude. He came to me before to sorta ask my permission to date Sammy. I told him 'no worries.' I didn't see a problem with him asking her out."

"B-b-but she can't stand him, I thought," says Gabe, confused.

"Exactly, so I told him good luck with all of that and sent him on his way."

"Damn! It was making them do that guest DJ promo thing together. Why did you suggest that?!" Gabe asks, animated again.

"What are you talking about? Man, you came up with that idea all on your own."

"Shit! She's gonna fall for him, isn't she? It's that fuckin' English accent."

"Yeah, Gabe, that's all that's about, the accent." Shaking his head, he walks away, leaving Gabe by himself.

Damn, Gabe, stop giving me the evil eye like that. I guess you are now in the know. The Englishman likes me and asked for Jonathan's permission to ask me out. There's no one left on your side to give me shit about it.

You'll be alright.

I'm sure you'll find someone tonight to help make you feel better.

CHAPTER 51

A PLEASANT CONTINUATION

What a difference a day makes. Yesterday I was nervous to face him and today I don't want to let him out of my sight.

I adore watching him do what he enjoys. He's magical at it. It was strange, too, but I thought just about every song that the Englishman played tonight was for me.

Yes, I am a bit self-absorbed; I know this, but every time I would look up at him, he would have a smile on his face just nodding his head at me. And then, of course, every time I looked at Gabe, he was giving me the evil eye.

I couldn't help but smile at him. That made him even more furious with me, which just made me smile harder.

Poor thing.

It was another good night, though. The crowd was so thick and I can now openly admit it's because of him, our new DJ man.

That's because he likes me, too, so of course I think he's the best now.

Closing time is done. It's time for the evening drink. It's now Gabe who's trying to fly out early. Is he really that upset? He knew I would never date him. Did he always expect to chase off all my new prospects with my brother on his side? I have dated before. He has never overreacted like this. What a baby. He's used this club to meet all kinds of girls and now I can't have a guy interested in me? He's just having a temper tantrum. I'll give him a couple of days to cool off then I'll talk to him. Ooh, I better wait until at least after my date with the Englishman to see if there really is anything there that would last. I don't want to get ahead of myself here.

Tomorrow is going to be an interesting one, with only the three of us on duty. Maybe Jonathan should come in and act as the buffer between the two of us and Gabe. It's going to be a crazy night, I'm sure.

I'll worry about that tomorrow. It's time for me to catch my ride home.

I'm all smiles again.

"Ready to go, Samantha?" asks the Englishman, right on cue.

"Yes, actually." I gather my things and say, "Good night, fellas. See you tomorrow, Gabe."

Salt in his wound, I know, but I couldn't help it.

He really is such a gentleman, Andrew. He opens doors for me, carries my things, and walks me to my front door. Very caring, and I like that. I've always thought of myself as an independent chick, but I kinda really like the idea of being taken care of like this by a guy. It's these little things that get me.

I found out on the way home that the phone call he received at work earlier was for a call back for a small part in an upcoming series. He unnecessarily assured me that it would not interfere with his DJ responsibilities in the club, because that was one of the conditions he added before he read for the part. Good on him. He seems really excited, so I hope it goes well.

He told me he would be around at 6:00 pm Monday to take me on our date, that everything was all set.

That was fast.

He gave no hints as to what we would be doing, so I have no clue what to wear.

He gave me another real kiss goodnight when he walked me to my door. It was better than the first one, if you could believe that to be possible. I can't wait for Monday's date.

Just as I'm thinking of him, he calls me to say he made it home safely and that he was thinking of me, too. We talked as if we hadn't seen each other in months. We talked for hours about anything we could think of. It felt as if I really was in high school again and it was great.

He is into a little of everything nowadays, he said. I don't know how he does it all. He told me that right about the time he signed a contract with us; he got hired for a modeling campaign that will begin next week. Said I could come with him to the shoot if I'd like. He said he wants everyone to know that he has a girl. Woah! That's moving way too fast, I said. He's calling me his girl and we haven't even had our first date yet.

"Yes, we have," he announces.

"What are you talking about? No, we haven't."

"We had a coffee and a sandwich and sat and talked

for hours. That was a date to me," he says.

"Are you serious?"

"I definitely am. That was our first date."

"Please explain to me how you figure that to be a date."

"Right, I asked you to have coffee, I chose the location, I paid the check, and we sat and talked to each other for hours about everything but work. So that was our first date, officially. Now *you* please explain to me how it wasn't."

"That's cheeky," I answer, which really makes him laugh.

Wow, he's got me. We have had a little date already. Who knew? He has been working on me before I even realized. Good show, because it worked. Obviously. But I'm still not gonna let him call me his girl. It's way too soon. I didn't even know we were on our first date then, even though that's when I realized that I liked him. He really needs to pull out all the stops now if he wants to impress me.

"I'll see you tomorrow. Would you like me to walk with you again?" he asks.

"No, better not. I think we better arrive separately because of Gabe," I say.

"Right, Gabe. I'd like to ask, did you two used to date?"

"Ha, no. He's just my brother's best friend. It's funny, because I refer to him as Shadow sometimes because wherever Jonathan was, Gabe was right there, too, you know, like a shadow. He had a little crush on me when we were in high school, so they say, but I always saw him as if he was my second brother, that's it. I still do. I was never attracted to him like that. He's sometimes more protective over me with guys than Jonathan is, and I guess he is pissed because you got Jonathan on your side first. It's usually the two of them ganging up on any guy that shows the least bit of interest in me. You must have flown under Gabe's radar because I gave you such a hard time in the beginning. I guess he never saw you as a threat, for lack of a better word," I over-explain.

"Okay, so he still has a crush on you," he says.

"What?! No! He treats me like a little sister, too, AND he goes home with so many different girls from the club, haven't you noticed that? He knows I would never be interested in dating him."

"Right, he still has a crush on you then, got it."

Whatever, Englishman. Whatever.

CHAPTER 52

THE DREADED TALK

It's Sunday again — my favorite. The only downer is worrying about how Gabe is going to act tonight. He can be a bugger about things, too. I'll wait and see what kind of mood he's in before I decide what tactic I will use. If he's grouchy, I will use avoidance. If he's super nice, I will keep one eye on him at all times, because he'll be up to something and can't be trusted. If he's down and blue, then I'll be his little bestie for the evening; men can be such babies with their feelings, I swear.

Walking into work went super-fast. I can't believe I'm here already. I must have been really lost in my thoughts. Well, here I go to face Mr. Gabriel and whatever mood he brings.

Of course I see him as soon as I walk in. Thank goodness I thought enough for Andrew and me to arrive separately.

"Hiya, Gabe," I say.

"Yeah, hi, Sam. So, where's your boyfriend? He didn't walk you in today?" he says, acting a little smart ass-ish. I follow him into the office.

"Gabe, don't start. First of all, he's not my boyfriend, he just asked me on one date. Second of all, what's up with the little boy temper tantrum? You're not really jealous. Besides *you* thought he was a good guy; your words, remember? You need to just stop being childish right now," I say, trying to nip this in the bud.

"You're wrong. I am very jealous. I've been in love with you since I've known you. You know this, but you never gave me a chance. So yeah, I'm pissed that he just strolls in and all of a sudden he gets a date, no problem. I mean, he's cool, just not cool enough for that." He starts to walk away, then turns and says, "I don't even get what happened. One minute you hated him then the next you two are going on dates? You knew I would be upset over this. I don't know why you're acting so surprised," he says, looking really wounded.

"Gabe, look, I am sorry if his being interested in me and me interested in him is hurting you, but you gotta know that I would find someone of my own eventually, someone that is not you. You play around about this, but you are not in love with me. You can stop that guilt trip. I know you way better than you give me credit for. Now, you are an important part of my life, just not that part, and I'd hate to lose you as a friend because of this kind of nonsense. But if you insist on behaving badly towards me for seeing him, then I'm going to pull away from you and all we'll end up being is just business partners. I wouldn't want that to happen, but I need to be allowed to live my life like you are able to live yours, as an adult who makes their own decisions. I care for you. We've been friends for such a long time and you are family to me. I would hate for you to allow something simple like this to come between us."

He stands there looking at me for a long moment, and I almost walk away because I think he's done with the conversation. But just before I do, he says, "Okay, Sammy, it's cool. I won't give you a hard time. You're right; I'd rather stay friends as we are if it comes down to it. I know how stubborn you can be when you decide to ignore someone. I don't want to be on the end of that. Do know, I really do love you, and I just want you to be happy."

I side eye him when he says this. He wants me just to be happy — what is he up to?

"Really, Sam, I mean it. Of course it would just be better if you were with me, but I'll let you live your life as you say. You're right. He IS a good dude. I'm cool with it. Seriously, I won't hassle you," he says.

I look at him again, first to make sure he's not just telling me what he thinks I want to hear. When I decide he's okay, I say, "Thank you, Gabe, that means so much. I love you, too." He smiles big right away, so I clarify, "But not like that. I told you, so get that stupid grin off your face."

"I knew you loved me girl…" he says, shaking his head up and down with that huge grin still.

"Oh my God, you're impossible," I say as I walk away.

Whew! Thank goodness that worked out. When did the Englishman get in here? Sneaky bastard, that one. Maybe he's the one I really need to keep one eye on.

CHAPTER 53

SUPER FLY

The night is going well. It's hard to believe that one person can make such a difference in so many things. Swooping in, saving the day when we didn't even realize we needed to be saved. His DJ name should be 'Super Fly' 'cause he's got the swagger as he comes in to make everything better. Yeah, Super Fly is way better than DJ Drew any day.

"Hello, lovely. I didn't get to say hello to you earlier, before we opened. It looks like everything went okay with you and Gabe then," says the Englishman.

"Hey. Yeah, he's okay," I say, looking at him suspiciously.

He laughs a bit at my reaction and explains, "I saw you two talking when I came in. It looked serious, so I just went up to the booth. I heard a bit though."

"You did? What parts?"

"The bit where I'm not your boyfriend."

"Oh, you heard *that* part, did you? Of course you did."

"Listen, it's okay. I get it. I'm not trying to rush you into anything. I'll give you some space if you need it. I want you to be comfortable with what we're doing. We have plenty of time for all the other."

Is he serious with this bullshit? I have never heard a guy talk like this before. Should I laugh? Should I stomp off? I have no clue how I'm supposed to react to what he's saying, so I say nothing. I just look at him.

"Why are you looking at me that way, Samantha? I'm serious. I respect you and I don't want to rush you. I want you to like me as I like you in the end," he says, and then starts to walk away.

Okay, I guess we're done with the conversation then.

I really do like watching him walk back to his booth, but that was the strangest speech ever from a date. Jeez, just listen to me. I go from *he's so great* to *he's so strange*. I better really slow it down to see if I really like this guy. Being super sexy is not always enough.

CHAPTER 54

CAN'T WALK HOME

The night is done. True to what he said, the Englishman gave me my space tonight. No sneak ups. Because of that, I think it really helps me get a little better grip on what I think I may want from him. I'm excited for our date tomorrow. I can't wait to see where he takes us. I still need to figure out what I'm wearing, though. Oh boy, here comes Gabe with a look that tells me he wants to say something else about our earlier conversation.

"Did you walk in today or drive Sam?" he asks, acting annoyed.

"I think you know I walked, Gabe. Why, what's up?"

"Well, a certain someone gave Jonathan and me a really hard time about letting you walk home alone after work the other day," he says, gesturing towards Andrew.

"Well, I guess he just cares about me more than you do," I say, not making things easy for him. He looks a little wounded again, looking at me.

"Yeah, I hate to admit; he's right on that one," he finally says. "Since you're gonna be spending most of your time with him soon enough, I thought it would be cool if you let me drive you home today."

I look over at the Englishman; he sees me and gives

his head a quick nod. I turn back to Gabe and say, "Yeah, okay. I'll let you drive me home, umm, thanks."

"Great," he says a little too quickly. "Let's stop by the diner first. I didn't get a chance to eat earlier and I'm starving," he adds.

"Really, Gabe?" I can't help but think that he's up to something.

"For old times' sake," he says, giving an exaggerated *wink, wink*.

He is such a troublemaker. What the hell is he up to? Is this some sort of test from him? Well, I can give a test of my own, but not to Gabe. This is as good a time as any to see if the Englishman is really okay with giving me 'space.'

"Okay, for old times' sake," I respond, but immediately feel the need to add, "Please know, THIS IS NOT A DATE, but you're still buying."

"What are you talking about? I know it's not a date. Chill out, girl, unless you want it to be," he says, looking at me out of the corner of his eye wearing a huge smile.

"Fat chance. But nice try though. Let me just tell Andrew not to wait for me."

"Yeah, okay. I have one last thing to do before I lock up, then I'm ready; in about ten minutes."

"Okay, ten minutes. Got it," I respond as I go towards the DJ.

Now I have to let the Englishman know that I'm getting a ride home with the dude he thinks still has a crush on me.

I walk over to him at the booth.

"Hey, Englishman, I'm going to catch a ride home with Gabe tonight, okay? We're gonna hit the diner."

He looks quickly at me to see if I'm joking with him, I guess. Then he says, "Yeah, yeah, it's good. Is everything okay with us then? We still on for tomorrow?" he adds.

"Yes, everything is fine with us, you don't get off the hook that easily. I'm looking forward to seeing what you've got," I add a smile and a wink.

"Right then, I better bring it," he says, giving a half smile back. "Remember, I'll pick you up at 6:00 pm. Oh, and give me a ring when you get home tonight if you like. Anytime is alright," he says.

"Okay. Cheers," I say as I walk away.

"Yeah, cheers," he says as he heads out of the club.

I know the deal. He only wants me to give him a ring so he can make note of what time I get home. I know how that works.

CHAPTER 55

THE ENGLISHMAN

That threw me for a loop. I was not expecting her to get a ride from anyone else but me today. I'm wondering if I put a screw into things with the 'so I'm not your boyfriend' comment. That's too simple. Perhaps she likes to play. Did I misjudge her?

I can't think on that. At least we're still on for tomorrow. I will get a better read on who she is then. I've been waiting to genuinely take her out and to spend some real time with her outside of the club more, since the coffee date and seeing her silly side at the employee party. Tomorrow, I get to show her a different side of me as well. With what I have planned, I think she'll really be impressed.

CHAPTER 56
DATE NIGHT BEGINS

"Cheers, Andrew, sorry I didn't give you a call last night when I got home. It was already late when we left the club and I didn't want to wake you. I hope you weren't waiting up. When you get this message it's no big deal, I didn't really want anything, I was hoping to get a clue though as to how to dress for tonight...well, I'll talk to you when you come then. Bye."

No answer. Okay, I will try not to take that too personally. I don't think he's ignoring me because I didn't call when I got home this morning. At least that's what I hope, anyway. Oh crap, it's 4:00 pm already. I need to get a shower and figure out what to wear before I run out of time. Something tells me he'll be here well before 6:00 pm and I need to get a move on.

Is that him pulling up already? It's only 5:40 pm. I'm a girl getting ready for a date, man, I need every minute I can get. I definitely need to clue him in on that for future reference if we go out again. I go to look out the window. Is he coming in? Oh good, he is. I can gauge what to wear from what he *has* on.

Knock, knock, knock.

"Hiya," I say as I open the door.

Kiss, kiss, one cheek, two cheeks. God, he always smells so fantastic. If I'm not careful, I might just find myself floating behind him with my eyes closed, a big smile on my face, smelling the scent of him as he walks down the street.

"Cheers, I received your message earlier. I worked a photo-shoot early this morning and then I was at the gym after that. I'm not really sure when you called because my phone was off both times," he says as he walks inside.

"How do you have time for it all?" I ask him. He just shrugs his shoulders.

"It just seems like so much," I add. He just smiles as I close the door behind him. "Okay, so you may need to make yourself comfortable. I'm not quite ready. Sorry. But while you wait, would you like a cup of something? I have tea or coffee. I could put the kettle on for you while I finish getting ready," I offer.

"Yeah, yeah, that sounds great. Just point me in the right direction and I'll start it myself, no worries. Would you like one, too?" he asks.

"Oh, yes please. I'll be right out, I promise."

"We have time," he says, and gives me that sexy smile.

"Great," I say, a little relieved. "Here is where the teas and coffee are and over here are the cups. You choose for me, I'll take whatever. I'll be right back, okay?" And I head off to the bedroom to get dressed as quickly as I can.

Finally ready. It was hard trying to look fabulous without seeming like I was trying too hard. I decide on a simple black dress that can go just about anywhere since I don't know what we're going to be doing exactly. I go into the living room, and he does a bit of a double take. Just the reaction I wanted.

"I made you a coffee. I remembered: sugar, no cream, right?" he offers.

"Yes, perfect, thanks."

"You have a great place. I love all of the photos and paintings. There's some great art here. You seem to live a very happy life. I like that about you most, I think," he says.

I take a few sips of my coffee and watch him as he looks around at things.

"Thank you. I am happy; I have good people in my life, that makes a difference," I say, noticing that he doesn't have a cup in his hand and ask, "Did you finish your coffee already?"

"Almost, I was waiting for you a bit. You look great, by the way," he says.

"Thanks." Him saying that made me happy, like a little kid. I was worried that I wouldn't be dressed properly for what we will be doing. "I'm ready to leave whenever you are," I say, now feeling bad about not being ready when he arrived.

"Right. So, I have plans for an early supper, if that's okay, then I have a few other plans for later. You don't have a curfew tonight, do you?" he asks as he turns, looking at me.

"No, no curfew for tonight that I scheduled," I respond. I'm all smiles.

"Good, because we may be out a bit late tonight," he says.

He's all smiles too.

CHAPTER 57
WHAT A NIGHT

Our first stop: dinner. This is the best little Italian restaurant. It's so small on the outside; I don't think I would have noticed it on my own. I've probably passed by here a million times and never knew this place was here. The wine he chose was delicious and something I would have never known to choose on my own, either. I have to be sure and ask him the name of it again later. I think this could be my new favorite.

He said he couldn't make up his mind on the menu and asked if I wouldn't mind sharing a few things with him instead. That worked out perfectly, because secretly I couldn't decide either.

We shared a portion of a fantastic chicken parmesan, thin and crisp, with a little side of pasta that had the best sauce I think I have ever tasted. We shared a small margherita pizza (my favorite pizza, by the way), a half-sized salad with mixed greens tossed in a balsamic vinaigrette topped with marinated grilled chicken and, to complement everything, a basket of nice warm crusty bread. It was like a mini smorgasbord on our table and I loved it.

After dinner, we walked to an art gallery co-owned

by Anne — a friend of his, he said. She's from London, too. I wondered silently about the two of them, but, as if he was reading my thoughts, he explained that she used to date his brother.

That was a relief; I'd hate to be on a date in the presence of an ex-girlfriend of his. Not that I am the jealous type, it's that it would be way too strange to be in the middle of something like that.

Oh hell, who am I kidding? I would be so jealous and, of course, would hate her instantly.

After the introductions, Anne told me that they were having a special showing of Sandro Botticelli on loan from the museums. "Seriously?" I couldn't help but ask, looking at Andrew in disbelief. How did he know that I loved art? He is one of my favorite painters. This was the best surprise. Being able to be a part of this once-in-a-lifetime viewing made the evening unforgettable, for sure. I can't imagine how in the hell they are able to host his work, but I don't care. I'm so excited, I have to fight from running throughout the gallery like a little kid.

The gallery had both *The Birth of Venus* AND *Primavera*; absolutely breathtaking. Seeing Botticelli's paintings in person was such a magical experience for me. I could have stayed there for hours more but the night was, "not over yet," he whispered. He still had at least one more thing planned, if I was up to it. What else could he add to this night? My feet were barely touching the ground as it was. I was having a great time, how could he top things off with anything else?

Once we leave the gallery, we walk through the

shops in this great little neighborhood and he stops to get us gelatos for dessert, then we continue on our way. As we walk along a bit more, he puts his arm around me. That makes me smile, too. It feels like we're a real couple already. I know I said that I didn't want to move too fast, but this gives me the idea of what we could be and it's nice.

We come to a little outside cafe and decide to stop and have an espresso as a kind of nightcap, and talk. I get the Italian theme so far and it's perfect.

Before we realized it was almost 10:30 pm. The time went by so quickly. I didn't think that we were out for that long. Most of the time must have been spent in the gallery; he really had to work hard to get me out of there.

He asks if he can keep me out for a bit longer because he still has one more place he would like to take me.

Seriously? There's more, still?

We have our coffees but we decide to stay no longer than ten to fifteen minutes since it's later than we thought. As we get ready to head to the next stop on his list, I can't help but take notice of how charming he really is. I feel a little mesmerized by this evening. Saying he thought of our date in great detail is an understatement. I'm so impressed.

As we sit at the cafe finishing our coffees, I think about what I know about him. He has so many things going on. He's a DJ, of course, but he told me that he is trying his hand at creating music, too, and has a few songs in the works with a couple of friends, which I think is cool. All of that started before he signed on to work at the club. He tries to go to the gym every day to stay fit, and fit he is. He's modeling and soon he'll be acting again. He invited me again to the shoots with him. He wants me to see him outside of the club, he said. He asked me to go to the filming studio on his first day, too. He wants me to see ALL the sides of him, to really get to know the full him. I gave him the joke that he must be Jamaican because of all of the jobs he has, that his daddy would be proud. He didn't get it. He chalked it up to American humor. I thought it to be hilarious and laughed quite a bit; I couldn't stop. The clueless expression on his face didn't help either. I tried to explain the joke and that it came from an older comedy skit show, *In Living Color*, but that really didn't help him understand at all. Maybe I'll show it to him one day.

After coffee, we walk again, to this small lounge. It is for dancing off supper, he tells me. Wait, he dances, too? That does it for sure; I'm so hooked on him right now. I hope he can't see my back teeth because of how hard I'm smiling.

He's doing everything right so far.

We dance for the rest of the night. His moves are so good and seem to come so effortlessly for him. He's so damn smooth. I love that he is not one of those guys who just says, "I don't dance."

We move so close, and I just breathe him in in every way I can. Then, without warning, he kisses me. This kiss is icing on the cake. I've been waiting for him to kiss me again all night. I can't be sure, but I don't think my feet are touching the ground at this point.

Yes, tonight is absolutely perfect.

We're on our way home. He's driving me back. I'm so attracted to him right now but I have to be strong. *I will not invite him in, I will not invite him in, I will not...*

"What are you thinking about over there? Your face is a little intense. You alright then?" he asks, catching me off guard.

"Yes, I'm fine," I say, slightly embarrassed.

Big dummy girl, don't let your face tell it all. Get it together. You're not inviting him in, damn it. No matter how charming, good looking, or good smelling he is. *I will not invite him in, I will not invite him in.*

I need to think about something else.

"I had a great time tonight. Thank you for everything, Andrew. It was perfect," I say.

"Andrew? I get called by my given name? It *must* have been a good night," he says teasingly, and it makes me fake pout a little, so he tells me, "I really enjoyed myself, too. I would like to take you out again on Wednesday if it's alright with you. Stix will be working that night alone and I'm free."

That worked. The pout is gone. "Okay, I *would* like that. Wednesday is good, I haven't planned anything yet."

"I was thinking of going to the cinema. Is there anything out in particular that you wanted to see?" he asks.

"I don't know. I will have to look. I could do a movie. I haven't gone to the movies in a long time, now that I think of it."

"Neither have I. I was also thinking that we could go earlier in the afternoon and maybe then we could get a theatre to ourselves."

"That sounds good," I say, shaking my head in agreement. Then I remember that I wanted to ask him about where we were tonight. "Hey, we were in such a great neighborhood. How did you find it? I've never really done anything in that area before. I mean, I've driven through, but never knew about that restaurant or lounge; it was a nice change."

"I live in that neighborhood. That's my part of town. I wanted you to see it," he says, a little more serious than I expected.

"Wait, what? Your neighborhood? Why didn't you say anything before, while we were there? I would've liked to have known that then. While we were still there, ya know. Why did you keep that a secret? You should've said something, seriously," I rattle off.

"No, no. It wasn't a secret. I just didn't want to be tempted into taking you to my flat. I'm trying to keep on pace," he says.

"Oh, right. Good idea then," I say more to myself than to him. Going to his place would have definitely been a dangerous thing.

When he walked me to the door, I got another kiss on the cheek. It's a good thing, too, that he didn't kiss me like he did on the dance floor earlier tonight — I would not have been able to resist him.

Lizzie's getting another late-night call about the Englishman when I get inside, that's for sure.

CHAPTER 58

GIRL TALK

"Lizzie, I'm falling hard and fast for the Englishman. I am really losing all control. That date he planned tonight was just perfect."

"Good, girl, you deserve a good man. Shit, I say it's about time. Go ahead. Fall hard. You're worth it," she tells me.

"I want it. I want him and I to work. I really, *really* like him. I don't think I've liked anyone this way before and we haven't done anything for me to; it's all so strange to me."

"I know, girl, but he seems to really like you, too. He called me early on Saturday to ask what you liked so he could plan a good evening for you."

"He called you?" I say a little louder than I expected.

"Well actually, Jonathan called me and then put Andrew on the phone, so…"

"He did? How in the hell did he get Jonathan to do that?"

"I don't know, but if he goes through that just to impress you on a date then he must really like you, too. I almost fainted when I heard his voice on the other end. Shit, his voice is sexy, too. If you don't want him,

I'll take him on."

"Alright, down girl, he's all mine. At least I hope him to be. But I can't believe he got Jonathan to call you for him. Jonathan never does shit like that."

"Yep, he sure did. Then asked me to tell him everything I could think about you, what you liked, what you didn't like, everything, so you have no secrets left," she laughs.

"That's how he knew I would love the gallery. I was wondering about that."

"Yeah, girl, he did his homework on you. He definitely wanted to make an impression."

"Well, he did that. The night really was perfect."

"Uhh, not too perfect. He isn't there *and* you're still on the phone with *me*."

"Come on, it was our first official date. I'm not that easy. He's got to know me a bit."

"Whatever. You're better than me, 'cause you and I would be talking to each other tomorrow afternoon if I was the one on that date with him 'cause I'd still be busy getting busy tonight and would still be busy getting busy tomorrow morning, too." She laughs again.

"Oh my God, you are impossible! I am not moving that fast with him. I want his respect and I don't want him to think I'm easy like that. You know how he has girls throwing themselves at him every night. I don't want to be like that. I'm different from them and I want him to see that."

"Okay, you go ahead. Keep your man that everybody wants. That's right."

"Bye, Lizzie, I think you need to go back to sleep."

"Bye, girl, you're right. I need my beauty rest so I can catch me a new man, too."

CHAPTER 59

THE CAT IS OUT ALL OVER

Well, it's Tuesday. The night when it's just the Englishman and me in the club; everyone else has the night off. No Jonathan, no Gabe, and no Stix; just the Englishman and me.

It's raining again. The Englishman was outside waiting to walk me with an umbrella. He was half soaked. He said he walked from his gym from around the corner this time. He had his gym bag but asked if I didn't mind if he left it at my house. He really didn't want to walk with it to the club. He would pick it up some other time, later. I'm still not sure if that was a strategic move or a coincidence. Why didn't he keep it in his car? Wasn't it parked at the gym? I didn't ask, but maybe he needed it for something else, I don't know. It did just start raining again, so it could be just the timing of things. But I've already learned how sly he can be, so I'm not totally convinced about the coincidence of it.

When we arrive at the club, I see his car in the lot. He must have parked here then walked to the gym and stopped to get me on his way back. I feel better about him asking to leave his gym bag after seeing his car here. Luckily it wasn't raining hard, and being under the umbrella together gave us the excuse to walk with his arm around me again.

Because it's still raining, the crowd is light at the club tonight.

Halfway through the evening, sitting at the bar talking with a few regulars, I hear a slower song come on, which I think is unusual for the middle of the night. Something tells me to look up. Just as I do, I see Andrew walking towards me. He walks over, grabs my hand and asks me to dance.

How could I say no? We walk, still holding hands, as I pay attention to the lyrics; he then pulls me in close when we reach the dance floor and move to the music.

> *...There goes my baby*
> *(Ooh girl, look at you)*
> *You don't know how good it feels*
> *To call you my girl*
> *There goes my baby,*
> *loving everything you do*
> *Ooh girl, look at you...*

While we were on the floor, everyone else seemed to just disappear until, in my mind, it was just him and me. It was as if every word was playing from him to me. That's how it was, again, in my mind, anyway. We danced close and slow. Damn, he's doing everything right so far and I notice again that I'm really falling fast and that scares me.

Maybe the girls were unaware how close I was because, later in the night, I overhear Angela talking to Lisa about me and Andrew together on the dance floor...

"Lisa, did you see Drew ask Sammy to dance to that slow song?" asks Angela.

"Of course, I think everyone saw them," says Lisa.

"Why would he do that? Do you think he likes her?"

"Ah yeah, Angela, he likes her. Why not? She seems like she could be his type."

"But why? I let him know I was interested in him before she did. I'm so upset! Do you think she likes him, too?"

"It certainly looked like she was liking him back, and why not? He's everyone's type. But why are you so upset over that? You're my girl, damn, but to be honest, I'd pick Sammy over you, too."

"Shit! I should've known he liked her. The way he smiled at her. But this is the first time I've seen her like someone back like this. Do you think they're serious?"

"Not your business, you know that, but I tell you what, you'll be alright. They're a way better match for each other, anyway," she says, and walks away.

CHAPTER 60

SLOW YOUR ROLL

Well, what a surprise: it's raining still. I haven't checked the weather report but I hope it doesn't last much longer. I have the next two days off and I want sunshine. Hey, what's taking my ride home so long tonight? I'm inside by the doorway of the club so I'm not getting wet, but it's really cool out and I want to get home and get under my blankets.

It was a slow one, so he should have been ready before me. I peep through the window of the door and have a look around. Here he comes now. He walks back inside with his umbrella at his side.

"Hey, sorry about that. I had to take a phone call and it went longer than I expected. Are you ready to go?" he asks.

"Yep, I'm ready. You know it's still raining out there, right?" I ask, because I don't understand why he wasn't using the umbrella instead of carrying it.

"Yeah, yeah, I brought the umbrella from the car for you. It's just outside here. I have you covered."

"Yes, you do. My hero once again," I say, smiling.

I guess being English makes you a little more immune to rain than the rest of us.

I lock up, we walk to his car that is now parked near the entrance, and I get my ride home. He's such a gentleman.

We have great conversations when we're together. He makes me laugh and I like that about him. Another thing added to the list of why I think he's great. He's perfect for me. But still, I need to make sure I take it slow and do things right. I don't want to move too fast and get too serious too early. I've done that before and I was kinda bummed when it didn't work out. I don't want that to happen now.

His phone call was from back home, he said. He was sorting out plans. He has an older brother who is coming to town with their younger sister in a few months and he wants us all to meet. That's serious. Meeting the family. He knows that he wants me to do that already? He does move fast. This is the brother who had dated the girl I met at the gallery on our date night. His brother and sister will be here in four months. Meeting the family is a scary thought. I might be ready for it in four months. Maybe. At least he gave me full warning.

He has the proofs from one of his shoots in a folder in the back. He wants me to see his work. Damn, these are great. He looks good. He's not like a pretty-boy handsome in these; he's a perfect kinda rugged, kind of a man's man, a Greek God kind of handsome.

"These are great Englishman, what are you advertising exactly in these?"

"Thanks, it's all of the clothes. The designer is an old mate from London. The one I worked with before. He's here briefly working on his fall line for a show. He's still up and coming in the States. I did some shots for him before I moved, and he wanted me on the new campaign here. It just worked out. Next time he's in town I will introduce you, yeah?"

"Okay, sounds good. I'd like to hear some old stories about you growing up, you know, listening to the Spice Girls and such."

He laughs.

I then say, "You know, you should frame some of these for yourself, if you could."

"It's funny you should say that. I was hoping you would ask to take one for framing to add to your photos at home."

"Really?" I ask really, really surprised.

"What? Am I doing the moving too fast bit again?" he asks.

"No. No, that's not it. I'm just caught off guard a little. You are always so clear with what you want from me already and you're not afraid to say it."

"I keep doing that to you, don't I? It's hard for me not to say what I want because I just know my feelings for you, yeah? I don't see why I should waste any time not letting you know. But I understand that I may be coming on too strong for you. I get that."

"I don't know if that's it really, you coming on strong. I just don't understand it; how do you know so certainly about me?" I ask him seriously.

"Know what?"

"How do you know that you feel so definitely about

me, that you want me in your life like this so fast? We've only just met, and remember, in the beginning I was so mean to you. So...really, tell me, how do you know?"

"I know because from the moment I saw you, there was something that I knew I wouldn't be able to shake. The entire time you were pissed because of the way I was hired, I was trying to figure out what I could do to get closer to you, to turn your opinion around about me. I have never been attracted in this way about anyone before. I like everything about you, and I unfortunately have seen enough tragedies in my life to know not to wait to tell someone that you care. I want to be with you, and I don't see what should get in the way of me telling you or showing you how much I *do* like you. BUT. But I understand if this is too fast for you. There is no pressure, I assure you, but know that I do want a relationship with you. You seem afraid of that; maybe it's because you've been treated badly in the past, I don't know. I do know that I will not do anything to deliberately hurt you. This you can trust," he explains.

"That's a lot to take in," I say, more to myself, as I turn to look out of the window.

"Let me ask you this, Samantha. Your feelings now, have you felt this same way about anyone else? The way I hope you're beginning to feel about me so far? I've told you this is the first time like this for me, so I know what we could have together will be great."

I think about what he asks for a moment and decide to answer truthfully. "No. No, I can see it. You're about right, it *is* the same for me; I haven't felt this way about anyone else so quickly. I have recognized that already. I just don't want to move too fast and wreck what you say could be a great thing."

"Please don't let your bad experiences dictate how you are with me. I am not those other guys. I've told you I really like you, full stop. It *will* be great between us, you just have to stop fighting it," he says, trying to assure me.

"I hear what you are saying. My heart says to start letting you in, but my head is saying take it slow. It's very confusing," I mumble.

"Right, and what does that mean exactly, yeah?" he asks.

"I'm saying I need to take it slow while I sort out what I can give back. Right now, I can't give you all of me, not everything. It's just really too quick for me to do that."

"I understand. Just keep giving me the chance, is all," he says, sounding very calm and sure of himself.

We've been sitting in my driveway talking for a few minutes now. I can't shake the feeling that I may be making a mistake pushing him back like this, but it's what I need to do. I can't move faster than my head will allow. I have to be smart about things. He's so right though. I have never fallen for anyone like this before. I'm usually the one in control, but not now; he's really got me under his spell. I can try to deny it all I want, but I know it's useless.

I have to stay strong though. I can't let my heart take over so soon (or my libido, for that matter).

I insist on taking things at my own pace. He seems to be okay with this and I feel myself breathe a small sigh of relief.

He gets out and walks me to my door.

"So, call me and let me know what movie you'd like to see tomorrow. I will go to the gym first thing so we can have all afternoon. Alright then? Goodnight, Samantha," he says.

"Yes, okay, goodnight," I respond automatically.

A kiss on the forehead and he's out.

CHAPTER 61

SORT IT OUT

Oh my God. I keep going around and around about this. Is there something wrong with me? There seems to be absolutely nothing wrong about him, but am I really ready for a relationship like this? He is so intense, so serious about us getting together already, and that scares me. Am I crazy for holding back? I feel so uncertain right now, going back and forth with this. He seems so perfect for me and yet I really feel the need to slow it down. I don't know why I'm doing this to myself. I hope that by the time I am ready for the kind of relationship I think he wants, he won't be moving on because he's tired of being pushed away.

There is no one I can talk to about this who will understand what I'm going through. Lizzie will say I'm insane and he's perfect. Jonathan will ask me what the big deal is, and Gabe would probably say to leave him alone. I just have to work this out on my own.

Maybe I'm just overthinking things and should let it go its course.

CHAPTER 62
DATE #2 – OH, NO, IT'S #3

It's Wednesday, my second day off of the week, and I just thought again about how that cheeky Andrew was sorting his schedule to have the same day off as me. He *is* a sly one. The stalker.

No sunshine again. It's going to be a perfect movie day.

I didn't really get any sleep last night again. What he said just kept rolling around in my head. I decided that I really just have to go at my own pace. If he is starting to care for me as he says, then he'll wait for me until I'm ready, too. I can't compromise, I just can't, or I'll be second-guessing our entire relationship.

Early again. Of course he's here already, but I am all set this time.

"Hiya," I say as I open the door.

"Hey, lovely, you ready to go?" he asks.

"Yeah, yeah, I'm ready. Just let me get my jacket."

As we drive along, he says, "I thought we'd try that new theatre that just opened up. They are supposed to have large seats that feel like you're sitting in your front lounge."

"Sounds good to me, I'd like to try it there, too. I

hope they have fresh popcorn."

"Right, I'm not a fan of the popcorn here. You're on your own I'm afraid."

"Funny, I'm not a fan of the popcorn in England. Who puts sugar on popcorn? Yuck!"

"You're making fun of the royal popcorn, you do realize that don't you?"

"You're funny," I say, then I turn to him a bit more seriously and say, "Thank you for not giving me a hard time. I appreciate you allowing me time to sort this *relationship* thing out on my own terms."

"Anything you need, I already told you that," he says with that smile of his.

The movie was great; a little bit of action, a little bit of romance, and a little bit of laughter. We grabbed a light lunch after and had some great conversation as usual. He told me a little bit more about his brother and sister who are coming, and he seems really excited about seeing them. He wanted to hang out a little more, but I haven't had a lot of sleep lately. A lot has been on my mind and I'm really tired now, so back home I go to get a good sleep while hearing the rain hit against my windows.

Alone.

CHAPTER 63

THE NEW INVITE

I had a great nap. I feel so much better now. It's nighttime but I feel as if I can take on the world. Too bad it's late and the rest of the folks are calling it a day. The phone is ringing. Where the heck is my phone? It's Andrew. Nice, I like that he's calling. I smile.

"Hello?"

"Hiya, love. How was your kip?"

"It was very nice, thank you."

"Hey, listen, I know I asked before about the shoot, but I wanted to ask you again; you know, about that new part. Would you come with me tomorrow morning when I report to set for that acting part I gained? I really would like for you to come with me the first day."

"Yeah, okay, I'll go with, sounds exciting. What time should I be ready then?" I say.

"Great!" He sounded a little relieved. "Thank you for that. Umm, let's say I will be by around 8:00 am. Is that too early for you?" he asks.

"No, that's not too early. Why would you ask that?"

"Honest? I have not seen you before 12:00 pm since we met that one time for coffee. You remember, our first date, yeah?"

"Haha. Funny man. But I can rise early just like you."
"Just like me, huh?"
"Yes, just like you."
"Good, then I'll actually be by about 7:00 am after I hit the gym, then we can grab a bite for breakfast before I have to check in," he says, then we say our goodbyes.

Oh great, me and my big mouth; I better go back to bed now so I can get up and be ready. So much for me taking on the world tonight.

CHAPTER 64
ALL QUIET ON THE SET

What does one wear as a visitor on set? I'm making it a jeans day. Jeans, a nice top and flats; oh yeah, and a cardigan, because I don't want to freeze in the air conditioning. Hair? Definitely down; hair down and make up on. I told him I would leave the door unlocked for him this morning and here he is, sitting in my front room having a cup of coffee, waiting for me.

Boy, someone is a little excited today. He sure jumped up from the sofa pretty quick when I walked into the room. Nice, he's wearing jeans, too. Good, I made the right choice.

"Hiya," I say as I walk into the living room, "ready to go?"

"Hey, Lovely, yep, ready. You ready then?" he asks, looking like he wants to make some kind of joke but doesn't.

He's moving in for his kiss hello. All manners. *Kiss, kiss*, one cheek, two cheeks. Man, smelling him is such a huge turn on for me. Thank goodness he has some place to be this morning or we could get distracted from leaving the house; well, I could, anyway. I think I could just rip his clothes off and have my way with him about now and forget that I'm a lady. I sneak a good look at him. Yep, it's a really, really good thing that he has some place to be.

He's holding my hand, riding in the car. He's never done that before. It's weird for me but I like it.

Breakfast was quick enough. He still has plenty of time before his call time, but he is so eager to get there. Give your name at the gate. It checks out. He's really hired because they actually let us in. He joked about that, but I can tell he's relieved that they actually opened that gate for him. He's like a little kid today. It's nice to share this with him. I'm glad he asked me.

The set is huge. This is the coolest thing I've ever seen. I get to watch the entire process, front and center. Make up, going over lines, making changes, and acting his scenes. He's good at acting, too. What can't he do? I think I'm beginning to be a little intimidated by him. By all of this.

I can't wait to see the finished product. I'm definitely watching this series when the network picks it up.

He's not going to live that make-up thing down anytime soon, though. Maybe next time we go out, I'll ask him if he wants to borrow my lipstick.

Boy, I crack myself up.

I'm sitting alone, laughing at myself, and a few people give me some weird looks. Oops. I make sure to stay quiet the rest of the time I'm here.

Hey look, they have stars I've seen before working on the show, too. That's Nvette Reed. This is so cool. I've seen her in so many movies and shows, I can't believe that's her. So he gets to intermingle with a few of the who's who. Good for him.

Oi, hey now, don't be flirting with my man, Ms. Nvette. I don't care how much of a big shot of an actress you think you are, I say to myself as I sit up in my seat, watching that actress pour it on when speaking with Andrew. Good thing he's not giving any of it back or I might have to be escorted out by security. She really needs to cut out all of that extra chit chat.

I just sit there watching everything with my arms folded, holding back a little attitude.

He pays her no mind and comes to sit next to me whenever he has a break in his scenes.

This is exciting and I am happy for him, but it looks like hard work and I don't know how he could possibly do both jobs. I don't say anything though. He's really enjoying the moment, and I don't want to mess that up for him.

It's been a long day here. He broke for lunch and now they're breaking for dinner but he's leaving. His contract says he's gotta be done for his other job as DJ SuperFly.

He's afraid that he doesn't have time to drop me home before he's due at the club. He asked me if I wouldn't mind dropping him at the club and then I could drive his car to my house. He has spare car keys and will just walk over when he's done to drive himself home, so I don't have to come out so late for him. I think I will anyway. It's the least I can do since he has been taking care of me so well after work lately

CHAPTER 65

ARE YOU SURE YOU'RE NOT A STALKER?

I woke up this morning to find the Englishman's car gone from my driveway. What happened? Why didn't I wake up to meet him? It must be the sound of the rain on my window again. Bugger! I wanted to surprise him. Well, he will be back at the set by now this morning and then he's at the club for the night again tonight, so I won't see him or probably speak to him before then. I missed talking to him last night. I should do something for him, but what? I know. I'll bring him supper. He didn't have time to eat before he left the set yesterday. I know he worked all night and will be working the same for today. I don't want him to get run down because he's not taking care of himself, working so hard.

I can't believe it's still raining. I'm so tired of saying that. I guess that just means I'm driving myself to work today. Do I have everything? Jacket, workbag, the Englishman's supper. Right, I'm good.

As I wait for the garage door to open to pull out, I think about how I haven't driven my car since the weather broke before summer.

Wait, is that Andrew standing there outside my garage in the rain? It is. What is he doing here? Extreme stalker. I've got to pull back into the garage to let him in without getting everything super wet.

He opens my passenger door and I say, "Hey, what are you doing here? I thought you'd still be at the set."

"No, I finished earlier than yesterday and wanted to get here because I thought you'd be walking in and I wanted to walk with you."

"Why didn't you call?"

"I don't know. I just thought it would work out."

"Look at you, you're soaked. How long have you been waiting out here?"

"Not long really, I just got here a minute before you began to pull out. I walked from the gym."

"So where is your car? At the gym then? Did you want me to run you by there before we go to the club?"

"No, I'm alright. It's supposed to stop raining by tonight. I'll just walk to the gym from your house."

"Are you sure? We can go by now or go by after the club. Either way it's no problem, really."

"No. It's okay. I'll just get it later, yeah?" he insists.

"Okay, but I still can't believe you didn't at least knock on my door."

"I know. I wasn't sure if I should. You didn't know that I was coming and..."

"That's a bullshit excuse!" I say cutting him off. "There

is no good enough reason for you not to have knocked. Standing outside like this, you're totally soaked. Not knocking or calling doesn't make any sense to me."

"I'm not that bad. Really, I'm good. Ready to leave? I think we need to go so we're not late though," he says.

He's acting really strange. I wonder if it had something to do with the set today.

"Okay, okay. You're sure you don't want to dry off? I could get a towel," I offer.

"No thanks, I'm good. Would you like me to drive?" he asks, changing the subject.

"No, thank you, I will drive you today, so sit back and relax, Englishman. You've been working hard these past couple of days. I'll do something to take care of you for a change. I even made you supper."

"You made me supper?" he says. This seems to light him up a little. "Brilliant, I'm starved," he admits.

"Good, I'll set you up in the office when we get to the club and you can then dry off, too — we have towels in the office bathroom."

CHAPTER 66

THE ENGLISHMAN

Can she tell that I've had a really bad day? She doesn't let on if she can. They wrote in a kissing scene in today's schedule. Only one scene that needed to be shot today and I kept mucking it up.

That damn kissing scene. It felt so uncomfortable. Maybe if I had time to prepare for it, or if I knew it was coming. It messed my entire day up. I wanted to leave to hang with Samantha so bad; it was that painful. Going to the gym was the best way I knew to get rid of most of my frustrations from the ruddy mess that happened on set.

I was planning to tell her when I saw her but, damn, she looks so good today it was just everything I could do not to make a move on her. I wouldn't have been able to control myself if I stayed at her house another minute.

She is so damn good for me. It was really good to see her light up when she saw me standing there. I wasn't sure how she would respond to seeing me, since I just showed up unannounced. I didn't want her to think I was coming on too strong, rushing her again. I'm surprised she didn't call me a stalker like she did before when she found me outside waiting for her to leave.

I just wanted to grab her, hold onto her, and just let the rest of the troubles from the day melt away.

I can't believe she made me supper tonight. That means that she's really thinking about me when I'm not around. That's good. She set me up as I got dried off, then left me to my thoughts. I think she *has* noticed that I've had a bad day.

Everything looks great. Chicken salad sandwich on whole wheat bread, green grapes, crisps, and a small mixed greens salad. Perfect. All I need now is a coffee.

"Here ya go, Englishman, I got you a Coke to go with your supper," she says right on cue. Coke is close enough.

Damn, she is good for me.

CHAPTER 67
WHAT IS UP WITH THAT?

He really seems out of sorts today. I can tell something is on his mind, but I don't want to bug him about it. He'll let me know if he wants to talk about it. Maybe it's the long hours he's been keeping that are finally catching up with him.

I can't believe how quick he was to rush me into work today. What was that all about? I cant help but wonder what the deal really is. He could've easily come in on his own if he really wanted to get here.

He looks worn out; the poor hard-working thing. Well, it's Saturday tomorrow and he doesn't have to be on set or at a photo-shoot or anything like that, so I'm going to *insist* that he gets some rest before he comes in tomorrow night.

"Hey, love." *Kiss, kiss* one cheek, two cheeks. He says when he walks out of the office, "Supper was just what I needed. Thank you again." A third kiss on the forehead and it's off to his booth. He does seem a little better; maybe he just needed to stop moving for a moment.

The crowd is nice for Friday night despite the rain and he's doing his thing again. Tired or not, we have a great DJ. When I look at him tonight, he looks as if he's miles and miles away. I wonder again what's on his mind.

CHAPTER 68

THAT SCENE

Another great night for the club comes to an end. Yep, he's a great addition; I still won't willingly tell the fellas that they were right, though. They don't need me to say it.

Stix is starting to do his thing, too. But I can still tell the difference when the Englishman gets off the turntables.

When the night is over, we all sit around having our drinks, talking about the day. Jonathan announces that he's taking a holiday with Lydia towards the end of the year, and will need his shifts covered. That would mean me. That would mean working the dreaded Ladies' Night *AND* my Wednesday night off. Ugh! At least he gave me a warning this time. *I need to start taking more vacations.*

His vacation announcement makes me ready to go home.

Since I drove, I offered to run Mr. DJ by the gym again to get his car but, because the rain had stopped, he said he would rather walk. So, the plan is I would drive him to my place and he would get out there to walk to his car. Walking is good for him, he said, because he had something on his mind he wants to sort through. No shit he has something on his mind.

If I knew which gym he went to, I would just take him anyway. But there are too many around for me to try to guess.

He was very quiet on the ride to my house and just as I pull into the garage, he blurts out that he had a serious kissing scene today.

"I had a character-changing kissing scene on set today," he confesses.

"Really? How was that, then?" I ask as casually as I can.

How does he expect me to respond to this 'I was kissing someone else today' information? *How was it?* was the best I could come up with.

"I had no idea that I would be going into that today. It threw me out of sorts. It was written at the last minute, they said, and I felt really uncomfortable the entire time. Because of that, we had to do so many bloody retakes. I had one scene, and it took three hours to get through it," he says.

"That's why you're upset today?" I ask him.

"Right. You could tell I was upset?" He turns and looks at me.

"Uh, yeah. You hardly spoke when I first saw you this afternoon, and you looked as if your thoughts were miles away tonight at work." Then I add, "But I don't get it. You want to be an actor, right? They do scenes like that all the time, even actors that are married. Why is this bothering you so much?"

"It bothers me because of how it happened," he

says. "I had no notice, no warning. I sense an ulterior motive in it somehow, and I'm not comfortable with the lot of it. Because of this, of course it ended up being the longest scene of my life. Honestly, too, it felt uncomfortable partly because I am beginning a relationship with you, and I was not sure how this kissing scene would affect things once you found out. I'm just thankful that you weren't there on set today watching. I would've never gotten through it if you were. I'm certain that the co-actress manipulated the producers somehow to get the scene changed like that. She has been a little forward with me and there was something in her attitude today that I couldn't shake off. She was all over me, and she seemed to really enjoy the director making me kiss her over and over again." He stops mid-thought and I allow him to take the moment, then he continues. "I wasn't sure how exactly to tell you. I worried about that the most, believe it or not. Telling you. To add to that, they decided to give my character more of a lead starring with her and it all jumps off from this bloody kissing scene," he says.

"Wow, that's a lot. First, your character is more important? That's great! Congratulations on that. But listen, if you're an actor, you're an actor full stop, right? That includes doing love scenes and doing them with people you may or may not like," I say as I make a face. "I get that, so I would expect something to come up eventually. You make for a great leading man. Granted, it is very early for us for a scene like that, but as far as I can tell it was just an acting scene to you. It meant nothing otherwise, so I'm cool with you having to do your job. I think you worried about me for nothing. I'm not that possessive."

"Well, this is all new for me," he says with small hand gestures, and I get the feeling he's talking about being in a relationship, not acting. I'm not sure and I don't ask.

But I do say, "I will, however, have to kick that actress' ass if she manipulates the scene with my man like that again. I did see her flirting with you before you guys got started yesterday. *She's* the one who's lucky I wasn't there today, not you," I say a little more forcefully than I meant to, which was enough to make him laugh.

That's good, right? I made him laugh a little. Lightened his mood a bit. I still don't get why that scene bothered him like that. I can't help but think there is more to the story. Like there is something he's not telling me about that chick.

It seems like he feels a little better now, since he told me, but he's still going to walk to his car to shake what's left about it off his mind, he said. What he doesn't really know is I actually *will* kick that heffa's ass if she keeps up flirting with him. I will need to keep an eye on her, I see.

"You sure you don't want me to drive you to your car?" I ask one last time as we stand in the garage.

"No, no. You're home now and I want you to stay. I really do need to walk so I can finish getting the muck of the morning out of my head," he says, heading on his way.

"Alright then. Just do me one favor?" I ask.

"What's that, love?" He turns to face me and walks back towards me.

"Get some rest tomorrow. I'm afraid you're going to run yourself down working so much." I try to look serious.

"Oh, so *now* you're my nan, huh?" he asks, laughing a little.

"No, smart ass, I'm not your nanny. It's just that you really have been doing a lot," I say with a pout.

"I'll get rest. No worries, love. Will talk to you later, yeah? Cheers," he says.

Kiss on the forehead again and he's gone down the drive. Just like that.

Then I hear him say, as he turns walking backwards looking at me, "Oi, don't think I didn't notice that you called me your man…" He gives that crooked grin, turns and continues on his way.

Oh, just great. Won't be living that down, I see. I notice myself smiling as I close the garage door.

CHAPTER 69

THIS IS VERY UNEXPECTED

As I was getting ready to go to bed, it seemed like less than ten minutes after Andrew left, the skies opened up again and let us have it. I think to myself, *I hope the Englishman made it to his car without getting soaked too badly.*

About ten minutes after that, I hear, *knock, knock, knock*. Is that someone at my door this late? It's Andrew. He got soaked, poor thing. I guess he didn't make it to his car in time after all.

As I open the door, I say, "Oh, look at you. You're soaked again! You didn't get far, eh?" I can't help but laugh.

"No, not far. But I knocked this time since you fussed at me earlier when I didn't," he says with a half-smile. "I'll take that ride now, if you please."

"Hold on, let me get you a towel first. You need to dry off a little. You stay right there; I don't want you tracking water all over. I'll put the kettle on, too, if you'd like; make you a cuppa before I take you."

"Yep, sounds good. It's been one hell of a day. I'm beat up from it. I'd rather have a stiff drink, though," he says. I try to act like I'm ignoring him about that last request, but I've got him covered.

Kettle on. Check. Bottle of brandy on the counter. Check. Biggest towel I own. Check.

"Okay, here's your towel."

"Thanks, love."

He's taking off his shoes. I look at all of the water in them still and shake my head.

"It must have really been coming down out there," I say as he tries to dry himself.

"Yep, cats and dogs."

"Here, I'll help you. Give me your jacket," I offer.

His shirt and pants are clinging to him, soaked through. He needed to take something off or he'd never get dry, and if I get any closer to him I'm going to end up soaked, too.

"I think I need to take these off. Can I use your dryer for a bit before we go?" he asks, not waiting for a response.

Oh my God, oh my God, oh my. He's undoing the button on his pants, untucking and taking his shirt off; every single muscle of his is glistening against the light. He is beautiful in every way.

I take a deep breath. I tell myself, *just look away, look away girl*. But I can't. He looks too damn good, and I end up stepping closer to him instead.

"Here, let me help you with the towel. I'll dry off your back for you if you turn around." I just can't help myself.

He turns as instructed. I let my hands move across his shoulders, barely touching him with the towel. As

I get even closer, the smell of him just takes me over again and the next thing I realize, I'm behind him with my arms wrapped around the front of his chest, laying my head on his shoulder. He turns around to face me without really moving me away and kisses me.

Feeling his bare skin is more than I can handle. I know I won't be able to control myself tonight. I want him so badly. The front of me is getting wet now and I don't care. He pulls me in even closer; I feel the difference in how he's kissing me and know that he wants me, too.

He has one hand holding the back of my head as he begins to kiss my neck, moving towards my chest, kissing me slowly everywhere. He slips my robe off my left shoulder, which exposes me a little, and he moves towards my breast. He lifts me up as I wrap one leg around him. Somehow, his other hand has made its way underneath my robe and I feel his fingers holding me into place. I lean my head back slightly, arching my back, enjoying the pleasure of his lips on my skin. Then I realize I can't. I cannot do this. In a panic, I attempt to pull away.

"Wait, wait, wait. Stop. We can't do this. Not now," I say, breathing a little heavy as I'm trying to push myself completely away from him.

He still holds me though, not letting go so easily. "I don't understand. Why are you pulling back?" he asks, looking a little hurt.

"I can't be with you tonight, we don't have any..." I pause, looking for the right words, but only come up with, "I practice safe sex," sounding a little embarrassed.

Okay, I'm very embarrassed. I feel myself get really red. He looks at me and puts on this sheepish little grin and he begins to kiss my neck again as he pulls me back in, closer.

"Condoms. That's it? That's the only reason you're pulling away?" he asks, almost in a whisper, paying my panic no mind.

"Yes. That's a big reason," I say in protest, still trying to stay in control as he kisses me.

"I have condoms here," he says.

"What?! You do?! Where?!" I try to pull back again, to get a look at him, but he's still focused on the kisses.

"In the gym bag I asked to keep here before."

That sneaky ass bastard! I knew it was suspect that he would ask to leave his bag here and just forget about it. Cheeky bugger! I should just kick his ass for that and send him on his way.

"You plotted to have condoms here?!" I ask, shocked. Accusing.

He looks at me again and says, "Looking back, I know it sounds bad, but I wanted to be ready when you were ready. We've never been to my place, and I didn't think it proper to ask if I could keep a box here just in case you wanted to shag me." Then he flashes that crooked grin at me again.

"You *are* a sneaky bastard," I tell him, as I get free and start to walk away.

He grabs hold of my hand and gently pulls me back

to him as he says, "Samantha, come here."

He holds me close again.

He begins to whisper in my ear. "I want to be with you..." Then he begins to kiss me again. *Kiss, kiss...* "And from what I can tell, you want to be with me, too..." *Kiss, kiss, kiss...* "And you did admit earlier that I am your man now..." *Kiss, kiss...* "So I fail to see what the problem is..." *Kiss, kiss, kiss...*

That was it; I couldn't fight him anymore. I help him finish unbuttoning his pants as they drop to the floor. He slips off my robe completely as he lifts me up again. I wrap both my legs around him, and he carries me into the bedroom.

He lays me down gently on the bed and leaves the room for a moment. I sit up, wondering *what in the heck?* When he returns, I see the outline of a small box in the darkness. The plotted condoms. Of course.

He places the now opened box on the little table next to the bed and comes and stands over me. I put my hands on his waist and wriggle my fingers of one hand into his waistband. I attempt to pull him near. Instead, he takes my other hand and pulls me up to stand directly in front of him. He looks at me. All of me. Taking me in, and I can feel the desire build as he does. I see the lust in his eyes. He lets out a slight breath and then places his hand on the back of my head, grabbing me gently, and pulls me in for a long, hard kiss.

I feel his hand moving across my body. When he touches me, I let out a little moan to show my approval. He lays me on the bed again and kneels over me. I wrap my arms around his shoulders, pulling him in closer as we kiss. After a moment, he removes my arms from around him and places them above my head, holding both wrists with one hand. He goes back to kissing me all over and I can't help but arch my back again when he does. I get lost in the moment of things. I get lost in his kisses. I get lost in his touch and after another moment, he grabs my hips, pulling me closer to him while he shifts his hips to get closer to me and begins to make love to me like no other man.

It feels good to finally give in a little with him and not act on guard all of the time. Being with Andrew was everything I could have imagined. Everything.

CHAPTER 70

GOT IT THAT BAD ALREADY

Saturday morning and the sun is shining. I look over to see Andrew still asleep. *After last night, there is no way I can go back to taking it slow*, I tell myself. I'm all in. I can't imagine how I went about keeping him at bay this long. He's got me really hooked, but I'm going to keep that a secret a little bit longer. Can't have him thinking I'm this easily whipped.

I go to get out of bed, but he secretly has hold of my arm. I didn't realize he was already awake.

He turns and looks at me, then smiles. "Hey, lovely, where do you think you're sneaking off to?" he asks in his morning voice as he rolls over more to face me.

"Oh, hey, good morning. I wasn't trying to wake you. I was just going to go turn the kettle on and maybe make us some food," I say.

"Do that later. I need you to stay here with me for a bit more, please." He pretends to beg, and it works. I lay back down beside him.

He pulls me near and wraps his arms around me. He kisses me on the shoulder and then on the neck. It's getting heated and I'm melting all over again. Yeah, I've got it that bad for him already.

CHAPTER 71

LEISURE TIME

Spending the morning with the Englishman was quite nice. We had a big breakfast together. I could see that he no longer let what happened on the set yesterday bother him.

We talked, we laughed, and we acted like we've always had this little morning routine together; it was nice. I'm happy. I didn't realize how much I needed his love and romance as part of my life.

He held me near while he read the paper, sitting on the sofa as we continued to lounge around. At least I know he's taking it easy like I instructed.

"Samantha, it says here that a couple of clubs and bars have been robbed at gunpoint during their business hours lately. The robbers simply walk up to the bartender, demand the cash in the registers with their weapons, and then vanish into the crowd. Although the businesses were packed with customers, the robbers acted so quickly no one knew what was happening until they had disappeared with the cash. Have you heard anything about this?" he asks as he puts the paper down to look at me.

"No. This is the first time. That's really scary," I say,

thinking how big of a target we could be.

"Right. I'm worried that your club could be on the robbers' list soon and the police have no leads," he explains.

"Wow, that could be a problem for sure, considering how busy the club has been lately. I'm going to talk to the fellas about installing some type of video surveillance. Definitely. I'm thinking that we should have something that won't put the staff in any danger by having to push a police call button. I want it just to record so it can be used to identify anyone who might come in to do that."

"Just do it straight away, it makes the most sense," he agrees. "Don't wait for a meeting with the fellas, they'll see it makes sense, too," he adds.

"Yeah, okay, I'll see about having it done early Monday. It's too late for this weekend. I'll put everyone on alert, though, in the meantime."

"Do me a favor, too — try not to help out as much behind the bar until this is sorted," he says as he tucks a piece of hair behind my ear, caressing my cheek.

"Really? Why?"

"I just don't want you to be placed in a position where you feel like you need to do something if these guys show up this weekend," he says in a tone that tells me that he simply wants me to listen to what he's asked and that's that.

Okay, Englishman, I'll listen. No behind the bar this weekend. Got it.

So now it's back to reality. We begin to get ready for

the rest of the night. We find his clothes still soaking wet, piled on the floor near the door, so he just puts on the gym clothes he had in his plot bag. I drop him off at his gym for a quick workout and to get his car. He'll be by later to ride with me to work, he says.

When I get back home, I put his clothes in the dryer and call Lizzie to officially admit that I am sprung. She'll never let me live it down, I know, but I don't care, I'm pretty damn happy about it.

CHAPTER 72

GIRLS' NIGHT IN

Lizzie knew it was gonna happen sooner than later. She could tell that I really liked him even though I was trying to deny it, and she knew that I wouldn't be able to fight off my feelings for much longer. She always just knows every damn thing. I tell her it's no good being friends with someone like that. She just laughs at me.

"I don't know why you tried acting all cool, calm and collected. You know you wanted to rip his freaking clothes off from day one," she tells me.

She's *not* even a little bit funny, I don't care how much of what she says is true.

"Why don't you come over to my house tonight after the club? We haven't had a girls' sleepover in f-o-r-e-v-e-r. Pack a little bag and tell your Englishman he'll see you tomorrow. He's got you now, so no worries, you're not going anywhere."

"What? Why do you want me to stay over tonight all of a sudden?"

"You being in love is depressing me and I want someone to eat ice cream with and talk shit about boys to."

"You're crazy," I say.

"You're only calling me crazy 'cause now you got a man."

"That's not true."

"Then come over after the club," she begs a little.

"Alright, stop whining, but he's gonna miss me, you know. He might have to talk to me for hours while you're asleep."

"Oh, I hate you and I hate your new man, too."

"Hater, hater," I say, singing a little. "I've got to go. I'll call you when I'm leaving the club."

"Don't forget me," she says. "Bye."

CHAPTER 73
GETTING BACK TO BUSINESS

My door is unlocked for Andrew when he arrives. His clothes from last night and my bag for Lizzie's are at the door.

"Hey, love. What's this then? Is this your plot bag for my place?" he asks with a grin.

"Oh, umm, no...sorry. I'm going to Lizzie's tonight after work. It's last minute. We're going to have a girly sleepover to talk about boys; you're included in that, by the way — the talking about part, that is."

The grin disappears. "Oh. One night with you is all I get then?" he asks, looking a little dejected.

"No, of course not. You have many, many nights ahead with me if you want them," I say as I walk over to him and give him a kiss.

He looks a little too serious now. I can't guess what he's thinking about, but I'll tell him later how I'll make it up to him— that should cheer his mood up *and* give him a little something to think about while he's alone.

"So should I drive since I'm going to Lizzie's, or do you want to still chauffeur me around everywhere?" I ask.

"What would you like me to do?" he asks.

"I want you to drive me, of course. That means you'll need to pick me up tomorrow, too. Are you free?"

"Yep. For you, of course I am."

Good answer. He's such a good sport. I might have thrown a little temper tantrum if he said that he didn't want to spend tonight with me after how we spent last night. I definitely have to make this up to him.

I'm a little worried about going in to work today. That article about the robbers really has me concerned. I hope Jonathan and Gabe see the importance of installing the cameras. Luckily, I was able to sort out a company to come first thing Monday morning already.

When Andrew and I tell Jonathan and Gabe about the thefts, they both agree that the security appointment stands. The three of us make plans to be there so we can be taught how everything works. The fellas want cameras installed at all of the public locations, though. Just installing cameras at the bar is not enough, which totally makes sense to me.

I ask Andrew if he wanted to attend the demo Monday. He's due back to the set then, he reminds me, so he won't be around until the afternoon. He tells me I can call, just in case I need him. That's a good thing; I don't think Gabe is ready for a full-on launch of Andrew and me just yet. I don't know why I asked him to come. I know not having Andrew around works out in more ways than one.

I know another thing, too: that chick on set better not try any more shit now that he's officially my man now, I know that much is certain.

CHAPTER 74

THE RAIN IS GONE

Another beautiful night; the rain seems to be done with us and the crowd is thick again. Our guest DJ winner is in the booth having a blast. I have Gabe and Jonathan stationed at the ends of the bar all night to stop anyone from being able to just walk behind there, robbing us. I'll have Gabe ask another couple of bouncers to come in tomorrow for the posts since Jonathan is off.

I notice mixed in with other songs throughout the night, the same line from the song *Stay*. He *is* sending me messages through the music. I knew it.

...All I need is you
Why don't you just stay with me
Stay with me...

When I hear it again, I look up at the booth and he puts his head down like he's really working on something, but I know better.

CHAPTER 75

EVERYONE IS HAPPY NOW

We're getting through the night without incident. I notice that I have a voicemail from Lizzie. I can't believe it when I check it. She canceled our girly night but didn't say why. After all of that junk talk. She needs to do better than that after giving me all of that whining to come over earlier. So I call her.

"Lizzie, what the hell?! Why did you cancel on me?!" I demand when she finally answers.

"Sammy, you'll never guess who's back in town. Guess who's moved back and called me to meet him for dinner, and it had to be *tonight*, he said, that he didn't want to wait?"

"What? What are you talking about? Oh wait, it's not Brian is it? Brian moved back to town?" I ask.

Yep, that's the ex-boyfriend. The love of her life, as she puts it, and now he's back, it seems.

"Yes, Sammy. I mean, you know we've been in touch a little since he left and he talked about coming back before. I thought it was just talk, though. He always said something was missing; he just couldn't get it together out there the way that he wanted to. I didn't want to get my hopes up about him coming back, so I would always just change the subject when he'd try to bring it up," she says, and then she goes quiet for a moment. I imagine her thinking about the time when he left and how it almost broke her in half.

She continues, "You know how long it took me to get over him when he left?" she asks, more to herself.

If she *really* had asked me, I'd say that she never did get over him, but that's probably exactly why she didn't.

"He said over the phone that he wanted to go over an idea for a change that could benefit both of us, but we had to meet tonight," she says, super excited.

"What the hell does that mean? Why do guys talk in riddles? Just say what you freakin' mean," I say, complaining.

"He moved back for me, Sam. He explained during dinner that he was crushed when I didn't ask to move with him. He said he didn't ask *me* because he didn't want me to leave a career that I worked so hard for and after he moved, he didn't want to be there anymore without me. YAY! I'm so happy right now. We both get our guy!" she says, sounding like she's jumping up and down.

I smile really big at that image and then say, "Oh my God, Lizzie, that's so great. Congratulations! I'm so happy for you; tell him if he hurts you like that again I'm gonna kill him."

"Shit, you tell him that message yourself. He needs to hear that from you directly 'cause you're the crazy one. Having you tell him, he just may believe it to be true," she says, laughing still. "Hey, maybe we all could do a double date. Like in high school, how stupid would that be?" she says, all giddy.

"Pretty stupid, Lizzie, 'cause in high school we both dated jerks. I don't want to do anything that reminds me of those times."

"You're the one who's being stupid now. You know what I meant. Listen, I've got to go. I've been in the bathroom for like ten minutes talking with you. He might start to think that I changed my mind about him and maybe I escaped out the back window."

"Okay, Lizzie, go back to your man, girl."

"Oh my God! I can't believe he came back for me, Sammy."

"Tell Brian I said hello when you come up for air. Bye, talk to you later."

With that, we hang up.

That was totally unexpected; Brian's back. Good on him, he should never have left without her. He knew Lizzie was the best damn thing he ever had. Coming back for her was the smartest thing he could've done. Boys can be so dumb sometimes, I swear.

Wait until I tell the fellas the news.

CHAPTER 76
CHANGE OF PLANS

Before I can tell anyone about Brian and Lizzie, the Englishman catches up with me.

"Hey, love, Gabe and Jonathan said that they were going to go over a way to install a large one-way safe at the bar to maybe help deter any other ideas of stealing."

"Did they need me to do anything?" I ask, trying to help stay on top of this threat.

"No, I don't think so. I told them you had made plans with Lizzie for after work tonight, so they know you won't be around."

"Oh, okay, um thanks. By the way, I just found out…" But before I could finish what I was about to say, the Englishman interrupts and says, "You know, Samantha, I had plans for us tonight before you told me about you going to Lizzie's," looking at me expectantly.

I don't respond yet because I'm still stuck mid-sentence, mouth open, taken aback about being cut off.

"I said I had plans for us, you know?" he repeats when I don't respond right away.

I decide not to give him a hard time, so instead I say teasingly, "Really? I can't imagine. What kind of plans? Stalker plans? Plot plans?"

"No, seriously. You making other plans like that really caught me off guard and bothered me."

"I didn't mean to bother you, you should've said."

"I am saying. Right now," he says matter-of-factly.

Okay, I can't help it now. He's giving me no choice but to call him out on this behavior. So I start with asking, "Why are you taking this so personal? It was not about you. I am a big girl, you know. I don't need your permission, and I definitely don't need someone who wants to control me."

He looks at me as if he can't understand what I'm saying. "That's your take on what I've said, really? You are a big girl, yes, but maybe you misunderstand how it works when someone is interested in sharing their time with you." He pauses and takes a deep breath before he continues. "Listen, this is new to me, being the chaser. And I'm not saying that you need my permission on anything. I'm definitely NOT trying to control you or dominate your time, even. It's that I would like a little more grace from you if we're going to really give being together a try. When I left this afternoon, there was no impression that we weren't going to be together tonight. You had time to call me before I came to pick you up and you didn't. I don't want to feel as if I have expectations of spending time with you that I shouldn't have, because that's what it felt like. I have no problem with you having other plans without me, trust this. In fact, I think it's important for you to do so. I only expect that you see *me* as just as important in the full scheme of things," he says as he looks at me with his serious face still.

Wow, what do you say back to that? I get it, I guess. But he doesn't need to give me this little lecture. After a short moment, I simply say, "I apologize." I look at him a little defiantly. "I didn't mean for you to feel that way. It was just as unexpected for me when she asked me to come over. She's my oldest friend and I didn't want to ditch her as soon as I found myself in a *relationship*. But you're right, I could've called you before you came to get me," I say, just as serious.

We stand there for a moment, eyeing each other. I keep thinking about what he just said and then I realize that I admitted to being in a relationship out loud. That sidetracks me. I'm in a relationship now, with Andrew, already. Wow. So yeah, I guess he has a point. When he left this afternoon, I thought we'd be together tonight, too.

I don't want him to be salty over this, so I decide to lighten the conversation by saying, "I promise to make it up to you when you least expect it." Giving him my sexiest smile.

He sighs, grabs my hand, pulls me near enough to kiss me on the forehead, and says, "It's alright, love, it's sorted now. But it had to be said because I really like you and I guess I just want you to be keen on me, too, yeah? Are you ready to go then?" he asks as he turns towards the door, still holding my hand.

"Yeah, about that. Umm, Lizzie canceled on me," I confess as I pull back a little.

"Oh, and what does that mean then?" he asks as he turns back, looking at me with that crooked grin of his.

"Well, I'm free to go with your plans if you still want me to," I say sheepishly.

To this, he just winks and says, "My plans it is then."

He doesn't take me home. Instead, we arrive at his place since I already had a bag packed, he said. I guess he doesn't understand that a bag packed for Lizzie's and a bag packed for his place are two totally different bags.

Good thing I came prepared just in case I didn't make it to her house.

His place is great. It's nothing like I imagined it would be, it's so much better. He lets me in and stands at the doorway as he watches me walk around. I think he got that move from me when I watched him look at my pictures and paintings.

His decor is very eclectic, very worldly, a good mix. I try to take it all in. His great taste is evident in the things he uses to furnish his place. He has a classic Englishman's style leather couch and it's nice and big. He has a dining table, which somehow caught me off guard. There are French doors that look as if they lead to a terrace. This is definitely not the typical bachelor's pad I had expected. I guess I pictured seeing milk crates as furniture and nothing much else.

I continue to take it all in. I'm not surprised, however, to see that there's no T.V. in his living room, but I am surprised to see that there's a piano; that's sexy.

"Do you play?" I ask, turning to look at him.

"Yeah," is all he barely says with a slight smile.

Okay, that's not too convincing. I wonder about his half response but don't ask.

He has a great stereo with an old turntable, tons of LP albums and CDs. There are a lot of books and he has a few great pieces of artwork on his walls, too. Nothing here is a surprise to me if I really stop and think about it.

As I slowly look around at each piece of art, I notice one small section of wall with nothing on it. It's completely bare and it looks out of place. He starts to walk towards me when I notice it.

"I have that space cleared for you; I noticed all of the pieces at your place were signed by you. All of those paintings are yours. I would love for you to create something for me," he says as he wraps his arms around my waist from behind.

"How did you notice that?" I say, completely off guard.

"Right, well, I saw your signature on my contract and recognized it on your paintings and then Lizzie told me that you were into art and that you painted often when she helped me with the clues for the date night."

I turn my head slightly to look at him.

"I know it's no secret that I called her about you before our date," he says, now kissing the side of my neck, pulling me in closer.

"Wow, you're full of surprises, aren't you? Always catching me off guard," I say. Then he turns me to face him and I place my arms around his shoulders. We begin to kiss and I wrap my legs around him again as he lifts me, but this time we don't make it to the bedroom.

He's got me — hook, line, and sinker.

CHAPTER 77

YOUR TURF

Sunday morning. I'm unprepared for how comfortable I am already at waking up next to him in his bed. It's as if I've been there so many times before. It almost feels like home. That makes me feel a little uncomfortable. I like that we've started a relationship but I've got to slow down. I roll over to see him awake, reading. He puts a big smile on his face as he turns to look at me.

"What? Why are you smiling at me like that?" I ask him.

"I'm smiling because you're finally here, at my place. It took you long enough to come around," he says, smiling even harder at me, playing with my hair.

"Seriously? That's all you got? It took me long enough to come around?"

He says, "Hmm," and pretends to think. "Well, yeah, that's it," he says with a kiss.

This makes me laugh, and it makes me realize that I couldn't imagine spending my Sunday any other way today.

We walked hand in hand around his neighborhood. We had a late breakfast at a local cafe and walked through the farmers / flea market. We brought back some fresh fruit, a loaf of French bread, some nice cheeses, and he even included a bouquet of flowers just for me.

    And we made love; again.

Damn, it does feel good to let go, so why can't I accept what we're starting as good? Why do I still have in the back of my head that I am moving too fast? Why am I telling myself to slow it down? Am I so independent that I can't have a good man in my life? What is wrong with me? In the back of my mind, I am afraid of everything to do with us. I can't explain it. He's always so certain about how *he* feels about us and that scares me, too. Is it because I refuse to be happy? Maybe it's just because I do want him to be my everything, and being so used to being on my own, I'm still really afraid of what being hurt by him would do to me.

    I have some issues to work out, I know.

    We took our time heading back to my place so I could get ready for work; then, off to the club.

I love watching him. Everything he does just reels me in. The sound of his voice, the way he walks into the room, looking at the muscles in his arm as he holds the door open for me, how his shirt hangs from his shoulders, the way he wears his headphones when he's in the booth, the way he holds his head off to the side a little when he's looking at me being playful, and I especially like the way his expression is a little devious when he whispers in my ear as he passes by at work. I just want to spend every moment with him.

We are together all of the time now; one day just blends into the other. We become almost inseparable. He's shown me that he's not interested in doing anything to hurt me like he said. Nevertheless, I know that I've still been holding back.

CHAPTER 78

IT'S OVER

The time is passing so quickly; the summer has changed to autumn, and that's almost over, too. Thankfully, it's almost a second summer with the unusually warmer weather so we still get to take advantage of enjoying the outdoors.

The club is still busy thanks to the changes with Andrew and Stix. They're both fantastic.

Life keeps us moving for sure. Andrew's schedule is as busy as ever. On our days off, the Englishman and I try to spend every moment we can with each other, even though he still has a lot going on. He tells me tonight that he wants to cook for me. He hasn't done that before. Cook for me. I get excited as I drive over to his place. Him being able to cook would just be the icing on the cake.

As I walk up to his door, the smells are deliciously making their way through, and I realize that I'm really hungry. Smelling good, that's definitely a good start. I knock, fifteen minutes early, of course, giving him some of his own medicine. He's at the door straight away.

"Hey, love, perfect timing, everything is ready. C'mon in," he says as he kisses me.

"Perfect timing, really?" I say, looking around.

"Yes, of course," he says with a little smile.

The French doors are open, taking advantage of the warm breeze from outside.

I get a look at the table and it's set up nice and fancy — for a dude.

Candles are lit. Salad is mixed. Wine is at the ready. So much for giving him his own medicine by arriving before our agreed time. I need to learn that if you're on time with Andrew, then you're actually late with Andrew.

"It smells delicious in here," I say as I start to take my jacket off.

"Thanks, love, I've made a chicken," he says as he takes my things and leads me to the table.

"You've been very busy, I see," I say as I gesture to the table. He laughs and kisses me again, then goes into the kitchen.

As he comes back, he says, "I've made for you herbed chicken, asparagus, and mixed greens." He then sets a beautiful plate of food with the chicken and vegetables in front of me. He pours me a glass of wine and gives one last kiss as he sits with his own plate.

We eat and drink and have a great laugh or two, as always. It was delicious, I must admit. As we finish, he tells me he would like to go out for dessert.

After dinner and cleaning up, we walked to another small club in his neighborhood. He said he wanted to show me where he got his first temporary job after moving to the States.

He also told me this is where he met my brother and Gabe, before the Vegas Nite thing.

He explained that the owner is from Italy; Lorenzo and his wife, Sofia, whom he happened to meet by chance one day walking back to his flat after having a bit of a rough day looking for a job. He says that he considers them very good friends now, but I wouldn't believe the story of the way they met if he just told me himself.

When we walked in, a very beautiful woman greeted us and obviously knew the Englishman; she was Sofia. She commented on how long it had been since he'd been there as they kissed on both cheeks like Europeans do. We chatted for a moment after he introduced us, then she directed us to the bar as we waited for a table. I excused myself to the restroom and when I returned, a man who I assumed to be Lorenzo was there talking with Andrew. Still hidden by the crowd, I was able to listen to their conversation a bit as I slowly walked up.

"I think I know your fidanzata, I've seen her before," says Lorenzo.

"Yeah? You think you know her? From where, mate?" asks the Englishman, curious.

"She is one of the owners of the club you work at now, right?"

"Yep, she is. You recognize her from seeing her just now? You've met then?" asks Andrew, sounding a little surprised. Then he adds, "She's sister to one of the mates that hired me."

"No, I don't know her. We've never met directly, but

I know who she is," admits Lorenzo.

"Yeah, who?" asks Andrew.

"There was a party a few years ago and they were there, the brothers and your date. A fellow was trying to show attention to her, but she wasn't interested, it seems, and told him no. He didn't take to that too well. It almost got ugly, but she handled herself, to put it mildly, and he learned his lesson for sure." He clears his throat. "She made a huge impression on everyone that night," he finishes.

"Right, so exactly what is it that you're trying to tell me with that story?" asks Andrew with a little laugh. "You're not really saying what you mean, I think. Go on, just say it then."

"Please understand, I'm not trying to speak badly about your date. I can see you really like her. She just seems a little, how should I put it? A little dangerous. I don't know. It's just that I want you to know what you are getting involved with, my friend, but at the same time, I don't want to mark your opinion about her either."

Andrew really laughs now. "Oh, right, I get what you mean. Dangerous, is she? I've heard all of the stories about that night already. I've even heard about the one where she lets the air out of tires or something like that." Still laughing. "No worries, mate, everything is good. I know exactly what I'm getting myself into. We seem to be a good match for each other, I think. I *like* the fact that she's a bit of a spitfire. She's not dangerous to me, at least not in that way. Now my heart, that may be a different story altogether," he says, still laughing at his own comments.

Lorenzo notices me then and says, as he gestures in my direction, "Well, she is a beautiful young lady. I am happy you found someone that suits you. I'm sure we all will be good friends."

Andrew turns then and sees me, too. He politely introduces me to Lorenzo, and I can't help but wonder if he doesn't like the idea of Andrew being with me at all, considering what I just overheard.

Things are awkward for me, but we three stay at the bar and talk a little. The entire time I can't help but wonder what Lorenzo is really thinking about me now. I want to bring up what I overheard, but don't. I can't believe he was there that night. I knew I would forevermore be 'that psycho chick,' but I had no idea someone already told Andrew what happened. It was Gabe, no doubt; I'm not surprised that he would say something. At least Andrew doesn't seem to mind that he's with the 'crazy' lady, surprisingly.

After a bit, Lorenzo leads us to a table labeled reserved just as it was finished being reset and leaves us alone.

We are seated close to the dance floor. We can see everything from where we are and the place is beautiful; I definitely get how this could easily become a favorite place to go.

There's a great band playing a funky slow style of jazzy house music. The Englishman said it was one of his favorite bands and wanted me to hear them. That was another reason why he brought me here tonight.

Their music is really nice. Just then, Lorenzo returned with a small cart and began to put together three dessert plates that already had small oval sugar tartlets on them. He began to mix together some sliced strawberries, dark red plums and blackberries into a glass bowl. He squeezed fresh lemon juice, added some fresh herbs, and sprinkled a little coarse sugar over the top. He mixed this together a bit and finally, drizzled in a small amount of brandy.

It smelled so good. I tried not to watch him the entire time because I still felt a little strange about what I overheard, but I was mesmerized by what he was doing. He placed the berry mixture over the tartlets and added a dollop of cream on the side with a few mint leaves. He served us and sat down with a plate for himself.

Before the conversations began again, Lorenzo unexpectedly turned to me and said that he wanted to apologize for having the wrong impression of me. I was caught off guard again; I didn't know what to say. He admitted to where he remembered seeing me from. Said that because of that night, he was really worried when I showed here with Andrew; but after actually talking with me, he has completely changed his mind about all of that. I looked at Andrew and he gave a little nod.

This was so unexpected but really appreciated. I respected him telling me this and I was able to relax. That definitely made a difference. I was enjoying getting to know Lorenzo now and enjoying getting to know a little more about Andrew, too.

Dessert was divine; the music was great and the conversation even better. Lorenzo and his wife moved from Italy, opened this place after a few years and have been living happily here ever since. He really was a nice guy, so I didn't hold on to what I heard at the bar. He was only looking out for his friend. I probably would have done the same.

"So, has Andrew told you the story of how he began here with us?" asks Lorenzo.

"No, actually the only thing he has said is that he worked his first real gig here when he moved to the States," I respond.

"It was quite by accident," Andrew says.

"Fate, I'd say — that was no accident," adds Lorenzo.

"So how did it happen?" I ask.

Lorenzo starts, "It was early one Friday night. I was outside the club on the phone in a fury. Our regular DJ had just called out for the night, and it was less than two hours until opening. I was in a complete panic."

"I was walking home after supper and heard him saying that the DJ booth had everything set up but there was no DJ, that it was the start of the weekend and he needed the DJ to come in and do his job," says Andrew.

"What?" I say. "You're kidding, right?" I ask, looking back and forth between them.

"Not kidding," Andrew assures me. "I stopped, pretended to be tying my shoe, so I could listen a bit more, and then told Lorenzo that I could do it, that I could DJ for him if he was really stuck," continues Andrew.

"I thought he was crazy. I thought he was playing

with me. Trying to take advantage of my bad situation. He had to really convince me before I gave in and gave him the job for the night. I really had no other choice but to give him the chance. I was stuck, you know? I tell you, though, it was the best chance I have ever taken," says Lorenzo.

"That's how he got a job with you?" I ask, laughing a little.

"He was fantastico," announces Lorenzo, using his hands as he talks. "As the night went on, I heard people talking about him as he played, and they knew who he was. They knew he was this guy from London and I couldn't believe it. I heard people calling their friends to come down and then we were busy, really busy."

"Your brother and Gabriel were there and talked to me at the end of the night. Jonathan said he knew who I was, too, and was glad to hear me here in the States. Somehow we got on topic about me possibly working at your club. I told him I was working on another appearance, that I'd invite him to come out when it was all sorted. We exchanged numbers so I could let him know when it was on. That was the Vegas Nite event. In the meantime, I went to your club to check the place out, to see if it was someplace I might be interested in working. I didn't see you then, but the rest of it you know," says Andrew.

"Wow, that's some story," I admit. "You're right, it's pretty unbelievable."

"I made a very good friend that night," says Lorenzo, getting up, clearing the dessert dishes, bidding his goodbyes, then leaving with the cart.

I look at the Englishman; he's looking at me. I can feel myself blush a little. He grabs my hand, stands up, and leads me to the dance floor.

Finally.

The song the band is playing is not fast. It's a bit slow and funky; but still too quick for slow dancing. I get to see the Englishman's moves again and he is so damn charismatic. I find this extremely sexy and enjoy watching him. Everything he does seems to have a hypnotizing effect on me.

We dance for a good little while and I begin to actually feel tired. Never thought I'd hear myself think that while dancing, but I need to catch my breath.

We decide to take a break and head back to our table. I have a seat as he stops to order us drinks from the waitress passing by.

Yes, I definitely need another drink. I need to cool down for a minute; he's got me totally hot over here.

Just as he's placing our order, we hear a guy from the band say that they are taking a fifteen minute intermission, but not to worry, because they will be back on stage for another set before we know it.

"Right on time," Andrew says as he winks at me.

The sound system comes on in the club and a song for dancing close starts to play.

"This is perfect," Andrew says as he quickly grabs my hand again, leading me back to the dance floor.

I don't recognize this song and the lyrics don't begin until he has me in his arms.

*You got me thinking
(You, you)
Of you for you
Got me telling my mama
(You)
And my friends all about you
In my daydreams are you
Touching, holding, kissing
(You, you)
As I'm sweaty with, came right on time
(You, you)
Hey you, every word in this song
Girl, every word in this song's
Gonna be about you...*

He pulls me in close, then pulls back a little so we are face to face. He is staring at me sensually, moving slowly, arms around me, holding me tight. I breathe him in, looking into his eyes. I continue to listen to the lyrics and, with everything, I begin to get hypnotized by him again.

*...You don't stress me
At times you test me (you)
But I pass for (you)
So I promise I'm not leaving
Only a fool would leave or try to deceive
I give my word to
I would die for (you)..*

He pulls in close again then begins gently kissing me on my neck. This drives me crazy. I'm in his spell as I continue to listen to the message in the song (he always has a message to me in a song, he admitted.)

...Girl, I live for said I breathe for
(You, you)
I adore no one but
(You, you)
Came right on time (you)
Girl, every word in this song's
Gonna be about you...
You inspire me...
You...

It's over. I'm so in love with him already. I've had no other choice. He's doing everything right. He's perfect for me.

Yes, I can finally admit it; I am in love. I'm done. Truly, I have no more reservations about us and since I'm being honest with myself now, I'm really tired of continuously trying to slow things down. That shit is exhausting.

I've lost the battle and I'm okay with that. There's truly nothing left for me to hold back from him. He can have it all.

CHAPTER 79

A PLOTTED REVENGE

I found a while back this great little black sequined shirt dress that I love, love, love, and decide to wear it when I'm ready to start some trouble for Andrew. It's perfect for the club scene. It's see-through in strategic locations, with a shorter hem and beaded sparkles everywhere. I'm wearing it tonight because it's get-you-back time. I owe Andrew a plotted payback that he will be sure to remember.

CHAPTER 80

WHEN YOU LEAST EXPECT IT

Friday night. The crowd is nice. Not too busy, and not slow. Stix is playing more on the turntables, even though Jonathan and Gabe worked out with the Englishman to extend his contract with us for another year already.

They were actually approached by Andrew to do so. He said he wanted to show his commitment to the club above his other obligations. Again, I was not included in that decision, but was okay with being left out this time around.

I noticed before that Stix and Andrew began to cover each other for meal breaks during the evening. They justified that Andrew never had time to eat any more it seems, at least not until he settles in at the club. No explanation was needed.

His days *are* so long. I still can't understand how he does it all. It makes me exhausted just thinking about it. When taking his supper, Andrew usually just spends time with me and he rarely eats anything. I'm worried that this *will* catch up with him sooner than later. I tell him so. That's when he teasingly asks if I am his nan again. He's always laughing it off, but I'm not amused.

When Andrew is close to taking a break, he usually

puts on a song for us to dance to and he'll text me to meet him on the dance floor. Tonight, he chooses *So Beautiful*. It's perfect. As we dance, the lyrics seem to wrap around us and again, in my mind, everyone else disappears.

> *You're my baby*
> *My lover, my lady*
> *All night you make me want you*
> *It drives me crazy*
> *I feel like you*
> *Were made just for me, baby*
> *Tell me if you*
> *Feel the same way...*

He starts with his hands on my waist and we move together, slowly. I love breathing him in and I put my arm on his shoulder.

> *...Girl, don't you know, you're so beautiful?*
> *I wanna give all my love to you, girl*
> *Not just a night but the rest of your life*
> *I wanna be always here by your side...*

I pull away just a little to turn around, making sure to brush up against him as I move. He pulls me in closer and I feel his breath on the back of my neck. It's warm and deep. I can tell he's getting a little excited. I pull away just far away enough for him to watch me move.

...When you're not here,
You don't know how much I miss you
The whole time on my mind
Is how much I'm gonna get to make
You feel so good like you know I could...

I make sure to exaggerate the movement of my hips just a little more than I usually do. I turn back and he's doing exactly what I wanted; he's watching my every move. I turn around again as he reaches for my arm to bring me closer. I make sure to rub up against him each and every time as I turn. I can see in his eyes how much he wants me. Perfect.

We keep moving like this for the better part of the song. I pull away again just as the song ends. I take a quick look back at him as he puts one hand up to the back of his neck and shakes his head at me, then I turn and walk away, leaving him there on the dance floor. I see him go to the bar to get a soda before he returns to the booth. I go into the office.

I kick off my shoes, sit on the edge of my desk, in a location he is sure to recognize as the office. I pull out the small box of condoms I bought, matching the brand he plotted and left in his gym bag at my house. He's not the only one who notices things.

I hold the box up to my chest, lower one shoulder of my dress and bite my lower lip as I snap my pic. I send it to him as a text and type one word: suppertime.

I quickly go to the door and crack it a bit to watch

his reaction as he reads my text. I see he does a double take and then takes a small step backward, so Stix can't see what I sent, I assume. I then see him lean forward and say something to Stix, as Stix nods his head in response then Andrew leaves the booth and crosses the dance floor to the bar. He seemed to do this in about two steps. I smile to myself and keep watch to see when he's coming, to make sure no one else comes in first, so I won't be caught in any compromising positions trying to be cute.

CHAPTER 81

THE ENGLISHMAN

Tonight, Samantha is really driving me mad. The way her little dress swings across her hips as she moves her body and the way she's actually moving those hips. How she stands just out of my reach, the way she happens to brush up against me when she moves and turns around. She's teasing me and it's making me want her bad. Closing time is hours away and I'm not sure I can take much more of her toying with me like this. The song ends right on time. She really enjoys teasing me, I see. The way she looked back at me smiling.

I need a drink. I think that I may need to add a little rum to my colas tonight.

Back in the booth and I can't focus. Where did she disappear to? I don't see her on the floor anywhere. A text. What does she have to say for herself? Bloody hell. That picture. She plotted condoms in her office? Cheeky.

Alright, I'm trying to keep my cool, but knowing she's there waiting for me is a little too much. It's all I can do to stop myself from jumping over this booth and running across the dance floor into that office. Suppertime is it? I've got to make one stop at the bar on my way to her. I need to slow myself down enough for us to have a drink and then willingly give in to her plot.

She did say that she was going to get me when I least expected it but it's right on time.

CHAPTER 82

IT'S A JOINT BENEFIT

Andrew leaves the bar with two shot glasses and heads towards the office. I rush back to the edge of the desk, trying to put on my sexiest pout as he opens the door. He locks us in. Good boy.

As he approaches me, I sit up near the edge of the desk and arch my back a bit, leaning back with my hands on the desk supporting me. He stands in front of me and I'm able to wrap my leg around him. I like doing that, wrapping my leg around him, pulling him closer. Nothing is said. He grabs my thigh, leans in forward, kisses me passionately, then pulls back a little and hands me my glass. "I thought a sex on the beach shot was appropriate for our supper starter," he says with a wink and a smile.

Sweetness overpowers my nose. I really don't do sweet drinks and it makes me hesitate. He takes his in one gulp, so I slowly follow his lead and drink. It goes down surprisingly warm as I feel the heat of it spread through me. Liquor does this to me sometimes.

I don't know if it was my imagination or if I'm really into what we're doing, but my entire body begins to become extra sensitive to everything around me. First it is to temperature; I instantly feel the warmth of his body next to mine. Then it's his smell; if I thought the way he smelled turned me on before, smelling him now exaggerated that desire tenfold. Next is to the sounds of the room. The music from the dance floor is muted in the background, but the sound and rhythm of his breathing seems to be everywhere I turn; it hypnotizes me. And, finally, his touch; I can't get enough of his touch on my skin.

He kisses me again as he goes to undo my buttons. He slides his fingers tenderly across my skin, opening my dress. When he does this, the top half of my dress slips off my shoulders, falling with a slight thud on the desk because of the weight of the sequins; revealing that I have nothing on underneath, up top.

I'm almost naked, with the top half of the dress now gathered around my waist. He moves his hand up my inner thigh, teasing a bit. He then begins to move his hand around, gripping my bottom, pulling me closer to the edge of the desk as he leans more into me. I let out a little moan. I can't help it, the anticipation of him is too much.

I wrap my other leg around him, keeping him close. He pulls his shirt off and I begin to slide my hands across the muscles on his back and shoulders, and around the front over the muscles on his chest, then sliding down to the button of his pants. I close my eyes as I feel *his* fingers move. His kisses progress to my neck then to my chest.

I feel as if I might lose control.

He pulls me forward, off of the desk, and when I stand, my dress falls in a pile on the floor. He turns me away from him. His movements now are slightly more aggressive than they have been making love before and I like the roughness of it.

Somehow, we end up against the bookcase next to the desk. His hands grip my hips, pulling and holding me up to him, bringing me up on my toes in one motion. I must have been too focused on the pleasure of things because I barely hear him when he whispers "shh" in my ear. I feel his hand pulling the back of my hair, turning my head to the side, and he kisses me passionately again as we both enjoy the benefits of my plotted revenge.

CHAPTER 83

YOU'VE BEEN WARNED

"You know how to do a payback, love," he says.

"Yes, I do," I warn.

"Oh right, I've been advised of that before," he says laughing.

"Good, just so you know," I say in my extra serious voice.

"You're with me now and I wouldn't do anything to upset that," he says with a kiss.

"Yeah, yeah. Okay. I get it. Won't hurt me. Yep, got it."

Shaking his head at me. "Subject change, yeah? Let me ask you: did you lot have cameras installed in the offices as well? Because that would definitely make for a great home film, the two of us just then."

"What?! Seriously?! No, there are no cameras in the offices. You want to make home movies now?" I ask.

"With you? Absolutely," he says, not skipping a beat.

"Well, you're out of luck on that one. There are no cameras in here."

CHAPTER 84

THE SET UP

I don't get to go on a regular basis, but I get to visit the set here and there with Andrew as we settle into being with each other more. He is so good at this acting thing. He's great as his character and I'm not saying that just because I am his biggest fan; I'm saying it because he's actually that good.

That chick, however, is testing me. Nvette. I see her trying her best to catch his eye. Always flirting and messing around. Lucky for him, he's not having any of it still. So what she's been in a few movies and such, she totally acts like a diva the world can't live without. Clearly, with that, she thinks she is running the show.

She's a good actress, too, but her personality and attitude are awful. She doesn't seem to be a very happy person. I've heard her sometimes on the sidelines using her mobile phone. All she does is argue and plead with the person on the other end. How tragic.

There are so many people that work behind the scenes at these things. You would never know that simply from watching the show. A good part of being an on-set spectator is having access to the catering. I don't remember seeing food on the set when Andrew first started with the show, but it's something of a big deal now. At least now I know he can get some good food in him during the day.

I see one of the caterers and recognize her, but can't place her. I know I've seen her before. I decide not to go to her and ask; I just quietly keep in my spot, watching what they're doing with the show.

CHAPTER 85

THE ENGLISHMAN

I enjoy this acting thing. I like the direction of the show and I really seem to be settling into my character now. I'm quite proud to be a part of all of this, and I'm happy to have Samantha's support with it. I bring her with me when I can, but when she's not here is when I seem to need her most, I find.

"Dreeew, I need your help," announces Nvette, sauntering over just as the crew gets ready to film the last scene for the day.

Bloody hell, here we go.

"My help with what, Nvette?" I ask, a little put off. I'm over these tactics she keeps trying on me.

"I need you to help me with this wardrobe they have me in. This dress, I can't unzip the back of it, and I need your help when this scene is over," she says, acting helpless.

"No ma'am, I will not. You have people for that. I know, because you have people for everything. You can bloody well believe that I will not be helping you get out of that ruddy dress."

Looking a little taken aback, "Gee, there's no need to respond like that. I'm only asking for a little help from a friend. I don't know what you were thinking, but that's all I meant," she says with a pout, rubbing my arm.

I can't help but laugh at this as I pull away. "Not you. You're not just asking. You must think I'm daft to fall for that. I'm not interested in any bunny boilers. Thanks, but no."

She looks at me suspicious-like. I'm not sure she understands, so I explain, "You know, like that movie *Fatal Attraction*, where the bint was delusional about the guy leaving his missus for her, so she takes the pet bunny and boils it on their cooker."

"But they slept together. They had a wild, steamy love affair. That's why she thought that," she says a little quieter.

"I'm definitely not interested in having any love affairs with you, Nvette, and I'm in no way interested in having sex with you under any circumstances, either, so you can stop with these antics of yours," I say rather firmly.

"I know you like me, Drew. I could tell when we started having more scenes together. You don't have to try and hide it from me, I get it. I won't tell anyone if you want to keep things secret at first; at least until you can get rid of your little girlfriend," she insists.

She's crazy. A nutter. She is not listening to a word I say to her. So I tell her one last time. "There is nothing that's going to make me leave my lady for you. It's not going to happen between us," I promise.

Places everyone is announced.

Her look hardens and she narrows her eyes a bit as

she says quietly, "Careful, Drew, you don't want something horrible to happen to your character now, do you?" Then she walks off to her post.

CHAPTER 86

YOU DO YOUR THING

The Englishman definitely works hard. I am proud of what he's doing. I think that I'm actually more impressed with the fact that he moved all the way here, alone, and was not afraid to follow his dreams. Good on him. I'm not sure I could have done something like that.

His schedule is becoming crazy busy, and he now has an additional day off at the club; Tuesdays. It's a little tough because that was the only day at the club that we worked without Jonathan, Gabe, or Stix and I liked having him to myself like that, but on Tuesdays it's just me and Stix now.

When the Englishman does work both on the set and at the club, he sometimes comes in looking so agitated, but it doesn't last. When he gets into the booth, I see all of his troubles from the day just melt away like magic. He never says anything, but I know something there is troubling him.

CHAPTER 87

HERE'S THE FAMILY

I don't know why I'm letting my nerves get the best of me. It's just a dinner. Just a dinner with Andrew's brother and baby sister. And I'm terrified.

I've been standing outside his door for about five minutes now, afraid to actually knock and go in. I hear the elevator open and when I look, it's Andrew with a case of wine. Thank God it's him. I don't have to go in solo. And thank God there's going to be plenty of wine.

"Hey, lovely, what are you doing standing out here? Why didn't you go inside?" he asks.

"I was way too nervous and I didn't know you had gone out. I'm really glad now that I waited out here to get myself together. I guess I needed you to come and rescue me again."

Laughing, he says, "There's absolutely no need to be nervous, they're excited to meet you."

I know he's just trying to reassure me, but what's so funny? I watch him come towards me down the hallway. I like it when he rescues me, I decide, so I play the 'poor little me' role a little more and say, "But you weren't here," and give my best pout. He gives another little laugh at me. When he walks up, he gives me a long kiss, then tells me, "No worries."

He knocks on his door and leans against the wall next to it, watching me with a huge grin on his face. I can't help but roll my eyes at him. He's getting way too much enjoyment out of this.

As we wait for someone to open the door, he tells me, "I just went down to the restaurant to pick up a few bottles of that wine you liked," gesturing towards the box in his hand.

"Oh, thank you. You got me wine; I have a feeling I'm gonna need it."

"You'll be fine, trust me, yeah?" he says with another smile.

"Yeah okay, if you say so," I respond, not really believing him. I'm still really nervous even with him standing with me.

"What's this? Sweets?" he asks as he finally notices the dish in my hands.

"Yeah, I brought dessert. I made a trifle."

His sister opens the door just as I say that. She looks just like him, but more, more gorgeous.

"Brilliant!" she says grinning. "I haven't had trifle in forever."

"Samantha, this is my sister, Grace," announces Andrew.

CHAPTER 88
ON THE SPOT

I feel so out of place. I don't know what exactly Andrew has said about me and I am so, so, so nervous. I've never been like this meeting someone before. I am usually so confident, but when it comes to Andrew, somehow all of that confidence goes out the window and, besides, I really want to make a good impression.

After opening the door, Grace grabbed me by the arm and pulled me inside with Andrew in tow. His brother is there in the kitchen. He's a bit thinner than Andrew and I can tell immediately that Andrew looks up to his older brother.

"Edward, this is Samantha," Andrew calls out. His brother turns and a huge smile spreads across his face, which immediately puts me at ease.

Edward greets me, grabs the dish from my hand, places it on the kitchen counter, and turns to give me a kiss on each cheek. He looks at Andrew, pretends to smack him upside his head before he goes back to cooking, then says, "You are more beautiful than he described. Junior truly didn't do you justice. He said that you were just lovely, which is such an understatement."

Okay, love the brother.

The Englishman takes me by the hand and leads me into a corner of the kitchen. "Junior, huh?" I say, letting him know that I did not miss his nickname. He just nods and pours me a glass of wine, which I down almost immediately, and this makes him really laugh at me.

"Slow down with this, yeah?" he says, still smiling as he pours me another glass. I take a deep breath and tell myself that I can do this. I take another sip, slowly this time, and Andrew gives me a hug and kiss before going to help his brother.

Dinner smells amazing and I automatically think that Andrew learned how to cook from his brother. Who knows if that's true or not; I don't ask.

CHAPTER 89

FUELED BY ONE MOTIVE

I enjoy spending time with Andrew's sister, Grace, and his brother, Edward. They make me feel like I am a part of their family immediately. "Of course," Andrew says. "Why wouldn't they? They love you, and what's not to love? Besides, they can see how crazy mad I am over you."

They're in town for another two weeks. With Andrew's crazy schedule, I end up spending a lot more time with them than I originally expected. We're together every afternoon. I couldn't leave them alone with Andrew away working all of the time. Yep, we get to know each other pretty well. They're fabulous.

Andrew does manage a day off during the week and he wants to take his sister and brother to the seaside. We find a great little beach town to pal around in. It's a little too cool to spend most of our time on the beach, but there are plenty of small shops and cafes to get lost in. I'm so happy to see Andrew with his family; they seem really close and I can't imagine how tough it is for them to live so far away from each other.

Halfway through their holiday, when Andrew is on set, Edward, Grace, and I decide to have a late lunch at an outside cafe and the conversation quickly turns serious. Edward has something he's been wanting to share with me almost since we met, he says. Grace is unusually quiet. In fact, she barely looks at me and this starts to worry me. I immediately expect to learn that Andrew is married with a family in England or something devastating like that. What he has to tell me is not at all what I thought; it's much worse.

Edward explains that he sees how Andrew acts when he is with me and thought I should know about the family 'secret.' if you would. I learn why Andrew wastes no time in saying or doing what he wants. It's not everyday aspirations that influence him. Nope, tragedy is his motivator.

I'm told that there was another brother, William, the eldest of the three boys. He and his girlfriend Maxine dated for a long time and William had talked about the possibility of getting married, but did nothing more than talk, everyone thought. He was a bit of a flirt with the ladies and said that he had plenty of time to settle down if and when he wanted it. Maxine was lovely in every way, Edward explained, and he couldn't understand why she had always put up with his brother's nonsense.

The tragedy of it all came when she passed. Maxine didn't drive and was out of the city for a girlfriend's bridal shower. William was sorted to pick her up, but got sidetracked talking with another girl at the pub, so

Maxine ended up getting a ride home with one of the girls at the party. It was dark out by the time they left. It was raining, so the roads were slick, and the driver had been drinking a bit. They ended up having an accident and both girls were killed.

Of course, William was beside himself after the crash, blaming himself for not driving her and such, but the worst of it came when the doctor's report stated that Maxine was pregnant when she died. She hadn't told him so beforehand.

Edward pauses for a long moment, lost in his thoughts. I look at Grace and she, too, is in another world. Then he starts again, "No one knew this part, except Andrew and I of course, but before her crash, William had indeed bought a ring to propose to Maxine and he just kept delaying it. He never got around to asking her and that killed him. He just kept saying that she died without really knowing how much he loved her. It was difficult seeing him after the news of the pregnancy; the guilt of it all just overwhelmed him. A few days after her funeral, William crashed, too, and died. The police ruled it as a true accident, but Andrew and I know in our hearts that his crash was no accident; he died on purpose," Edward explained.

"It was hard to move forward because us boys were really, really close. Andrew and I handled it in very different ways. Me? I broke off my relationship with Anne because I was afraid to go through even a little bit of the pain William felt with his loss. I couldn't brave any of it. So, I ended everything that I thought could hurt me." Edward stops and looks at me directly before continuing, "Andrew was at the university studying music because of William's encouragement but quit after his death. We tried to get him to finish because he was so close, but he simply said that there was no point to it anymore and refused. William was so proud of our younger brother, bragging on him every chance he got. Andrew loves music, yeah, but would have never begun at the university without William's insistence." He turns, looks away and gets lost again.

Edward starts, "He used to play the piano all of the time, but I don't think he has since William. I was shocked, you know, to see that he has that piano in his flat." He looked back at me expectantly, asking, "Has he played for you then?"

"No," I say quietly. "He hasn't." I think back to how the Englishman responded when I asked if he played when I first went to his apartment.

"I was hoping he had, but I'm not surprised..." says Edward, trailing off.

He continues, saying, "Andrew, when he quit the university, decided that he had to immediately do everything he ever thought or dreamed of, which included moving here to the States; *Waste not one moment because you never know when it will be your last*," he says in a way that I assume was supposed to be Andrew talking.

Hearing about their brother explained everything. Andrew always idolized William, even when Andrew was in diapers, and that's how he got the nickname Junior.

He was a junior William in every way. Edward said that Andrew and his best mate were just as bad with the ladies as William was before, and he never was really in a relationship that he cared too much about until I came along. Edward then warned that Andrew would be furious if he knew that we were discussing what happened to William and asked me to wait until Andrew brought it up on his own before I said anything. He only told me now because he sees how serious Andrew is about me and thought I should know.

Andrew did say to me before that he had seen enough tragedy to learn not to wait to tell someone how you feel about them. I didn't get it then, but I totally understand it now. At least I know why he moves with such certainty when he talks about us. He's learned this lesson through his brother.

CHAPTER 90

THAT WASN'T SO BAD

Edward has been spending most of his evenings with Anne; the one he dated before, the part owner at the gallery. They seem as if they both really care for each other still. I can't help but think how heartbreaking it will be for them when Edward has to leave again, but he decided that he can't be afraid to live his life any longer.

Grace has been by the club almost every night and loves to dance as much as I do. I see the big brother peeking out of Andrew every time a guy approaches her, and I think it's hilarious. He's not amused, but I can't help but give him a hard time about it, of course.

Lizzie and Brian also come out to hang with us at the club, and sometimes when we go out to dinner. They are now engaged, to be married as soon as they can plan it, I imagine. I am really happy to see those two back together again. Yep, all is well in my world.

Brian and Andrew becoming good friends is an added bonus.

The holiday is over for Edward and Grace. Time for the family to go home. I see how this brings Andrew down. He really misses being around them, I can tell.

To lighten things up a bit, plans were made for Andrew and me to go to England to see them; to meet more of the family and for Andrew to meet some of mine. We agreed to do so as soon as possible. I love London; I can't wait to see it from Andrew's perspective as a Londoner. As soon as possible works for me.

CHAPTER 91
YOU'RE GIVING WHAT NOW?

"Listen, Samantha, you know I'm not one for waiting to show how I feel, yeah? And I know sometimes you think that we are moving too fast, but I disagree. I think we are right on schedule. With that, I've made you a key to my flat. I want you to know that I mean it when I say that I want you in every part of my life. I have nothing to hold back from you, or to hide, for that matter," explains the Englishman.

"Andrew, I don't know what to say, but I don't think that I feel comfortable taking this key from you," I say.

"Take it. That's it, innit. Nothing to think about," he answers.

"But you know that I don't have a key to my place made for you."

"It doesn't matter. That's not what I'm doing it for, yeah? When you're ready, you will. No worries," he says as he kisses me on the forehead. Then he says, smiling, "Don't think I haven't noticed that you're only calling me Andrew now."

"Am I?" I ask, trying to think back.

I remember now, with his brother Edward here, there

were too many Englishmen around for me to keep up with. Calling him Andrew was the only way I could keep track. I guess it just stuck.

CHAPTER 92

I GIVE IN, REALLY

My relationship, love affair, partnership with Andrew is like nothing I could have ever imagined. It sounds corny when I think about it, but it gets better every day. Every now and then in the back of my mind I'll still think that we are moving way too fast to be healthy. But, in fairness, I can't compare what we have to any of my past relationships, because he is so unlike anyone I've been with before, and knowing now about his brother, William, I understand why he does the things he does.

I'm so in love with him and, yes, that still scares me. It's been picture-perfect. I catch myself watching him, wondering what it is that I'm missing. What is it that I am not seeing that I should be protecting myself from; reminding myself that no one is this perfect. I come up with nothing, so I willingly continue to just allow myself to go with the *'I'm so in love'* flow.

CHAPTER 93

SNEAKY, SNEAKY

I've had a copy of Andrew's house key for a while now and have never used it. But today I have planned that I would. I want to surprise him with a few things while he's on set before I head into the club, covering for Jonathan's vacation tonight. I'm finished with the painting I secretly started for him ages ago. I hope he likes it. It's too much pressure when someone asks you to create something for them. It's been a huge task and I worked on it for what seems like forever since he asked. I'm going to take it to his place and hang it on that empty wall. I also think it's time that I give him his very own copy of my house key. He's right, he has continuously shown that he is not planning on doing anything to hurt me. I decided once and for all that I would put my total trust in him; he's earned it. I have another little surprise that I'm going to put in a strategic location but won't tell him about that until later.

I'm all smiles thinking about how he'll react to what I've left as I sneak back out of his place.

PART IV
THE SET UP

CHAPTER 94

THE ENGLISHMAN

Things are going well with Samantha. She is so lovely. She finally stopped fighting her feelings for me, I've noticed, since meeting Edward and Grace. I'm always thinking about her when she's not around. It becomes a distraction on the set when I have scenes with my co-star, Nvette. It's getting tougher for me to work with her and I find myself getting so angry at having long scenes with her.

I'm still put off by her working in that kissing scene on my first week. I know it was her doing. Nothing can convince me otherwise. She is always making passes at me and tries to flirt. She's not one for taking hints.

I don't want to gain the reputation of being mean or difficult as an actor, so I just try to keep as much distance between us as possible. There is something about her that I cannot trust.

We just found out today that a major cable network picked up our series and all of our contracts were extended. It all happened very quickly, but it's a great surprise.

It's Wednesday night; Samantha is working at the club tonight for Jonathan while he's away on

Holiday, I know. The cast wanted to go out to celebrate, but I told a mate that I already had plans to go into the club to see my girl.

Standing behind me, Nvette overheard and convinced the rest of the cast to go to the club tonight as well; to celebrate the pickup of the show. Not how I wanted to spend my evening. I didn't really want to be anywhere after hours with Nvette around. She's been too aggressive lately. I should call Samantha and let her know they are coming.

"Great, babe! I'll have a special V.I.P. section set up for you guys. Congratulations! I'll see you soon."

CHAPTER 95

IT'S A HAPPY TIME

It suddenly gets a little busy for a Wednesday night. But luckily, I have everything set up for Andrew, his co-workers, and the cast before the crowd came in. I am so happy for him. He works so hard. He deserves this break. I knew that show would get picked up.

I can't wait to help him celebrate later. My little surprises seem to be right on time. Here he comes now. Good, he's solo so we can have a quick celebratory drink before he has to go off with the others.

"Hey, babe. Congratulations! I'm so happy for you. Cheers!" I say as I give a big kiss.

"Yeah. Cheers, and thanks, it's great news," he says, sounding agitated.

"Really? You don't sound like you mean that right now," I say, pulling back to have a good look at him.

"I'm just a little put off because I wasn't planning for the crew to come here tonight to do their celebrating, I just wanted it to be you and me only," he says, rubbing the back of his neck, looking exhausted.

"Oh, it's cool. You know they wouldn't let you out of the celebration. You're a big character. And no worries, I'll take good care of you guys. I want you to have a good time. This is exciting. Be happy. Besides, you're *here* and I get to join in, even if it's in a small way," I say, kissing him again.

"Yeah, yeah, you're right. I am glad that I'm here rather than off someplace else. I just want to keep the two worlds as separate as possible. That is my work, and this is my private life."

"Wow, okay. But you work here, too, so why separate? Why so much?" I ask.

"I don't know how to explain it, really. I just feel protective of what I have here with you," he says.

"Okay then, Mr. T.V. Star, whatever that means," I say, making a face at him.

What's going on with him? The way he's acting now is just strange.

CHAPTER 96
THE ENGLISHMAN

I am unbelievably pissed that she manipulated her way into this part of my life. Nvette. Samantha is trying to convince me that this is a night to celebrate because everyone has worked so hard. She's right, of course. I just wanted to spend the evening here, just with her, without anyone else.

Talking to her now does make me feel better. It's nice how she's excited for me. She told me earlier that she's going to be calling me Mr. T.V. Star now.

Cheeky.

I wonder if she realizes how beautiful she is.

I'm so focused on my time with Samantha that I don't see Nvette walking up to us. When she comes, she stands right between Samantha and me with her back to Samantha.

"Excuse me, Nvette, I'm sure you see that I am in a conversation with my missus here and you just stepped in between us. That's very rude," I say as seriously as possible.

"Oh, did I? I didn't know. I thought she was just one of your little groupies or something and you couldn't wait to be rescued from her," she says, as she looks

Samantha up and down.

That look on Samantha's face says everything. I've never seen her look that way before. I need to get Nvette away from here straight away. Samantha is heated.

"Nvette, we are having a private conversation. You met Samantha on the set from the very first day. I know you recognize her. Now please go, we want to have our privacy," I insist as I try to get her to walk towards the V.I.P. area.

She turns and looks at Samantha again. "Oh no. I didn't realize. Honest. I didn't think you and your girlfriend were still together since I haven't seen her around lately," she says in an exaggerated way.

Oh bugger. She's making things worse. Samantha is now starting to take off her earrings. I need to step around Nvette so I can get next to Samantha. I need to stay in between the two of them, I think. I'm not sure what Samantha's about to do with that look still on her face.

"Look, the rest of the crew is over there. See them? I'll be over with all of you shortly. I'm not finished here. I'm in the middle of catching up from the day with the missus and need my moment with her," I say, still trying to get rid of Nvette as fast as I can.

"Alright, alright already. Just don't be too long or I'll have to come back and get you, Drewy," she says as she turns and wiggles her way over to the V.I.P. section to be with the others.

Fuck. I knew I didn't want her coming here. Samantha is furious like I've never seen. She's giving me a look like I had something to do with that. She's telling me to go over with my little friends because if that bitch comes back over here like that again, she's going home in an ambulance. I believe her, too, so I apologize and try to convince her that I won't let that happen again, and that I had no idea she was going to act like that. Assuring her that I'll do my best to keep Nvette away.

So, that's what her spitfire looks like. I've never seen her so *angry*. That was a little scary, to say the least. I do as she says and go with the rest of the gang.

CHAPTER 97

DON'T MAKE ME OPEN UP THIS CAN

"What the hell, Andrew?! What is up with your fucking co-star? I will beat her ass if she keeps disrespecting me like that. I will definitely send her home in an ambulance for real. That bitch is lucky that it's busy tonight because it was about to go down before you shooed her away. Don't play games with me like that."

"Samantha. Samantha, listen! I am sorry for that, seriously. This is exactly why I didn't want them to come, yeah? I want to keep them out of this part of my life. There is no excuse I can give for her treating you like that. All I can say is I'm sorry," he says.

"You need to go over there with your little friends, Andrew, because if she comes to me and disrespects me again..." I start to say.

"She won't, she won't. I'll make sure of it," he assures me.

"Yeah, okay. I've got to get back to work. It's too busy to be playing with her. If you see her making her way back to me, you need to call the paramedics right away is all I have to tell you." I am pissed beyond belief.

"Right, I know you're busy. I'll take care of it," he

says with a big long kiss, then he's off to his party.
 I see her watching him. This chick needs to get her sights off of my man before I hurt her.

CHAPTER 98

TROUBLEMAKER (AKA NVETTE)

Look at him over there with her. He can do better than that. I can give him better than that. We would be perfect together. He needs to be with me.

She keeps looking over here as if I would be threatened by her. She doesn't know who I am, I guess. She doesn't know who she's playing with.

Look at him. God, he has no idea how sexy he is. I know he wants me. When we were doing that kissing scene, he would mess up at the end on purpose so he would have to redo the scene over and over again. It was just one scene, and he made sure to make it last as long as he could. I don't care what he says, no one can tell me he's not into me after that.

My life would be so different if I had him as my boyfriend. I've made the decision to get that man no matter what it takes. I need him to save me. I need him to be mine.

Good, he's coming over, finally.

CHAPTER 99

THE PARTY'S OVER

I'm glad it's busy so I can divert my attention from what's going on with Andrew and that chick.

I have Stix announce our new promo. It's a chance to win a V.I.P. status package for a party of ten. I'm thinking it would be great for a bachelorette party to win or something like that. I look over to Andrew's party and he's sitting with a couple of fellas from his show, and I look to see that *she's* far away from him at the bar. *Good*, I say to myself, *nowhere near my man*.

I see her a little later as she submits her name for the V.I.P. promo. Hmph, big-time movie star I see. I look back at Andrew and he's watching me now, so I make a face at him to lighten the situation a little. He forces a smile. I don't like that, but I try to shake it off. Back to work for me; it's too busy of a night to focus on what's going on with him right now.

By the time I have a minute, the party's over. I ask Mike at the bar if he has seen Andrew.

He says, "Yeah, he left with a few of the guys a while ago. I thought you saw him. He looked pretty wasted. Must've been some celebration."

What? He left? No goodbye. And wasted? I've

never noticed Andrew to be even a little bit tipsy before. I chalked that up to him being a teenager in the pubs over in England. But wasted? So, how did he get home then? My place is close enough to walk to, but he has no key yet. I'm glad I drove in today. I'll have to go by his place to check on him. It's not like him to leave like that; this is all so odd. I'm not sure if I shouldn't be worried.

CHAPTER 100

FACKIN' 'ELL!

Finally finished at the club. Andrew's car is not in the lot. That really adds to my worry. I drove past my house to be sure that he didn't end up there in some drunken stupor and just wound up maybe sleeping in his car or outside or something like that. Nope. Not here. Good, I guess. I'll try his place.

Okay, very good, his car is here. Maybe he *was* a little too drunk. He's not parked in his regular spot. I can't wait to give him a what for if he drove like that. He definitely should know better. I walk over to his car to make sure he's not still there passed out. I see his registration and insurance card on the floor and wonder if he got stopped along the way.

I look up to his unit and it seems as if all of his lights are on. Odd again, but at least he's home. If he's alright, then I'm gonna let him have it for all of this anxiety he's giving me.

I open his door with my key. His clothes are all over the floor but, wait; there are women's clothes, too. What the bloody hell? I hear slight noises from his bedroom, and I walk slowly to the doorway. **UN-FUCKING-BELIEVABLE!!**

This is why he wanted to separate his *work* life and his *personal* life, huh? No wonder she didn't think he still had a girlfriend, and that's why he was looking so damn worried when they came to the club. I think I'm going to kill him.

He's half sitting, half lying on the side of his bed facing enough in my direction to see me and she is straddled across him just grinding away. I. Want. To. Kill. Them. Both.

He certainly seems as if he is drunk. The noises he's making are disgusting, slurring and grunting. I've never noticed noises like that when we were together.

I am sick to my stomach.

I can't believe I gave in to him. Damn, he really had me going. I can't see anything but red. I'm strategically thinking of my next move when he finally sees me standing there.

That's right motherfucker: you're busted and I'm gonna kick your ass. But I can't move. Looking into his eyes kills me. I am now totally devastated. Everything is swimming around in my head at once. I can do nothing but stand there.

He looks as if he just woke up from a dream.

Now he's trying to push her off of him, but he's struggling even with that. Drunk ass. I stand there unchanged. Glaring at him. She turns, sees me, too, and jumps up, runs to grab her things that are in the bedroom as she tries to cover up. I'm unchanged, unmoved, glaring, and wanting to kill the bitch.

He finally stands and staggers in my direction. Still,

I'm unmoved. I wait just until he's within arm's reach and then I punch him dead in his face. I stay long enough to see him fall back and hit the floor. Then I leave before I end up in prison.

CHAPTER 101

THE WATERWORKS

I can't believe I ended up being this chick. I'm driving home with tears streaming down my face. I can barely see because of my crying. I beat on my steering wheel as I scream to myself, *"FUCKING ASSHOLE!"* It feels as if I've been stabbed several, *several* times in my chest and gut. And I feel so damn stupid.

I can't stay home. He now has my key. DAMN IT! I ran out of his place so quickly I didn't remember to take it before I left. I'm going to grab some shit and hide out at a hotel for a couple of days until I decide what I'm going to do. Damn it, Jonathan, not a great time to take a holiday. We're both due to work Ladies' Night tomorrow. I gotta get these waterworks under control before I see his ass again. I don't want him to see me this weak.

CHAPTER 102

THE ENGLISHMAN

I feel like bloody hell. My head feels like I've been run over by a bus. I woke up on my bedroom floor, alone and naked.

When I wash up, I notice that I have a bloody black eye. Last thing I remember really is seeing Samantha standing in my doorway and Nvette nude on my lap. Before that, I only remember being at the club having a toast or two. Nothing in between makes any sense. I don't know how I ended up in my flat with fucking Nvette. Were we having sex? No, absolutely not. There is no way.

I've tried calling Samantha a hundred times and it goes straight to her messages. I've gone to her place and the club looking for her. Nothing. I'm at a loss. I don't know what to do. This is all wrong. I was not with Nvette. I'm sure of it. But how to convince Samantha that she didn't see what she thought. I don't know.

Bloody hell, this is a complete mess.

I can't stop thinking about that fucking bitch, Nvette. I couldn't go to the set today and face her. I just keep envisioning my hands around her neck, squeezing the life out of her for doing this.

I *knew* she was up to something, but I had no idea it would be something like this. I have to find Samantha. I need to speak to her before tonight. I have to explain to her that it was not what she thinks. I was not having an affair. I can't explain what was going on, but it was not that, I know.

The only thing I can think to do now is go back home and try to figure out how I'm going to correct this.

I go straight to my bedroom to look for some clue as to what really happened. Nothing. My things from last night are still all over the place. I go into the front room to clean up and that's when I see it. The painting from Samantha. That's what she meant by having a surprise for me last night. It's perfect. Bloody hell. I'm really fucked.

I try calling her again. No answer. I gotta have some coffee; maybe the caffeine will help my head feel a little better. I can't have a hangover; I don't remember drinking that much.

I stand in front of the painting, trying to figure out what I can do when I see the key tied to a thin red ribbon hanging over the right corner. Her house key. I put down my coffee, grab the key, and I'm out the door.

I'm at her place but she's not. It looks as if she never slept here last night. Damn. I thought she was here just ignoring me when I stopped by earlier. She could be anywhere. I've got just enough time to pick up some things before I'm due at the club.

Her car is here already. Good. Maybe she'll allow me to talk to her before the night gets going. I walk into the club and I immediately understand that the message playing in the music is meant for me.

> ...Played with my emotions
> You gets no devotion, (and you gets no love, gets no love, gets no love)
> You can't get no love from me
> You can't even be my friend (be my friend)
> And you gets no love again
> Whatever you do, it will come back to you..

Nice play, that one, is my first thought. I know that she is not in the mood to speak with me. This music is not coming from the booth, but it's through the house speakers. I see Michael and ask...
"What's this then? Where is this coming from?"
"That's Sam's playlist. She's playing it from the office's system. She's been blasting stuff like this all afternoon," he responds.

> ...Tell you why we can't hook up (you gets no love)
> 'Cause I had about enough (you gets no love)
> Hearin' all the lies you tell (you gets no love)
> Boy, I thought I knew you well (from me)
> People think that you are my man (people think you're my man)
> They don't even understand...

Yeah, I'm really, *really* fucked.

CHAPTER 103

YOU GETS NO LOVE

I hear him outside the office. That fucking accent. He has left like a million messages insisting that he needs to speak with me about last night. I know what I saw. There is nothing to talk about. Damn, I'd hate to have to change my number because he won't leave me alone, the stalker. I'll give it a few more days; see if he'll catch the hint.

Shit, someone's on the doorknob.

"Sam, what the hell?! Why is the office locked? And why are you blasting this 'I hate you' music all over the club?" yells Gabe.

Oh, thank God it's only Gabe. I turn off the music and open the door. He looks at me and immediately moves me in and locks the door again. I barely see Andrew as he leaves the bar on his way over to me. But then the door is closed. Good on you, Gabe, for locking it, too.

"Shit, Sam, what's wrong? What happened? Why have you been crying?" he asks, concerned.

"It's nothing," I say.

"Bullshit! It's not nothing. What happened? Is it Andrew? I'll kill him! What did he do to you?" he asks.

"I saw him with another woman last night. It's done between us. Over!"

"Wait, what? Another woman? Are you sure? 'Cause he seems like he's really sprung with you," he says, now in a different tone.

"Oh, that's real funny, Gabe. You're taking his side now, are you? Thanks, and yeah, I'm certain. I saw it myself. I caught them at his place, so I guess he had us both fooled."

"No, Sam, I can't believe that. I see the two of you together and, and there's no way."

"Great, first you give me a hard time when I start to date him and now you're giving me a hard time when I tell you it's over. What's worse, is you telling me that you don't believe I saw him cheating."

"It's just that he doesn't seem the type."

"Gabe, you're not helping," I start crying again.

"Oh, hey, I'm sorry. I didn't mean to upset you more."

Shit, I hate being this chick. I've gotta snap out of it before I leave this office. That asshole.

CHAPTER 104

GABRIEL'S TURN

"Yo! Andrew! I need to speak with you, man. Let's go out back for a minute."

"What the fuck, Andrew, what happened? Why would you cheat on Sam like that and then let her see you in the act? I mean, really man, what the fuck? I thought you really cared for her. How are you supposed to continue to work here with this going on?"

"Gabe, truthfully, I don't know what happened, yeah? I know what Samantha thinks she saw, but I was not having sex with that girl. I'm not interested in her like that, and I wouldn't do anything to put my relationship in jeopardy with Samantha," promises Andrew.

"Okay man, but you did," I remind him. "You left with that chick, and you took her to your place knowing that Sam would probably go there after work."

"No. No. That is not what happened. No way," says Andrew insistently, so I listen to his side of the story.

Andrew explains everything he knows. He tells me about how, in his opinion, it all began with this Nvette at work and some kissing scene on set the second day. How she always made passes at him except when Sam visited. How he thinks that Nvette manipulated the crew into coming to the club to celebrate the pickup of the show. Explaining how she treated Sam when she arrived last night and then how he found himself at his place naked with her straddled on him and Samantha standing in the doorway.

He said that when he saw Nvette on him, he was trying hard to push her off, but it was a straight up struggle, she wouldn't be moved. Nvette saw Samantha after a moment, too, and quickly got up on her own. Once she moved off of him, he could barely stand up and as he walked over to Samantha, she just stayed in the doorway watching. He was trying to talk to her, but he couldn't form the words right; he couldn't really speak, he was slurring everything. He knows that he couldn't have been drunk, especially not that drunk. He can't explain how things ended up the way Samantha found them.

Saying that he doesn't like Nvette personally and in no way has he been attracted to her. He never wanted to have sex with her before, so why now? What would make him want to be with her? There isn't that much alcohol in the world, he said. He really can't explain any of it reasonably without it seeming like he's making up a bunch of excuses, but he insists that he's going to figure out a way to sort it out. He needs to find out what the hell really happened.

Either he's a damn good actor, like I heard, or he really believes that the Nvette woman set him up. Either way, he's done. I know Sam. She won't easily forgive him for what she saw unless he's got the gods on his side.

He's worse off now than he was when he first began to work with us. I'm not sure of what parts of what he's said to believe. But I'm simply leaning towards the fact that he's a man that got caught with another woman by his girl.

"By the way, nice shiner," I say as we head back into the club.

"Yeah, Samantha," he admits.

"Oh, I know, buddy," I say. I can't help but laugh at him as I walk back inside.

Yeah. That part he remembers.

CHAPTER 105
THE ENGLISHMAN

Speaking with Gabe puts me in a slight panic. He told me how much Samantha had been crying after seeing that situation last night. I want to go to her. I want to explain that I'm not the guy she thinks she saw last night. I want to tell her, let her know that I only want to be with her, but she wants nothing to do with me now. I have never been in a situation where I wanted someone in my life and they wanted no part of it. It's a bit crushing.

Life has its funny little ways of coming back at you.

Damn it. This situation is really getting me pissed. I need to find a way to speak with her.

I don't get any time to see Samantha before the club opens and we immediately get crowded. Ladies' Night is always like that. Stix is here, so I will be able to break away if I see Samantha about, but she has yet to come out of that office.

Later, I happen to look up and notice the back of her sitting at the far corner of the bar. This is it. This is my chance to speak to her. I need to give her my side of things.

She doesn't see me approaching or I'm sure she would've gotten up by now. She's drinking? She never drinks while working. Damn, that throws me off a little.

As I get near enough, I grab for her hand, but she moves away and turns towards me. I see tears in her eyes, and it kills me. What this has done to her. I can't see her like this.

I try to put my arm around her, but she pulls back, gets up, and walks away. I follow her; she notices and changes her direction. She's going into the loo. I hope she understands that that's not going to stop me from following her. I *am* going to speak with her.

She enters the woman's bathroom and I follow.

"Samantha, stop. I'm not going to leave you alone until you speak with me," I demand.

"Andrew, get out of the ladies' room, please. I came in here so you *wouldn't* follow me," she says quietly.

"No, I'm not leaving. You need to speak with me."

"I don't owe you anything. I don't need to do anything else for you. You took it all already," she says.

Damn, that hurt. Luckily it seemed no one else was in the bathroom but us; we have a little privacy.

Someone opens the main door to come in, sees me, and turns right back around. I go and lock the door. She's looking at me with tears streaming down her face and I can't take it. I go to wrap my arms around her and again she pulls back, putting her arms up to block me.

"Just tell me what you want to say Andrew, then get the fuck out and leave me alone," she says, not really looking at me.

"I know how it sounds, but Samantha, you did not see what you think last night. I promise you that. I can't explain what was going on, but it was not that. I would never do that to you. To us."

"So, now you think that I'm really some kind of a fool. Like I'm not smart enough to know what it was that I saw? Is that it, Andrew? You're dumbing me down now? No. You do not get to do that. You got caught sleeping with another woman and it's over between us. That simple."

"No. I'm not accepting that," I say, hearing my voice raise a bit.

Just then a woman comes out of the end stall and begins to wash her hands. She's watching us through the mirror. She looks familiar, but I can't place her straight away. She goes to leave the restroom but stops short of the door and turns to us and says, "Look, I've seen you two on set and here at the club a couple of times. You two seemed pretty happy together, so I'm going to tell you a little something. I know who you are talking about. You're talking about Nvette. I know her very well. She's my cousin. She told me before that she hated the fact that you weren't interested in her, not even interested a little bit," she says, looking at me. "She did everything to get you to notice her and you didn't. Most guys fall all over themselves to get with her, and you simply weren't interested. That drove her crazy. She felt that you would be *just what she needed in her life;* her words. To make things better, she thought. One thing you should know about Nvette is when she sets her mind to it, she always gets what she wants. She will do *anything* to accomplish it." This last part she says looking directly at Samantha.

She then unlocks the door and leaves. I'm speechless. My mind is all over the place. I now recognize her from the set. She's one of the caterers. Kate's her name, I remember after she leaves.

I look at Samantha; she looks more confused than ever. I go to reach for her, and she pulls away once more, then walks out, leaving me in the women's room alone.

Bloody hell, this shit has to get figured out.

CHAPTER 106
MEET ME IN THE LADIES' ROOM

How did I not see him walking up to me? His smell, his touch, his voice. It's all too much for me to handle right now. I need to do better staying on guard or he's going to pull me back in.

I can't believe he followed me into the ladies' room. I thought for sure his Euro manners would have stopped him from doing that.

Nice eye, winky.

Damn, I hit him pretty hard. He's got a huge black eye. Good. All I kept thinking was that I should hit him again in the other eye when he was talking to me. He must really think that I'm a damn fool, that I'm really, really dumb to try to pull that *'I wasn't doing what you think I was doing'* shit on me.

Why does he keep on insisting that I did not see what I thought with him and that bitch? He said that to Gabe, too. And that other chick, the cousin, what was that? I think I need to check something out based on what she said, or this whole situation is going to drive me insane.

How did things get like this? I was so careful not to

give in to him until I was sure that I wouldn't get hurt. Damn him.

I can't think straight. My head is spinning.

I am successful in physically avoiding Andrew for the rest of the night. I can't say the same for his eyes though. He seems to watch me everywhere I go with that intense stare of his. Then, when I least expected it, I hear him say over the microphone, "Going to slow it down a bit, yeah. Since it's ladies' night."

I just wanna hold you in my arms...

"This one's been on my mind tonight and it goes out to that certain young lady who is very special to me."

...All alone by the phone
Waiting on you to call on a busy weekend,
Tell me have I seen when I stayed around,
Around the town, waiting on you to tell me what to do,
'Cause I'm happy being with you...

He plays something that almost makes me want to forgive him, but I fight it.

...Touching you, holding you
Is all I really want to do
Day and night I just can't get enough...

All I can do was listen to the lyrics and, damn, those lyrics make me so angry with him. How could he have done this to what we had?

...I want you more, and really need
For you to just believe in me,
And I'll be giving you all of my love...

I turn to look up at him in the booth and he's watching me. I'm not surprised. What is he really expecting from me? His stare, these lyrics; I can't take it. I need to find out what can be done about releasing him from his contract. I won't spend the next year or so listening to messages like this. It will drive me absolutely insane, for sure.

...Baby, I can't seem to make it without you...

Damn it. I've gotta get out of here.

CHAPTER 107

QUICK, GET OUT NOW

It's almost quitting time. I worked out earlier with Gabe that I'd leave before the end of the shift. I need to leave before closing. I can't face Andrew again and, worse, I can't have him following me. I don't know if he actually would, but he has shown stalker qualities, so I can't risk it. I need to be alone as much as possible to sort out how I'm going to handle him working here still.

As I head out, just as I'm out the door, something clicks in my head about what the cousin said and what Gabe told me earlier about his conversation with Andrew. Damn it, I need Gabe to check into something for me. I gotta go back inside.

It takes a minute to find Gabe, and I'm worried that I might run into Andrew. Luckily, he stays in the booth. I don't think he noticed that I came back inside. Good.

I talk to Gabe, the entire time keeping an eye on Andrew. I explain to Gabe how I need his help and why. He says he will look into it for me. Good. Maybe I will get closure from this mess sooner than later. I waste no more time. I'm out.

CHAPTER 108

THE ENGLISHMAN

I can't mess about finishing up tonight. I want to finish speaking with Samantha. If I don't catch her tonight, then I'll have to wait again until we're at the club. I don't want that. I need to speak with her one-on-one without all of these other distractions. Wait. She's leaving now? Bloody hell. She really wants no chance to speak with me again. I knew she was angry with me, but I guess I didn't realize how really hurt she is. Sorting this out is going to be my priority.

I see her return almost straight away. I pretend to be distracted, working, but I'm watching her still. What is she looking for? Oh. Gabe. Of course. She's telling him something about me. She's looking at me the entire time as they talk and then he turns and looks, too. What is she plotting? Then he turns and looks at the bar and nods just as she leaves again.

CHAPTER 109

SOLO

I make it without incident to the hotel. I haven't told anyone where I'm staying. I mean, no one knows that I am not home. I need to be alone to deal.

I'm sure Lizzie knows by now because of Gabe, but I'm not sure about Jonathan, since he's away on holiday. I see that I have a million messages in my inbox, but there is no way I have the energy to listen to them. I can't take hearing *his* voice and I don't want to have to answer a bunch of questions that I don't have the answers to for Lizzie.

I am going to drink this entire bottle of wine I have with me, feel sorry for myself, and do as much crying as I can because, when I wake up in the morning — okay, the afternoon — I want to be a different person, dammit.

CHAPTER 110

THE ENGLISHMAN

It's back to the set today. I am so distracted by Wednesday night that I don't know how I'll be able to focus on any of my lines or scenes today. Then there's Nvette. I don't know what I will do when I see her. I've played that moment over and over in my head and each time it doesn't end well for her.

I must keep my anger towards her under control. I have to keep telling myself this.

Walking in, I recognize how it's *crucial* for me to find out all that I can about what happened. I have to ask my mates that were there. I need to know, how is it that Nvette and I left together? How did I become that drunk without remembering anything leading up to it? I'm not sure, but there is the possibility that I won't like what they have to say.

That doesn't matter anymore, because I need answers either way.

There's her cousin. She gives a nod hello. I keep moving towards my dressing room; I can't stop.

There's a knock on the door. I hesitate to answer because if it's her, I don't know how I'll react with her standing there in my face after what she's done.

After a short moment, they knock again. It's just the director's assistant. She's telling me the director would like me to stay later today to try and make up some of the scenes I missed yesterday. That he's not keeping the entire crew. He only wants to do scenes that are primary for my character. She runs down the names of those who will be staying and, thankfully, Nvette is not one of them. So, I agree. Now I need to work the time out with Stix and Gabe for the club.

CHAPTER 111

KIND OF BLUE

At the club, in the office, as I get ready for tonight. My excuse for staying in the office today is because I'm behind on checking the socials. No hater music blasting again. I'm in another phase, it would seem. I'm on my headsets listening to *Miles Davis: Kinda Blue*. I think it is a fitting choice, anyway. Why headsets? Because I can't hear that accent when he arrives. I think it would kill me. I'm trying to stay strong, but it's not really working. I need to stay in my own little world until I'm okay.

Gabe comes into the office, and it scares the crap out of me. I don't hear him until he's right behind me because of the headsets. I couldn't hear him enter. I told him yesterday that he needed to have his office keys. He lets me know that Andrew may not be in tonight. He needs to make up work missed yesterday at the set.

He didn't go to the set yesterday? I didn't expect that. I wonder what he was doing during the day then, and I'm glad I didn't stay home. Gabe tells me that he will start looking into that info I asked him about last night, but it may take a few days.

A few days will feel like a lifetime…

CHAPTER 112

THE ENGLISHMAN

There she is, the bitch. She doesn't see me at first, thankfully. I go for a coffee at the catering area as a distraction to get myself sorted.

The cousin comes up beside me. She whispers for me not to react to whatever Nvette throws at me today, that she will try and make me respond in a threatening, aggressive way towards her. Me doing so would put me in trouble with the producers. It's all a ploy to get me under her control, she says. Phase two, if you would. Phase one was to break me up from my girlfriend.

The director's assistant announces that the director is ready to begin the day's filming and the first scene's roll call includes me.

"Please don't fall for it," Kate tells me. "Whatever you do, do not let her get to you." And then she goes back to work as she watches me walk to my placement for the scene.

"Oh, there you are Drewy." Nvette says. "I missed you yesterday."

I say nothing. She tries to give a kiss as I approach, but I pull away from her.

She gets close enough, though, to whisper, "How's

your little girlfriend now that she knows about us?" She smirks at me, then turns and says loudly as she walks away, "Too bad she had to find out like that. I hope she's not too angry with us."

If I didn't know better, that would have worked. I would have charged at her. I look back at the cousin and mouth a very grateful 'thank you.'

Getting through today's scenes was the hardest thing I've ever had to do. But I did not let Nvette bait me, no matter what she tried. As she leaves for the day, she calls my name and then blows me a kiss — a show for the rest of the crew, I assume.

Now I need to work on getting to the bottom of what happened at the club. I can now speak to the lads without worrying about her popping about.

CHAPTER 113

WHY IS *SHE* HERE?

No Andrew tonight at work. I have mixed feelings. Stix is doing great on his own, but still, it's not the same. I miss him in the booth in spite of myself.

The crowd is good again. Tonight we're full and I'm at my new post, sitting at the bar, even though there's work that I should be attending to. I can't quite get motivated.

There is a small queue outside, and a manager is needed at the door because there is some *woman* giving the bouncers a hard time about not getting in straight away.

Well, here's my motivation to do something I suppose. I go to see what the issue is.

Are you fucking kidding me?!

It's her.

Nvette.

She has the nerve to return to the club after what she did Wednesday night? Just as I'm about to go crazy on her, I feel someone grab my arm. It's Gabe. He pulls me back and whispers the warning, "Whatever you're about to do, she's not worth it." I supposed he got the 'manager needed out front' call, too.

I take another step back to evaluate. He's right. There are too many people here. I almost walked right into another trap of hers. I am smarter than that. I think quickly about what to do. I need to teach this bitch a lesson on how to plot someone's demise. I tell Gabe to go ahead and let her in, but to keep her close to him. I don't tell him this, but I need time to work on a plan. He looks at me real quick, worried like, but I just walk away.

I go into the office to think. I truly want to kill her. I can't believe she has the nerve to show up here. She came knowing Andrew was still on set. Sneaky bitch. What was she trying to do? Get me to beat her ass to get sympathy from him? She'd have tons of witnesses to say she did absolutely nothing to warrant my aggressions. I can't believe I almost let my emotions get the best of me like that. Shaking my head at myself, I think; *I can't believe I almost fell for that shit.*

Reflecting, I get lost in my thoughts.

Sitting here, I realize I'm looking directly at the contest entries for the V.I.P. promo and remember that she put her name on an entry card, and then something good comes to me. I feel a creepy little smile spread across my face.

PART V
I GOT YOU BACK

CHAPTER 114

IT'S ON NOW

I know what to do to get my revenge. I leave the office and call Gabe over. I let him know that I'll be alright with her being here. No worries. He can stop keeping her close. He told me he let her in the V.I.P. area to keep her from starting any trouble and asked his friend, who happens to be her cousin, to keep an eye on her. The cousin is a friend of his. Um, really? I never paid attention to that before. I ask if they'd been friends long. How come I'd never met her? He reminded me that he's introduced her more than once, but instead of calling her by her name, Kate, I called her Birdy.

Did I? Oops. My bad.

After about an hour or so, I tell Gabe that Nvette seems a little drunk and that maybe we should cut her off soon. He looks at me to see if I'm being...vengeful. But I act as normal as possible, and he slowly agrees.

Good, because I am being vengeful, dummy. He should really know better.

Look out bitch who plotted to take my man. It's time to teach you a lesson.

CHAPTER 115

LET'S GET PHYSICAL

The night is going well considering I still feel awful and I'm still thinking about Andrew. It's starting to get late, though. I'm planted at my new post again, sitting at the bar. The cocktail waitresses stopped taking orders from Nvette in the V.I.P. area as instructed (good girls). So, Ms. Thang decided to come to the bar for her own drinks. Where is that cousin? I thought she was supposed to be keeping an eye on the little diva wannabe. I look around and see that Kate and Gabe are in a deep conversation near the V.I.P. section. So much for that.

Everyone knows that Nvette has been flagged. She's starting a fuss. The bartender looks over at me and I give a small head shake, telling him no, not to serve her. She sees him looking at me and then puts it together. She stomps over, giving me a what for. I sit there acting intimidated by her rant.

Oh me, I am so afraid.

She's loud and her hands are all in my face, but I stay calm. I find it comical that she can be so easily manipulated. Doesn't she realize I am doing the exact same thing to her now, that she tried to do to me earlier at the door? I see Kate coming over to intervene. Nvette must have seen her, too, because she stepped up her show. Just as her cousin grabs for her, Nvette pushes my head back with her finger, telling me how sorry I'm going to be, that I'm not going to get away with treating her like this et cetera, et cetera, and so on.

A very public physical threat. Fantastic. That's even better than I could have hoped for. Thanks 'diva.'

She's pulled away. The bouncers remove her from the club. Gabe comes rushing over. Great timing there, champ.

He gets the lowdown on what just happened from Michael the bartender and jerks his head in my direction, then gives me a strong look of suspicion. I give him a *yeah, you know me, so what?* look back at him. I see him grab hold of the cousin's hand. They walk up and, as he stands there talking to me, she wants to make sure I'm okay before she goes back to see what's going on with Nvette.

He checks on me, too, to make sure I'm "*okay.*" All show, I'm sure, because he is glaring at me when he gets up close. Then he asks so only I can hear, "What the hell are you up to, Sam?"

I give him my best *'I'm innocent'* look, batting my eyes and all. He shakes his head and walks away with Kate in tow. I look at them together and wonder if that's where I recognized her from before. Did I recognize her from being with Gabe? Is he the reason why she shared Nvette's motives about Andrew when we were in the ladies' room? Why would she side against her own cousin? If they are an item, that would make some kind of sense, I guess.

Just then, I hear him. That damn accent is going to do me in. He's asking for me. Damn it. This, I was not expecting. He rushes over to me before I can react and wraps his arms around me. Oh my God, everything about him has my head spinning. I fight so hard to stay strong. I feel the tears roll down my face. He's saying that someone called him when this thing began with Nvette. Luckily, though, he was already on his way in. He tried to get here as quickly as he could. He is so sorry that I have to go through this. He doesn't know what she's doing this for. He's going to do what it takes to stop this nonsense from her, blah, blah, blah.

I don't want to hear any of it from him.

As he holds me, he must notice that I am stiff and unmoving. He slowly pulls away and looks at me. I scowl at him, tears still coming. He takes a step back and I get up and walk away, not saying a word.

CHAPTER 116

GIRLFRIENDS DON'T HOLD BACK

I'm so glad I decided not to stay at home these past couple of days. My phone won't stop ringing. A lot of the calls are from Andrew still; he doesn't leave messages anymore, but I see the missed calls. I now have everyone else reaching out to me, too. Gabe is calling, asking what it is that I am planning with that chick. He reminds me that he knows it's not my character to sit there and let someone assault me like that without reason and asks if he should be worried. No, scratch that, if he should be scared, 'cause he feels a little scared of me right now.

He's not funny.

I should call him back and ask him what the deal is with him and the cousin, but I can't be bothered with that right now. The only person's call I decide to respond to is Lizzie's.

"What the hell, bitch? Why do I have to hear about everything that's been going on this week from GABE?!" she asks, really annoyed.

"Lizzie, stop. I know I should've called you before, but I just couldn't talk about things with anybody yet."

"Yeah, well, I'm not just anybody now, am I? You

should have called me! And where the hell are you?"

"Why'd you ask me that?"

"'Cause I know you're not home. Andrew called me today asking if I knew where you were staying, and he told me about Wednesday night, too. He's going crazy, you know."

"He called? Oh, he *did*, did he? Well, how about I don't care about what he's going through."

"Okay, girl. I get that. I'm not an enemy here. The only side I'm on is your side. You know that, right?"

Sighing, "Yeah, I know, I thought that you were going to tell me that you didn't think he would do something like this, like everyone else."

"Ah hell, are you okay?"

"No. No, I'm not okay. He broke my heart, and he keeps on insisting that he wouldn't have had anything to do with that bitch, let alone sleep with her in front of me. He seems very good at putting that message out."

"I know. He told me that, too. He says he would never do that to you."

"I know what I fucking saw!" Saying this comes out way louder than I expected. It startles me.

Silence.

Sighing, "I know what I saw. I was there, too…" I say, more to myself.

"It sounds like you're not really sure, though."

"What?" Like really, what is she saying? Is she kidding me right now?

"Remember, I know you. I hear it in your voice. You're not so sure, I think. Are you doubting things? What's up? Tell me. What are you thinking?" she asks.

Somehow, she's right.

"Damn it. I don't know. I can't make any sense as to why he would do anything like this, and I keep replaying it all over and over again in my head. Something just doesn't fit, and I don't know if it's because I don't want to believe that he would cheat on me, or if it's because I keep hearing that it's not what it seems," I explain.

"Just because he says he didn't doesn't make it so," she says.

"I know that, but there are other things, too, that aren't making it add up right."

"Like what?"

"Like, why he was so worried that the cast was coming to the club. Him leaving without saying goodbye. His being so drunk that he needed help leaving the club. The way his car was parked in the wrong spot at his house with all of his papers on the passenger floor, and then those weird noises he was making. I can't shake all of those things out of my head."

"Okay, I'm going to play the devil's advocate here, because I know you to be a smart girl, so humor me, alright?"

"Yeah, okay, give it to me."

"Maybe he was worried they were coming because he *was* having an affair with her; maybe he over drank because he couldn't deal with the stress of the situation and maybe, just maybe, he was enjoying himself so much and that's why he was making those noises..."

"I thought about all of that out, too, and trust me,

I've seen him enjoying himself and he never *ever* made sounds like that. It was like he was struggling. And when he saw me, 'cause he saw me before she did, he looked as if he was trying to push her off of him but couldn't."

"Okay, so you thought it all out. Are you saying that you're taking him back because you don't believe that he cheated on you?"

"Don't do that," I say.

"Do what?"

"Don't talk to me like you feel sorry for little ol' dumb me."

"That's not what I was doing and you know it."

"It sounded like that's exactly what you were doing. Just don't. I feel stupid enough all on my own, but also, I'm hurt, I'm angry, and I still want to commit murder on somebody."

"Okay, okay, I get it and I'm sorry, but please don't commit murder; you don't look good in orange."

"Why is everyone trying to make jokes?"

"Okay, okay for real. Tell me something. I want to know, what the hell are you really up to though?"

"What do you mean? I'm not up to anything with him."

"No, not with Andrew, this other situation. I know better, 'cause Gabe gave me the other low down and *I KNOW* you've got something cooking with that woman. I want to know now, before you cause some real trouble and I have to come bail you out of prison."

"I'm not doing anything. I have no idea what you mean," I say, as neutral as possible.

"You are such a fucking liar," she says.

I don't have anything else to say in my defense.

Okay. So, he's still looking for me. Good. I hope his ass is suffering at least half as much as I am. Thanks for the info, Lizzie.

CHAPTER 117
WHO'S GOT V.I.P.?

It's Saturday and I don't think I'll be able to avoid Andrew much today. He's off during the day from the set and I'm certain he will be in way earlier than he needs to be to start his shift. Hopefully Gabe can give me some info before then.

"Hey, Angela, I need you to do me a favor please," I say quietly.

"Yeah sure, Sam, what do you need?"

"I have the finalist for the V.I.P. contest and I would like for you to call and let them know that the winner will be pulled tomorrow night, but they need to be present to accept. Very important, they need to be here no later than 9:00 pm," I instruct.

"Okay, I can do that. I'll be all professional like, too," she says.

This makes me laugh a little. "Yeah, good idea. Be very professional. Remember to identify yourself as the V.I.P. server from the club and that they're finalists and that they need to be present to win."

"Got it."

"Also, tell them that they and one other guest will have V.I.P. access before the contest, but they both have to be here no later than 9:00 pm — be firm with that."

"Okay. Should I have them announce that they are contestants when they come in?"

"Yes, of course. Go use the office phone so you can have a little privacy when you speak to them. Oh, and thank you, Angela."

"No problem, Sammy," she says as she heads to the office.

Perfect timing. Here comes Gabe. He looks like he has news for me.

"Where's Angela going?"

"She's sorting out the V.I.P. finalists."

"Oh, good. Listen, I have that info you wanted me to look into. When do you want to go over it?"

"Umm, let's wait for Angela to finish with the contest calls and then go into the office so there'll be no distractions."

"Yeah, alright. Call me over when she's done."

"Will do."

Now I'm nervous.

CHAPTER 118

NEW EVIDENCE

Why does Gabe feel he needs to give me a disclaimer before he shows me what I've been asking about? I mean really.

"Okay, Sam. Listen. I need you to stay calm when you see this. I need you to stay professional and calm. Now, the only reason I'm showing you anyway is 'cause if I don't, you'll go looking for it yourself on your own, I know."

"What the hell, Gabe, I'm calm."

"Yeah, well, the probability that you won't be real soon is at like 110%."

"Jesus, Gabe, just get on with it already. I'll be calm, I promise."

"Yeah alright, sit down first."

"What?"

"Sit down or I'm not showing you."

"Okay, now you're just being a pain in the ass," I say as I sit down.

It was definitely something the cousin said that night in the ladies' room that kept me wondering: *she'll do anything to get what she wants*. So, I had Gabe ask Andrew what the absolute last thing was that he remembered. He told Gabe that he was offered a drink to toast the pickup and extended contract of the show by Nvette. She had a tray of drinks for just about everyone. He was a little hesitant, but with everyone else sitting there she told him to stop being a baby and just have one drink with her. That it wasn't going to kill him. He took the drink like everyone else had and they all took turns toasting.

"He took the drink, or she handed it to him?" I asked.

"He didn't remember that when I asked."

"That bitch drugged him," I said, certain of it.

"It's a little worse than you think. You just have to watch the footage. I pulled the bar, the V.I.P. and the parking lot."

The way Gabe has it cued, the first thing you see is Nvette walking up to the bar by herself. She's communicating with Michael the bartender and he makes her what looks to be about ten drinks. She asks for a tray. You can tell by her hand gestures, so the bartender goes to get her one. When he's not looking, she dumps some kind of powder into one of the drinks. She finishes just before Michael turns back around with the tray. She takes a cocktail straw and stirs, but leaves the straw in the drink as Michael helps her load up the tray. She then turns around and walks away with the tray.

I say out loud, "That fucking bitch really drugged my man." Gabe gives me a warning look. I roll my eyes and sit quietly, waiting for what else he has to show me.

The next footage is in the V.I.P. You can see Nvette

walking up the V.I.P. steps towards the fellows on the crew. This includes Andrew. You see her talking, then some of the guys start taking drinks off the tray. Not Andrew. So, she goes over closer towards him; she takes the straw out of the glass and then pushes that drink towards him. He shakes his head 'no' but you can see her and the other guys give him a hard time about it. He takes the drink reluctantly. Nvette gives the toast to the group and they all drink. She watches him. A few more people say a few words and a few more toasts. The glasses go back onto the tray and Angela takes the tray away. Andrew sits down at one end with the fellas and Nvette goes over to the opposite side with some of the other crew members. As the night continues, Andrew does not drink anything else. He's just sitting there. He starts to look like he's beginning to feel the effects of that drink she gave him. People begin to leave and they say something to Andrew. He does look as if he simply drank too much. A few of the guys help him up and Nvette comes running over. He leans on the guys, trying to talk, and they laugh. She pats his jacket pockets and pulls out his car keys. She then starts to direct the guys helping Andrew. He moves as if he's really out of it but walks outside with the guys' help.

By this time, I'm seeing red, and I want to go find that bitch right now, but Gabe is watching me like a hawk. I know if he suspects me of thinking like this, he won't show me the rest of the footage. So I pretend to be calm and unbothered. I take a deep breath. I make sure not to say anything else just in case I let my true thoughts about what's going on slip out.

Next, Gabe switches to the parking lot. You can see Andrew's car clearly. The guys help get Andrew into his car on the passenger side. Nvette gets in on the driver's side and, after a long delay, pulls away. Because of that delay, I piece together that his registration and insurance card must have been used to get his address.

That's it! It's over, and I can't do anything but sit quietly with my hands folded in my lap now because of Gabe. I don't know what to think about the things I just saw. It's hard to process it all.

No. I can't process it and I'm not sure if this changes anything about me and Andrew, because seeing these videos does not make what I feel about that night go away.

Gabe speaks first.

"Listen, I know this was a lot to take in, but I got to let you know that I have to tell Andrew what we found."

"No," I say in almost a whisper, still processing what I saw.

"What? Sam." He looks at me as if I've lost my mind just now. "He has a right to know what happened. He's going crazy trying to figure this out."

"No, let me do it. I should be the one to tell him, but I need to do it in my own way. Give me a week," I ask.

"A week?! Hell no, Sam, that's too damn long. He should know now, tonight!" he insists as he paces around.

"Gabe, please! Let me tell him and give me at least a couple of days then. I need to sort all of this out in my own head without adding his part in, too."

"What the hell is there to sort out? She drugged him and took advantage of that situation. That's what you walked in on. Now you know why he said he wouldn't do anything with her. He was right. This shows that. He's innocent!"

"He's not totally innocent," I quietly say.

"What the hell are you talking about? You're talking some crazy shit right now, Sam."

"What I mean is this, okay. My feelings haven't changed. He is still guilty. He allowed himself to get in that situation."

"He allowed himself? Do you hear what you are saying right now? You really are crazy, you know that? I don't know what goes on in that head of yours, but you need to snap out of this. What you're saying doesn't make any sense, unless..." He stops mid-sentence, thinks for a second then says, "I know you have something else up your sleeve, Sam, and you need to let it go. Just let it go. You know the truth now. He did not cheat on you. It was *her*. He didn't allow anything. It was all her! You know that now and you have to tell him," he says, a little more animated than I would have expected.

"I will tell him, just give me a couple of days. I promise I'm not up to anything. I need to do it when I'm ready to face him. Please, Gabe," I almost plead.

He just stares at me, saying nothing.

After a moment of this, he says matter-of-factly, "You have until Tuesday. If you haven't told him by then, I will."

"Thank you."

"Thank you? Yeah, right. I don't know what you really have going on, but it better not blow up in your face. You need to be careful with this, girl."

"Got it."

Just then, I hear his voice. Damn it. He's in way too early.

CHAPTER 119

WHATEVER IT TAKES

Gabe leaves the office and leaves the door open without me noticing on his way out. Almost immediately, Andrew stands in the doorway and knocks.

Of course it's him, and I have nowhere to escape. Everything is starting to look different for me now that I am digesting the fact that he was drugged.

Damn, he looks so good tonight and that catches me off guard. I think I did a little double take.

He smiles to himself a little and says, "Hey, Samantha, I just wanted to see how you were feeling after last night and everything else that's been going on. You alright then?"

"I'm fine," I say a bit monotone.

"Listen, Sam, can I come in to talk?"

Sam? He's never called me that before.

He doesn't wait for me to answer, and he comes in and sits down in front of the desk.

He tries to smile as he says, "I keep finding prezzies all throughout my flat from you and I never get the chance to thank you." He seems really uncomfortable, and he's searching for what to say. He tries the smiling thing again and continues, "I tried to call you every time

I discovered one, but then I remembered that you won't have anything to do with me anymore."

I don't say a word; I just look at him.

"Listen, I know that you have been hurt by what has happened and I'm sorry for that," he says, looking at his hands.

This makes me cry. Ugh! I so hate being this blubbering little girl. I have no control. The tears just start streaming down my face again and he sits forward. I get a good look at him; he looks as if he hasn't slept in weeks. This makes my heart ache for him, and I have to fight to stay seated in my chair as he continues.

"Please know and understand that I would never intentionally do anything to hurt you or to jeopardize what I had with you. I know it's hard to explain, but that was not me. I did not do this."

I really begin to cry. He gets up and comes around the desk to me. He sits on the edge of the desk and puts his arms around me.

"Whatever it takes, tell me what I need to do to win your trust back."

I try pulling away half-heartedly, but he holds me in close to him anyway, not letting me go so easily. He holds me tight and kisses the top of my head. Then he whispers, "I'm so sorry for all of this. Can you ever find a way to forgive me? I don't want to lose you. Not like this."

I let him hold me for a good little while. It feels good, but I still don't say anything. How could I? I am now more confused than ever. I want to hate him, but I don't. And I have no clue what to do about *us*. I really do miss him. I know now that he did not start this, but there is one final thing I need to check to be sure that he really did not participate in this 'affair' thing.

Until then, I have to keep my head. I have to follow through with my plans so this can finally end. I need the closure. I force myself to pull away, I get up and I go lock myself in the office bathroom until I hear him leave.

CHAPTER 120

CLUE ME IN

"Hello, fucker," I hear.

That's Lizzie! Thank God. I come out of the bathroom to find her closing the office door behind Andrew.

"What are you doing here?" I ask, totally surprised.

"My girly needed me and so here I am. Are you okay? I saw him leaving just now, and he looks a mess. Shit. Just like you," she says.

"Gee thanks, nice to see you, too." I make a face at her. "But yeah, I'm going to be okay. I guess he finally got his chance to apologize to me directly and said he wouldn't have done anything to lose me like this and, and he may be right."

"Wait, what? Is he smooth talking you that easily?"

I shake my head 'no.'

"What the hell? Then tell me what you know, the whole story, right now. What in the hell did you find out since we spoke last night?"

"Well, I asked Gabe to look at the video footage at the bar from that night because of what I told you the cousin said. I had the feeling that she was trying to tell me something and, hey, did you notice if Gabe was dating anyone? I think he's dating her, the cousin. I saw them holding hands yesterday."

"Wait, Gabe has a real girlfriend? No. Nope. You're not going to change the subject. You're trying to distract me from the video. Just tell me already."

I don't answer. It's hard to form the words.

"Tell me!" she says again.

"She drugged him. That bitch drugged him. That's why everyone thought he was drunk and why he didn't say goodbye before he left," I confess.

"Holy shit!" Lizzie says as she sits down. "Brian knew it! Brian said that she had to have done something to him and I didn't want to hear any of that, but he was right. Holy..." She trails off. "I know you want to kill someone. Shit, I want to kill someone, and it didn't happen to me. How is it that you're still sitting in here?"

"I really just found out a few minutes ago."

"Oh, well, that explains it then. Getting your battle plans ready?"

I shake my head 'no.'

"No? I don't believe you. You know that, right?" She sighs and says, "Okay then, so now what? Did you just tell Andrew, is that why he was in here in the first place?"

"No. I didn't tell him."

"Uhh, what? Why not? Don't you think he needs to know? I don't understand. Why aren't you telling him? This is proof that you are plotting something." She narrows her eyes, looking at me. "What the hell are you still up to, Samantha?" she demands.

"Why does everyone keep asking me that?"

"'Cause we know your ass, that's why."

"Whatever." I go to sit down across from her. "I just wish you guys would stop always accusing me. I'm the victim here, remember?"

"So is he, it sounds like."

"I'm not going to give him that pass until I confirm that he had absolutely no participation in sexing her, damn it."

"What?!" she says, looking at me as if I've lost my mind. But I don't explain any further, so finally she says, as she shakes her head up and down, "Okay. You don't think like the rest of us, I know this about you. If you don't tell me, then I can't testify against you. That's a good thing." Then she starts to shake her head from side to side. "You know that I have no idea what you mean with your little code talk here, but I'm sure you'll tell me something when you're ready to clue me in." She then looks at me for a minute. "I can't with this, you are being too weird. This is way too much to deal with. I feel stressed and it's not even me he cheated on, or not cheated on, or whatever. I need a drink. Let's both get a drink; we need alcohol," she says, as she gets up and begins to pull me out of the office towards the bar.

CHAPTER 121

THE ENGLISHMAN

Lizzie's here. I'm glad she has the support.

"Hello, fucker." That makes me laugh a little and there's nothing to say or do to that but shake my head at it.

I can't help but notice that something's changed. Samantha didn't seem as angry with me just now. She didn't really pull away from me when I reached for her, either. I actually held her, which was something. I know this is such a bloody mess, but I didn't realize how much this situation really got to her. The way she cried when I wrapped my arms around her caught me off guard. I really have to do something about that damn Nvette for causing all of this.

Everyone at the set is saying they didn't see anything unusual, that I was just toasting with them. No one noticed how much I was drinking either way. When they saw me 'sloshed,' they assumed I just had too much to drink, so they helped get me to my car, and Nvette was the one who volunteered to get me home. They thought nothing of the events that night. When I didn't show for work the next day, they assumed that I was suffering from a bad hangover.

I know she did something to me. I don't know how or when, but that doesn't matter to me anymore. She's guilty and she needs to pay. In the meantime, I need to work on getting my missus back.

And I really need a bloody pint.

CHAPTER 122

WATERING HOLE

Lizzie drags me to the bar before we notice that Andrew is there. I go to leave, but Lizzie holds onto my arm and makes me stay. He doesn't say anything. He just looks at me for the longest moment as his expression goes from warm and friendly to really angry. He looks away as if he's calculating something, then walks back to the DJ booth.

CHAPTER 123

TOO LATE, SO SORRY

A day has passed since I saw the *'Nvette drugged Andrew'* videos and I have processed them as well as I can. I don't know if I am still upset with him or not. Yes, he was drugged, but I have in the back of my mind that he shouldn't have allowed himself to get in this situation to begin with. I can't offer how exactly, but still, in my mind, he should have done something to avoid all of this; it's still his fault, in a way.

It's been a rough afternoon for me and on top of it all, I'm starting to beat myself up about what I'm feeling. I'm starting to really get upset at myself because I have been thinking about how much I miss him since he held me last night. I believe that I do really love him and have thought of the possibility of us getting back together once or twice, now that all of the dust is settling, but I want to be smart about everything. I don't want to be a fool.

Dammit, I'm so confused. I don't know whether I'm coming or going anymore with this.

At least Lizzie will be at the club with me again tonight. I need her there, I told her. Without hesitation, she said she'd be here; she's got my back, and she's bringing Brian, too. Good, I need all of the backup and support I can get to work things through.

I know I can't live like this. I really need to do something to help sort this all out and move forward.

I've now decided once and for all that I seriously need to get that bitch back for all of the bullshit she's caused.

At the club now and I am on the ready. I've got my plot all sorted. The V.I.P. contestants are starting to arrive. But she's not here yet. I have to stay in control if I want my plan to work. I cannot let the watching of those videos mess me up and wreck the next steps.

I need another drink; where is Lizzie? Being next to her will help keep me in control.

It's 8:30 pm, thirty minutes to go before we get started with the contest. The V.I.P. area looks great. We're really taking care of them tonight. I hope those who don't win will still consider booking a V.I.P. reservation for their events now that they have had a little taste of being pampered. I see the cousin, Kate. She stares at me as she checks in. She looked as if she was about to come over to me, but changed her mind and instead just went straight to the section set aside for the contestants and their guests. Still no sign of that Nvette yet. I see Gabe with Brian as they go to the V.I.P. and they seem to be hanging out with Kate. I think to myself that it's strange that I never really noticed him with her like this before all of this. I guess they're closer than I thought.

Keep calm, keep calm, is what I keep telling myself over and over as it gets closer to 9:00 pm. Then the Englishman catches my eye. He looks like he's up to something himself. I walk away; he can't distract me right now, not while I'm on this mission.

It's 9:10 pm. I've waited a bit before getting started, but she still has not arrived yet. Change of plans. I will use her lateness against her instead; this may work better to my advantage anyway.

Lizzie and Brian are now by my side and Lizzie knows about the V.I.P. contest going on tonight, but she doesn't know that Nvette is one of the finalists. I point out the cousin and Gabe in the corner and we both agree that there is more to that than Gabe's regular 'friendships.' We are convinced that they're dating. She wants to go and give him a hard time, but I need her with me, I tell her, so she sends back Brian over to bother them instead.

We are in the section with the contestants, having our own little party before pulling the winner. It's 9:40 pm when Angela comes to me and says that the woman from the other night is giving her a hard time for not being allowed in the V.I.P. area.

"She says she's a contestant, she was invited, and should be let into the party even though she's been told she's too late, that she missed the cut off," Angela says, sounding very worried.

I look over Angela's shoulder. It is Nvette. Perfect. I see that the cousin is watching between me and Nvette, but doesn't move. I go to walk over, and Lizzie grabs my arm to stop me. She recognizes the actress and knows she's the one who I caught with Andrew.

I look at her and tell her it's okay. "I'm not going to do anything, I promise."

She says she's heard that shit from me plenty of times before. I assure her that I wouldn't do anything here at the club, and she reluctantly lets me go, but I see her signal to Brian, and he stands up, waiting for us.

As I walk over to the section's entrance, I look up at the DJ booth and see the Englishman is in his own world. He is focused on his music and hasn't seen what's going on yet. Good.

I feel that Lizzie is following close behind me. She doesn't trust me. Then I think otherwise. Of course, she's not going to let me take on this bitch alone. I stop directly in front of Nvette at the top steps of the V.I.P. entrance, looking down towards her.

"Is there something I can help you with, Miss?" I ask as professionally as possible. I see Angela is by my side now. Lizzie is still directly behind me, and I notice Kate standing with Brian, both watching.

"Don't play your little games with me," she says loudly. "You know who I am."

This is working out way better than what I had planned already. *Excellent*, I say to myself in my evil villain voice, and it takes everything for me not to do that evil genius thing with my fingers.

"I'm not sure what game you are referring to, but I am not playing with you. This section is closed. There is a private party going on at this time," I advise.

She steps up onto the first step and says, "I was invited to this party, but your employee won't let me in. Now tell me, really, you're not playing games? You know I am on that list!" she says, still talking loudly. Just then, Kate comes to the top of the steps and tells Nvette to calm down, that she's making a scene for no reason.

I then say, looking at Nvette directly, "Everyone who was invited was told several times to be here no later than 9:00 pm to ensure access," I say looking at my watch. "It is now 9:45 pm. You missed your opportunity, full stop."

She's having a little hissy fit. Her cousin is right next to her now, trying to calm her down. I can't focus on her or I might lose my cool, so I look up at the booth and see that Andrew is watching us now. I look back at Nvette. She is out of control, and I can't help but give a little smirk. She loses her mind when she sees that, yelling and screaming at me. In spite of her cousin's attempts to pull her back, she steps up again and is almost face to face with me. I want to just punch her in her mouth so badly, but I stay in control. I have another quick look around.

Lizzie, next to me now, looks at me as she narrows her eyes and gives me a look that's telling me that she knows I'm effin' starting something, but I just look back at her as expressionless as possible.

I know it's hard for her to understand what I'm going through. She is worried about me, she said earlier, but I see that she is following my lead and has pulled back from reacting herself. Lizzie is no one to play around with either, when it comes down to it. It's good that she's keeping her cool, too. Yes, that's good, that's very good. I would hate for her to get mixed up with this chick because of my plots.

I know I have to remain calm. Easier said than done, though. If I let my anger take over, she'll win. I see the DJ booth directly from where I'm standing and see the Englishman pull off his headsets and leap over the side of the booth. He is making his way over here fast. I've never seen that look on his face before. He looks as if he could kill someone, and this is the first time I think that I could be afraid of what *he* might do. It kinda scares me. I did not take his reaction to all of this into account.

I see Brian leave the V.I.P. area and Gabe follows close behind him. He and Gabe head towards the DJ to cut him off so he doesn't get involved.

Nvette is still yelling and screaming. Her arm is waving in the air and she's pointing at me. I snap back to reality and hear her threatening me. She moves closer and pushes my head with her raised hand like she did the other day when I was sitting at the bar. I don't react. This was the hardest damn thing I ever did in my life; not react. I want to fucking kill her, but I don't do a damn thing except act afraid again. I don't allow myself to respond to any of this. It looks as if she's bullying *me*. The hotshot actress who didn't get her way into the V.I.P. area and now she is raising holy hell about it.

The club seems to have come to a standstill. I notice

people taking pictures and videos with their phones. Lots of witnesses to show how I am just the little innocent victim in all of this. Perfect. This makes the second public incident against me in *my* club by little Ms. Nvette.

Lizzie grabs Nvette's arm and stops her from putting her hands on me again. That's my girl. That seems to make Nvette go even crazier. I want to laugh at how easy it is to manipulate her into behaving the way that I want. Lizzie now moves more in front of me, not letting go of Nvette's arm.

Just before Andrew gets in the middle of things, I see Gabe and Brian are there but are having a bit of a struggle holding him back. Gabe's talking to him, trying to calm him down, I assume. Kate is trying to get Nvette to leave, still attempting to pull her back, all the time saying things to convince her to stop; how she should not be doing this.

It seems like forever in my mind, but in reality it's probably only been seconds since this commotion began. The bouncers have finally moved in. There is now one bouncer at the top of the steps to protect me and Lizzie — our own little bodyguard. The biggest one, he's with the fellas, helping to restrain Andrew, and a third bouncer has picked up Nvette and is removing her from the club. Brian is on his way back to us to check on Lizzie. Passing by the guys, the cousin says something quickly to Gabe and Andrew, then she follows Nvette out of the club, and that's the end of it. The show is over.

Everyone who doesn't really know me comes up

to me with real care and concern. They're so worried about me. *How nice.* They want to make sure I'm okay. I act as if I'm really shaken by what just happened; poor little me. I'm a good actor, too. Andrew is still fighting to get free, but Gabe and the bouncer are still holding him back. Andrew is pissed. I can't take looking at that, so I just turn and walk away. Lizzie grabs my arm really hard and pulls me in the direction of the office.

"I know you're fucking up to something and you better tell me what it is right now!" she demands as she closes the office door behind us.

I just look at her without saying a word, turn, and walk into the office bathroom to check myself in the mirror. I can't believe I held it together long enough for that scene to play through. I deserve a fucking Academy Award for that performance.

Lizzie continues in on me. "There is no way the Samantha I know would ever let someone put their hands on her like that without striking back tenfold. And yet, this is the second time you've let that girl do this to you. What the fuck is up?" she demands again. "Not to mention the little fact that *I* was about to punch her in that movie star mouth of hers myself, so you owe me explanations and I want them now."

I come out of the bathroom. I look at Lizzie for a minute before I decide to clue her in and then say, "Look, if I go off on her, it would seem as if I was the jealous girlfriend who couldn't get over the fact that I caught my boyfriend sleeping with this woman. I'm not going to give her the satisfaction of ruining my relationship and ruining my character," I continue. "So, I'm using her own medicine against her."

"What?" she says in disbelief.

"You know that she came to the club two days after everything that had happened with her and Andrew?" I ask. "When she knew he was still at the set working late."

"I know, yeah. That's the first time she smushed you in the head."

"Yeah, exactly. She tried to get me to react to her out of anger out front before that. She was causing another scene with the bouncer trying to get inside, but Gabe caught me before I did anything stupid when I first saw her. So I got to thinking instead: what if I turn the tables on her, would she fall for her own tactics? Now, I'm giving her a bit of her own medicine and, yep, she's falling for it. The stupid cow," I say as I look at Lizzie, and I notice that she looks like she really wants to slap the crap out of me now for getting her involved in my mess.

CHAPTER 124

LAST CHECK

I actually feel a lot better now that I got rid of Nvette tonight. Gabe wants to ban her from the club, but I stop him, thinking that I may need at least one more show like tonight before I'm done. He stands his ground and says, "No way, she's done here." He reminds me that I'm not the only one involved now. He says he thought, too, that Andrew was going to really kill someone tonight, and it took forever to calm him down enough to let him go.

I say, "Good, it's about time he did something." Gabe looks at me like I have really lost my mind this time. I don't know why he seems surprised at that. I know he thinks I'm crazy already, he should not be surprised by anything that comes out of my mouth; he says he has no words for me so all he does is just shake his head and walks away.

My revenge is fabulously working better than I originally planned, but then I stop and think about Andrew in all of this. I didn't mean what I said about him finally doing something. It really scared me, though, seeing him like that. His reaction and how angry he was. Do I want to involve him like this? What if he gets angry again and can't be held back next time. Am I ready for those consequences?

Oh, God, here I go again with the back and forth. I can't think straight with the videos Gabe had shown me still playing in my head. The Englishman seems to be innocent, yes, but I still have to know for certain what his part was. I need to know exactly what it was they were doing at his apartment. He got angry, though. If he didn't react like that tonight, I'd think for certain that he had an equal part in this sex affair thing with her, drugging or not.

I'm no good at work; I can't focus on anything I'm supposed to. I need to get into his apartment without him knowing. I have to do one last check before I believe that he is totally innocent of this situation and forgive him for what happened.

I do need to get out of here before I drive myself crazy. The Englishman has been keeping his eye on me all night, since that scene played out. That isn't helping things. Besides, it seems to me like he's been planning his own plot and I'm not sure I want to see what he's up to.

I glance at him, but *she drugged him* is all I think about when I look at him now, which is destroying me. I fell for her plan to break us up and I can't stand myself for that. It was like I was waiting for him to do something to let me down and she unknowingly took advantage of that.

I find Gabe. I tell him I need to step out for a minute. I need some air to clear my head. I remind him Lizzie and Brian can help out if he needs it. Then I assure him

that I'll be back in time to help close up.
    I leave without looking back at Andrew. I know he is watching me, and I don't want to lose my nerve, because I'm now on my way to his place.

CHAPTER 125
IT'S THE PREZZIE

I arrive outside his door and place my ear up to it to be certain that no one else is there. I knock, wait, then unlock the door and go in. I look around. He still has the painting I made hanging on his wall where I placed it, but the key is gone off the corner. I feel myself tear up a little and I tell myself to stay calm. I take a couple of deep breaths and keep to the mission.

I go into the bedroom for the last thing I left for him. The stuffed bear which is disguising a small video camera. I look around but it's gone. I don't see it in the bedroom anywhere. I panic a little. Where could it be? I go back into the living room and it's sitting in his chair face down. That's good.

I relax a little. It's motion-activated. Being face down will save me a lot of time and trouble. I'm hoping it was left in the bedroom where I placed it that night. If it was, I will be able to see everything that happened. All I need is the memory stick and I will be able to go home to learn what I want to know. I take it, place the bear back the way I found it, and head back to the club.

CHAPTER 126
IT'S THERE IN BLACK AND WHITE

I help with the cleanup and the lock up. I told Gabe when I returned to the club that I needed him and Brian to help keep Andrew from approaching me. I told Gabe that I still needed time to tell Andrew what we found out and that it was way too much to deal with after everything else that went on tonight. He was cool with that, and the fellas are doing a great job playing interference. I get out before speaking with Andrew again.

I can't wait to get to my house. I park my car around the block so it seems like I'm still not home. I go in, grab my laptop, and hurry back out of there just in case.

Once I'm at the hotel, I relax a little. I grab a bottle of wine that I picked up earlier, then go straight into work mode. I set up my laptop on the desk, pour a large glass of wine, and start looking for the footage I want.

He must have found the bear early on, taken it into his front room, and left it face down, because there wasn't much for me to sort through from the past two weeks.

I begin looking at the last thing recorded, and I see a very frustrated Andrew grabbing and throwing the bear across the room at the chair I found it in, then everything goes black. That throws me for a loop. I don't know what it is that I really *expect* to find watching this, but I do see some things that I wouldn't have predicted. Him throwing the bear like that was one.

I pause, take a drink, take a deep breath, and keep going with my mission.

While reversing the footage, I catch a glimpse of Andrew playing his piano, so I go back to where he starts and watch. This holds my attention for a long time. I've never seen him play and he was moving so passionately over the keys, but I can't hear him; there's no sound with the video, just the colorless images. I think of him and his brother William for a moment and my heart begins to ache for him again. I almost forget what I'm on task to do.

I reverse the footage a little more and see Andrew just sitting at the piano, his head in his hands, and this time I notice a glass and a half-empty bottle of vodka next to him. For the first time, I get a sense of what he's been going through, too.

I can't take any more of these little insights into Andrew's pain, so I reverse the footage completely. It begins with me placing the bear in the bedroom and waving to myself after I turn the camera on. I look as if I think I'm sooo clever. Stupid girl.

Seeing that old me, the one in love, makes me cry all over again. The tears start streaming. Damn it, I hate being this crying chick. This was never me. He's really got me good, that Englishman. I am such a blubbering mess.

The next scene is Nvette coming into the bedroom. She takes a good look around at things, but I can't tell where Andrew is at this point.

She leaves the bedroom and returns with him leaning on her, barely able to walk straight. He falls onto his bed, and she takes off his shoes and socks. Next, she goes to unbutton his shirt and I can see that he's protesting but can't push her off. She lifts him up a bit, gets his shirt off, and then he falls back on the bed.

She is now climbing over him in a straddle position, helping to undo his pants. He becomes really animated with his protests, but still she overpowers him and somehow gets everything off. She grabs his things and leaves the room. I assume when she leaves that she was placing their clothes in a trail along the floor, except for the few things in her hands, because she comes back into the room nude.

I stop the video. I am not sure if I am prepared to see what happens next. Do I really want to know if they actually had sex?

I drink about three quarters of my bottle of wine before I decide that I can't take not knowing. I just *HAVE* to see it and can't wait any longer to know what really happened.

I play the video and watch with my eyes half open through my hands, which are now over my eyes. I'm squinting, not really wanting to see, but I can't seem to stop myself from watching.

She puts the rest of the things down near the bed then walks over to him. It looks like she is trying to wake him. He half sits up, looking completely out of it. She straddles him again but only halfway down his lap. He is trying to move her off of him without success. She looks back towards the doorway quickly and then scootches closer onto him and starts a grinding motion. He's trying to get her away from him, but isn't strong enough. I appear in the doorway watching them.

I rewind the video to see everything again. This time, though, my face is so close to the screen that I almost hit it with my nose. I want to see if she actually mounted him or if she was pretending to be sexing him. He's not aroused; at least it doesn't look as if he is. She scoots and grinds. That's it.

I now know that she's just pretending to have sex with him, and I am pissed as hell because I fell for it. I fell for it all. He was right this entire time. He was not with her. He did nothing but try and fight her off when he was aware of what she was doing.

Damn it all. I feel a huge headache coming on.

I'm at a loss. My head is really spinning and I'm not sure if it's because of the wine or because my thoughts are bouncing around in my head like crazy balls. I don't know what to do with this new intel. I look back at the screen just in time to see myself punch Andrew in the eye.

What the hell am I going to do? This entire thing is such a mess. I am so shocked at what I saw. I don't know why, but I really can't believe it. He was telling the truth.

The only thing he knew for certain was that he would never do something like that to what we had together. He's such an asshole for being right.

Seriously, what the fuck am I supposed to do now?

CHAPTER 127

HE'S BAAACK

I'm off today because Jonathan is finally back from his holiday. He calls me as soon as he hears what's been going on with Andrew and me. He wants to know where I am and, more importantly, he wants to know what I have up my sleeve. He knows about the Nvette incidents at the club, too. He threatens me a little, thinking that he can stop whatever I have plotted. If he thinks I'm plotting something, then he knows better than to think that he could stop me. I have more reason now to give this bitch a payback. I want justice with my revenge, and I want to make her suffer.

I haven't had a chance to tell anyone about the video I pulled from Andrew's apartment yet. I'm still dealing with what I saw. I don't know what to do and I really need some advice.

"Hey, Gabe, could you meet me for lunch at the coffee house today? I need help with something and I thought of you."

CHAPTER 128
I DON'T KNOW WHAT TO DO

Good old Gabe. He meets me without too much hassle. He's still a little pissed at me for not telling Andrew before now about what we found. Still, he knows I need his support.

When we meet, I tell him about the video I took from Andrew's apartment. He still looks at me as if he thinks I'm insane.

"Who are you?" he asks. I laugh.

"I had to know. I couldn't shake the fact that he never changed his story," I say.

"So, you haven't told him anything then?" he asks.

I don't answer.

"I can't believe you. What are you still waiting for?"

Again, I don't answer.

"Sam, you have to tell him. He is torn up inside over all of this. The dude knows without a doubt that he didn't do anything with her, but yet he still loses you over this. He has to know, and you have to be the one to tell him, and now."

"Me?! Why must it be me? I thought you would tell him if I hadn't already."

"It needs to be you now, because it's you he loves.

You two need to sort this out together and telling him yourself is the perfect way to start."

"Who are *you*?! How the hell did you get so smart about all things relationship all of a sudden?"

"Seriously, Sam, you need to tell him, and you need to tell him right away," he says, as if that's that.

I look around at the other people in the cafe. Some are couples that are enjoying each other's company, and I ask myself if I could ever go back into a relationship with the Englishman after all of this has happened. In spite of him taking no part, having no control, I still feel as if I wouldn't be able to trust him anymore. I can't seem to get past the feeling of betrayal from when I saw them at his place like that.

I have issues, I know.

Gabe seems to be reading my mind, because he says, "It's not his fault. He didn't do anything. *He had nothing to do with this*. He's more of a victim than you are. There is nothing you can hold against him. He knew that he did not cheat on you. He knew it in his heart. That's saying something. If you're sitting there thinking of holding him accountable, then you're letting her come between you two as if she did have sex with him. And guess what? She wins."

I look at him. It's like he has been invaded by a body snatcher and someone who has been in a real relationship has taken him over.

"You know I'm right," he says as he gets up and walks towards the restrooms, and I realize: yes, damn it, he *is* right. I hate that.

CHAPTER 129

CAN YOU?

I ask Gabe to do me one more favor. I ask him to have Andrew meet me at the club on Wednesday, our day off. I decide that's when and where I'm going to tell him about what I found out, and I can let him see the videos if he chooses.

Andrew agrees to meet without hesitation. He has a shoot scheduled early evening, but said he would come directly after that, Gabe tells me.

CHAPTER 130

SO BEAUTIFUL

It's finally Wednesday night. I'm at the club, waiting to speak with Andrew. I'm so nervous. I have no idea how he is going to react to what really happened. It's getting pretty late. I start to think that maybe he's not coming after all. Gabe came into the club tonight for support, he said. If I needed him, he'd be there to help. Good old, Gabe.

I'm sitting at the bar drinking up some liquid courage when Gabe walks over.

"How are you holding up, Sam?" he asks.

"I'm not doing so well. I'm really nervous. I don't know what to expect," I admit.

"You'll be fine. You didn't do any of this either. I think he'll be relieved to find out what really happened to him," he says.

"I guess."

"Well, you look beautiful tonight. If anything, he'll be so distracted, he won't care what's coming out of your mouth," he says, trying to make me smile.

"Thanks, Gabe. Thanks for everything. I really appreciate it," I tell him.

"Really appreciate it, huh? Then come on, let's

dance," he says as he takes my hand, and I let him lead me to the dance floor.

I need the distraction from my own thoughts.

As we get on the floor, I realize that Stix just started to play a slower song. It was *So Beautiful*, the song I teased Andrew to the day I plotted my revenge on him here at the club. Hearing that song kills me. I can't do this. I need to just go home before I lose it again. I stop dancing and try to walk away, but Gabe won't let me. I tell him I need to just go. He asks me to have this one dance, and if I still want to leave, then he won't stop me.

Out on the dance floor, Gabe begins to talk to me about the Englishman.

"Listen, Sam, you know how much I care for you, right?" he starts. "We've known each other for a very long time, yes? You've been told that I've always liked you. That's true, more than you know," he says as he pulls back a little to look at me directly as he talks. "I would like nothing more than to have had a relationship with you." He clears his throat. "We've talked about that a little bit before, and I know you don't feel the same."

I go to say something in response, but he cuts me off by saying, "I know you don't see me like that. It's okay. I get it. You don't need to say anything now."

He starts looking around a bit. I watch him a little. I really had no idea he felt that seriously about me. I thought maybe it could've been just a little crush a long time ago and from that they just teased, but I never thought it was more than that.

He looks back at me and gives a little smile. "I saw

how you and Andrew looked at each other when you were together. I know I would never have that with you, even if I were lucky enough to get you on a real date. He's really a good dude. I'm serious. I mean that. He's the right one for you. I see how much he cares for you and how in love you two were before all of this bull*shit*." He pulls in closer again and in almost a whisper, he says, "You would never feel that love with me, I know. I also know that no other man would be as true to you as he has been. You two were meant to be together. You need to give him another chance after you talk to him. You know deep down that I'm right."

I can tell this is really hard for Gabe to say; he looks a little sad when he looks at me again, but he continues on anyway. "I'm going to say it again; he's a good man, Sam. He loves you very much. I would not be saying 'give him another chance' if I didn't see that you two were a good fit. You don't really allow yourself to be loved like that and then walk away from it unnecessarily. If you don't give it another try, he will always be in the back of your head and you know it. You'll never again really allow yourself to be in love because he will always be the one on your mind."

I pull back now and look at Gabe. I can't help but begin to tear up at what he says. "You need to give him another chance. You need to give love another chance," he says. "You two were meant for each other, seriously." He pulls away slowly, holding up my hand as he turns. Surprised, I see Andrew waiting on the side of the dance floor. Gabe holds my hand up a bit more in a gesture to hand me off to the Englishman, and I allow him to.

When Andrew takes my hand, when he touches me, it all becomes too much. I can't help but let the tears fall fully now. Something so simple as a touch on the hand by him; just feeling his warmth and energy next to me again almost takes my breath away.

I *have* missed him so much and wouldn't really let myself admit it until this moment.

The song was ending just as Andrew took my hand, but that didn't stop him from holding me close and dancing with me slow. I could feel the entire club buzzing around us in fast motion, but I didn't care. I let him hold me. He held me tight, and I felt as if I would just melt into him. Breathing him in, feeling his strength around me, hearing his heartbeat; with all of this, I knew I'd have a hard time letting him go.

CHAPTER 131

THE ENGLISHMAN

I received a call from Gabe Monday asking me to meet with Samantha tonight at the club. She wants to speak with me.

Finally.

I had a job earlier and I couldn't come until after that. It's pretty late in the evening when I finally arrive. I was beginning to believe that Samantha might have left when I noticed her on the dance floor, slow dancing with Gabe. I watched them for a moment. It was hard for me to do because it seemed I might have lost her to him by the way they were talking with each other. He was doing most of the talking, though, I noticed, and I could see that she had been crying. I was ready to walk over to them when he stopped and turned to me, holding out her hand for me to take. I didn't realize he knew I was standing there.

She allowed me to hold her. There was no pulling away, no resistance. We didn't speak. I drew her in as close to me as I could, holding her as the rest of the world went on around us.

CHAPTER 132

KEEPING SECRETS

Andrew and I manage to get a small table towards the back of the club to talk.

He sits there very patiently, very attentive as I begin to tell him what was discovered about that night.

At first, I have a hard time finding the words to tell him what was seen on the videos from the club. I keep waiting for him to get that angry look on his face again. The one I saw when he walked across the dance floor the other night, when Nvette was here. Thinking about that makes me a little afraid to tell him everything, but, as I continue, he never changes his expression. Because of that, I find it easier to talk on. The words begin to build an ugly picture, giving him the details about what really happened before he left the club that night.

When I finish he just sits there, looking at me. It is as if he is replaying the entire scene over again in his head. He looks away into the crowd and still does not say a word. I don't know what to do. I reach for his hand and when I touch him, he gives a little jump like I have just awakened him. He looks at me again, but it seems as if he doesn't recognize me. That scares me more than any angry look he could've given.

He turns back to the crowd and speaks more to himself than to me. "How could you have known this and not have shared it with me straight away?"

I go to answer. I open my mouth, but the words won't come out, so I say nothing. I just looked at him.

He gets up slowly and walks away. I don't move. I watch him as best as I can through the crowd, and I see that he ends up at the bar. He doesn't leave the club — that's good, right?

Still, I don't move. I see how not telling him affected him. Me not telling him right away has affected him more than what he found out about that night, it seems. He did not bring up the fact that he was drugged or that he was right about not playing a part in any of this. He just asked how it was that I didn't tell him.

I know now, of course, that I should've listened to Gabe and let him tell Andrew the day we found out what happened, but I couldn't. I wasn't ready. I got lost in my own needs. I couldn't tell him right away. I still needed to know what happened in his apartment before I could talk to him again. I couldn't make any decisions about him and me because I needed to know more than half the story. I needed to know beyond any doubt that he had no part in any of this and I guess I didn't give much care about anything else.

I look back at the bar, and he is gone from where he was standing before. I look through the crowd and can't see him anywhere. The tears start again. I look down. I start giving myself a hard time about not telling him before now. I keep thinking that I would now lose him for certain because of my own selfishness. It's truly over with us then; I never got to the video that was in his apartment. It looks like she really wins in the end.

Just as I was thinking things were over, I hear his voice. He is behind me.

"Right, I know you've had a really hard go with all of this, but so have I," he says, rather seriously.

I turn, look up at him, but he's not looking at me; he's watching the crowd as he speaks.

"You should have never kept this from me. I've had a right to know. I knew I had no willing part in this and it was driving me mad, trying to sort out what really happened."

He looks down at me with that hard stare of his, and then he asks, "Why would you keep that from me? Why would you stop me from knowing? If you didn't want to speak with me directly, surely Gabe could have passed on the information, right? So, tell me, Samantha, really, why would you keep this from me?"

I know I am wrong. He feels betrayed by *me* now, and I don't have anything to say.

CHAPTER 133

THE ENGLISHMAN

When we sit, I think to myself that it's nice to be able to talk, finally. I expect that I will get to tell Samantha everything that has been on my mind for these past couple of weeks. She insists on speaking first. She has news about what really happened that night and I am ready to listen.

"You were right all along," I hear her say. "You were drugged."

But she found this out almost a week ago and didn't tell me. This I do not understand. This delay I can't get past.

I have to walk away. I need to gather my thoughts. So much is answered and yet she waited to tell me and, for the life of me, I can't process why.

I need the goddamn bar.

I should just leave, I think as I finish my second drink.

I'm not going anywhere. I need to know absolutely everything; so I can't just leave.

I also know I can't just walk away from *her* like that either.

Bloody hell.

Desperately needing answers, I walk back over to her and I must ask her again, "Why would you keep this from me, Samantha?"

CHAPTER 134

ANSWERS

The relief I feel hearing his voice behind me, even if he kind of catches me off guard, is everything. I want to jump up into his arms, but nothing is settled yet. I still need to answer for not telling him about the first videos and still, again, I need to tell him about the second video; the one from his apartment. On top of all of that, I have to sort out what I'm doing when it comes to him and the fact that I think I *need him* in spite of myself.

It's my turn. It's me now who has to figure out a way to work things out between us.

I am so thankful he came back.

I can't find a way to explain why I didn't tell him right away. Instead, I continue on about the second video.

"I used the key to your place only one time since you had given it to me. It was that afternoon when I left several things there for you as a surprise, you know. The painting, a key to my house, and the stuffed bear," I started.

He turns to look at me again, but I still can't tell what he is thinking. He's just looking at me, staring, expressionless. His stare is going straight through me, though.

I almost lose my nerve, but I make myself tell him everything.

I continued to explain that the stuffed bear was to be the biggest prezzie of the three. I wanted to surprise him with a homemade video based on that quick conversation we had early on when we were in the office, that night of my plotted revenge. When he wanted to know if there was a video recording of us, after we had been together. Because of that, I bought the bear, which had a nanny cam and included a motion sensor recorder. I wanted to record us at his place that night and surprise him with it. But I found him and Nvette together and it recorded them instead.

"After Gabe had shown me what he found on the club's videos, I needed to know what was on that recorder in your bedroom," I continue. "I couldn't talk with you without knowing exactly what happened once she got you to your apartment."

He still didn't say a word, so I went on. "I just recently worked up the nerve to go and retrieve the memory device the other day while you were busy here at the club. That was the second time I used your key. After I got it, it took me some courage to get the nerve up to actually look at what was recorded."

"The bear was a recorder? So, you saw what was going on in my flat afterwards, too?" he asks.

I just nod my head yes. I can only guess he's referring to the piano because there wasn't much else.

He didn't say anything more.

His head tilted slightly, and he then looks at me as

if he doesn't recognize me again. Neither of us speak; we just stayed there looking at each other.

Angela the cocktail waitress comes and drops off a couple of drinks. Startled, I looked up at her as she says, "You two looked like you *really* needed a drink. I hope you don't mind me interrupting, sorry." And just like that she was gone again.

"So, what was it that you saw on that other video then? Was it what you wanted?" he asks.

I ask him to please sit; I don't want to talk to him with him standing over me like this. It's making me uncomfortable. He hesitates at first, but he sits down across from me and I explain everything on the video between him and her. He looks as if a huge weight had been lifted off of his shoulders, but he still doesn't say anything and I don't mention the piano because of what his brother had told me before.

Again, we ended up just looking at each other, saying nothing.

After the longest moment, he speaks, breaking the silence between us. "I have known this entire time that I never did any of this with her. What I couldn't understand was how we ended up in my flat like that. Then I saw you standing there, looking at us, and all I wanted to do was get to you and..." His voice trails off.

I continue to explain that as soon as I saw the video and had all of the information about that night, "I asked Gabe to see if you would be willing to meet with me. That I didn't wait on. Once I had the complete story, I wanted to tell you. I wanted to let you know that you *were* right all along," I confess.

I finish my drink in, like, two gulps. His silence is killing me.

Shit, I need another drink. I start looking around for Angela, and he grabs my hand. I turned and look at him.

"Where does this leave us then?" he asks. "We both have to work through some things, I know, after this, but what were you thinking about us?" He looks back at the crowd on the dance floor. "Could there still be an us now that we have the truth?" he asks as he looks back at me.

I shrugged my shoulders and shake my head; I don't have any answers to his questions, and this makes the tears fall again. I really don't know what to do. He moves in closer and gives me a long kiss on my forehead. He then stands up and reaches for my other hand. He asks if I had walked to the club or driven. I'd walked. He asks if he could walk with me home so we could talk quietly along the way.

CHAPTER 135

OUR OWN PLOT

"She really had me boxed in, Nvette." he begins as we walk towards my house.

We walk together kind of awkwardly. A side-by-side, careful not to touch each other; awkwardness.

He says that he doesn't want to lose trust in me, but he can't shake the fact I didn't tell him straight away what I had found out about that night. He doesn't want to believe that I held onto the information out of spite. But hard as he tries, he can't think of any reason good enough for me to not have told him.

Even with my explanations, I had no real right to keep all of that from him. It was definitely selfish of me to do so.

I feel like a teenager whose boyfriend is breaking up with her. Officially, we had not been together for a couple of weeks, but his words make me feel as if I'm about to lose my best friend now. I have nothing more to say in my defense. He is right. Again.

He stops walking without warning; we aren't even halfway to my place, and I think this is officially the end. He steps to me, holds my face in his hands, looks at me for a moment, and then kisses me.

That kiss. It's everything I needed. It feels as if my heart begins beating again at this moment, and now it will officially be the end of things between us, it seems.

When he stops kissing me, I can't catch my breath. I start to tear up again, expecting him to say goodbye and walk away. But he doesn't. Instead, he tells me how much he loves me. He says that he wants us to start again. To help each other get through this. That, this *shit* of a situation could only make us stronger. We can not let Nvette win in the end by truly breaking us up.

I'm so relieved that he doesn't make this his goodbye.

What he was saying *is* convincing, but I tell him that I, too, am having an issue with trust. Although he did nothing but rightfully insist that he had no part in this plot, I still can't get over the feeling of betrayal when I think of finding them together in his apartment. The trauma of that is hard to shake. It broke me. "*That*, I don't know how to get over," I say.

"We weren't *together*. That's your first mistake, yeah? Stop thinking of us as together and look at it as it really was," he says, rather seriously. "That's how you start to get over it. None of that was me."

"You're right. In my head, I know this, but it's hard for me still. You broke my heart," I say.

"But why, though? That wasn't anything I did. I can't understand the issue," he says.

So, I explain, "Everything was going so well with us, that when I walked in on you, I couldn't help but say to myself: *you stupid, stupid, girl, of course he had you fooled, no one is that perfect.* You know? And that I was just dumb for giving you my heart. That's what made sense to me. Then I see the reality of what she did to come between us, and I can't help but think that I was even more of a dummy for easily falling for her tricks. It was as if I *wanted* you to do me wrong. I can't explain why, but I couldn't accept being *that* happy with you as right."

He looks at me and I still can't tell what he's thinking. I can't place his expression. He looks away for a moment, then he takes a really deep breath, looks at me again, and says, "Well, looking at things proper, I *didn't* do you wrong. I told you before that I would never intentionally do anything to hurt you, and now you know that for certain. I also have been very honest with what I've wanted when it came to you and me. I dunno, maybe I came on too strong, or maybe being with me is not what you really want. It crushes me to think that, but I can't force you to '*give me your heart,*' as you put it."

He begins to walk away, taking a few steps back in the direction of the club, but then he turns back around, clearly frustrated with me, and asks, "Do you want to be with me? Because I am very confused right now. Should I not be fighting for you?"

I just stand there looking at him, trying to find the right words to say.

He continues, "Of course I want us to be together, but not if you are not willing to go all in with me."

I realize that I am fucking things up here, so I give in and tell him how I really feel. "Being with you shows me that I've never truly felt love in a relationship before. I understand that now. You're perfect..."

"I'm not perfect," he interrupts.

I put my hand up to stop him from saying anything else and continue, "You're perfect *for me*. I couldn't have asked for more. I couldn't. And although being with you made me happy, being with you also terrified me to pieces."

Looking a bit shocked, he asks, "What are you so afraid of with me?"

"I'm afraid that I don't have control." I pause, trying to choose my words carefully, then say, "I mean, I really thought I had my life together before I met you. I had everything. I didn't need or want for anything, and I didn't really *need* anyone either. That's just the way it was. But now, none of that is true. These past two weeks have made me realize that I'm a mess." I laugh at this. "That I *don't* have my life together, I *do not* have everything I need or want, and *you* are the reason all of that is shaken up for me. Why things are out of control, and that terrifies me."

Wow. I can't believe what I just admitted to. I guess Jonathan was right after all. I was too independent for my own good, and it was stopping me from really being happy.

Andrew just gives me that hard stare of his and it makes me wonder if he is now really trying to see down to my soul.

I can tell that he's thinking about what I just said, but I still can't place his expression. I have no idea what's going to happen next. Then, without warning, he puts on that crooked little smile and says, "Well, then don't worry about any of that, because you equally have turned me into a mess as well. I think of you and I'm a person I've never been before. But I like the whirlwind you have me caught up in." He gives a devilish look and says, "Guess now we need to create our own plot to show her how she's failed at tearing us apart, yeah?"

Without warning again, he turns and continues walking towards my place.

Confused, because I never agreed to being back together, I slowly trail behind.

He slows down and allows me to catch up.

No one says anything as we walk. When we get to my driveway, he explains that our plan should simply show her that we are not defeated. That *she* is the one who truly failed. We can't give in to her in any way. Breaking us up was exactly what she wanted to do.

He asks if I think maybe we could try to continue on where we left off. He asks me to just think about starting our relationship again and what it is that I am willing to give. "There's no pressure," he says. If I couldn't answer right now, he understands. He doesn't want us to end this way but, still, he would understand, with everything that has happened. With that, he kisses me on the cheek, says goodnight, and then walks away.

I'm left a little dumbfounded. What is he doing? Reverse psychology? He says *'if I couldn't give an answer right now,'* but he didn't even wait one second to see if I would.

I watch him walk as far as I can see him down the street, still thinking about what he just said. In my heart there's hope, but there's still fear, too. I'm afraid now that I won't be able to let go of this enough to get back to who we were. To go all in. I know I want to be with him, but I don't know if I can let go of my fears. I'm still so confused and I don't know what to do. He was smart not to wait for me to give an answer.

I finally go inside and end up crying myself to sleep over it all.

CHAPTER 136

THAT'S NOT ENOUGH

It's Thursday. I have off today and I can't get out of my head what Andrew said to me before he left. *We need to create our own plan.*

By this, I think he means for us to get back together and show how happy we are. That Nvette was not able to come between us.

I've been thinking about this all morning.

That's just not enough for me. I still need to make Nvette suffer equally for the pain she's caused. It's not enough for her to see that we may be together in spite of her efforts. Seeing us together may have another effect. Seeing that might only make her try again. I need to end this, and I need my revenge. I need to cause pain in her world. I need to teach her a lesson.

I have an idea. I look at the clock and see that I have just enough time to make it to the studio before they quit for the day.

I called Jonathan and asked him if he wouldn't mind me using his truck for the evening. I lie and say that I have a few bulky errands to run. I couldn't let on that my car would be too easily recognized for what I really wanted to do.

I get Jonathan's truck in time to get to the studio with minutes to spare. I don't attempt to go into the lot; instead, I park in a parking area across the street so I can see the cars clearly as they leave.

I'm not familiar with each person's car, but I am in a spot where I can see the drivers as they wait to pull out onto the main road. Slowly, I begin to recognize the crew and those who were at the club celebrating that night.

There's Andrew. I swear he can see me sitting here and I get really nervous. He turns in the direction of the club. He's moving pretty fast. He still has to work tonight. I guess that's why he seems to be in such a hurry. I watch his car a little too long; I almost miss Nvette leaving the lot. Luckily, I see her at the last second. Even luckier, her car is flashy enough for me to catch up to when I finally pull onto the road myself. With Andrew pulling out first, at least I don't have to worry about him seeing and following me while I'm following her. That would have been another mess.

She pulls into this little condo complex, which throws me off guard. It's extremely average for Ms. Superstar. I expected a guarded entrance at the very least. I didn't see which unit she went into so I sit across the road and wait to see if I can get anything else from following her today.

Good thing I waited. I see Nvette coming out of her unit walking two tiny little dogs. But she seems to be arguing with someone and she looks like she may be trying to walk away in a hurry. She stumbles. I wonder what the heck is going on. Right as I think that, this huge, rough-looking guy comes out of the same unit and grabs Nvette by the arm really violently. I thought he was going to hit her, but he must have realized that he was out in public because he shoved her away from him and went back into the condo. I almost felt sorry for her, but that didn't last.

I recognized him immediately as the dude I had the problem with right when we opened the club. That same guy who grabbed me by the arm because I wouldn't accept his drink. I remember the warning the bartender gave me about him that night and something clicks about Nvette. I can't help but get the feeling that somehow what she did with Andrew is connected to trying to get away from this guy. It didn't make a difference. There were other ways she could have asked for help.

She walked her dogs quickly and then went back inside. A few minutes later, that biker dude guy comes out, hops on the loudest motorcycle I've ever heard, and leaves. I can see Nvette watching him from the side window. As soon as he turns the corner, it would seem, Nvette comes out in a different outfit. Less than a minute after that, she is flying down the road in the opposite direction and I follow again, of course.

She pulls up in front of this busy new restaurant, uses the valet, and goes inside. As I park, I see her come out of the restaurant and walk down the block to a small liquor store. I get out and go into the restaurant to check it out. They have a twenty-minute wait, I'm informed. As the hostess tells me this, I see that Nvette has put her name on the waitlist. I have a look around and, not recognizing anyone, I assume she's here to eat alone. I decide to order food to take with me. I might as well, since I'm here. I pay for my order, then walk to the same liquor store up the block. I don't want to miss anything.

In the store, she's getting help from the clerk on which wines to choose. She hasn't seen me yet. I hear her say that she's going to the farmers' market Saturday morning and wants to choose something that goes well with different cheeses. She is having a small party at work and wants to impress a few people. Just then, as luck would have it, my phone rings and it's Andrew. *What great timing*, I think to myself, a little annoyed at my ringer. I turn my back to her and I answer the call.

"Hello?" I say innocent enough. "Andrew, hiya, you've finished for the day already?"

I want to make sure she hears exactly who it is that I'm talking to.

He called to say he was thinking of me and then asked if I wouldn't mind coming by the club during his supper break to talk more. He said he would really like to see me. Good thing I couldn't decide what to order for takeout so ended up getting two entrees. I guess I could stop by and give him something to eat while we talk. I'm sure he didn't grab anything between gigs, as usual, and we do have a lot to work out, so I agree to stop by the club.

As I end the call, I turn around to see Nvette staring at me, watching my every move, and it makes me smirk at her. She's still with the clerk. He continues talking to her, not paying any attention to me. I choose my wine on my own, go to the cashier, pay, and leave.

I am standing at the bar near the entrance of the restaurant, waiting for my food, when she walks in. She checks her status on the waitlist, then heads towards the bar and sees me right away. Perfect. She looks so spooked. Luckily, I was there before she walked in, so it seems like she followed me instead of vice versa. She didn't know what to do and I just stand there watching her. She's saved, as it would seem, by the server bringing me my food order. I take my things, walk past her, and leave. She has the strangest look on her face, and I love that.

"Hello Lizzie? Girl, what are you doing Saturday morning? Do you want to meet me at the farmers' market at 8:30 am? Great! See you then."

I hop into Jonathan's truck, dinner and wine in hand, and head to the club.

CHAPTER 137

THE ENGLISHMAN

I've had a rough day. Knowing everything that happened that night and going into the studio was too much for me to sort through. I wanted to murder Nvette all over again. Luck would have it, though, we really didn't have many scenes together today. Every time I looked at her, a voice in my head would scream, "THAT BLOODY BITCH DRUGGED YOU, MATE!" She could tell something was off with me because she made no attempts to speak with me out of scene. That may have saved her life. I couldn't leave the studio fast enough when the day was done.

It's a tough situation. She's been trying her best to have something with me since that night. Pretending that we're lovers. I am such a bastard to her, but she won't let up. I'm under a new contract since the show has been picked up, so I can't quite quit. Besides, I really like everything about the job except for her. I don't want to give her the satisfaction of making me leave.

I tried to stop by Samantha's house before I was due at the club. I really wanted to see her, but she wasn't home. When I pulled up to the club, though, I saw her car and expected that she'd be inside, but she wasn't.

I want to settle what I said last night about us getting together again. I don't want it to wait. I need to talk to her tonight.

    So I call her.

CHAPTER 138

WE NEED TO TALK

I'm at the club earlier than the Englishman's usual dinner break, but I knew if I went home first, I wouldn't come back out.

I'm here to finish talking things out. Yes, I do miss him and, yes, I know we still have things to settle before we can officially get back together. I'm not kidding myself anymore, I know I want to get back with him. That's no longer a question. Now, it's just where do we pick up from?

When I enter the club, I go into the office first. Jonathan is there and we talk for a minute. Gabe brought him up to speed, so he knows everything, too. In his own way, Jonathan told me that I shouldn't let what that chick did stop me from being happy and, from what he saw, really for the first time, I was truly happy when I was with Andrew.

Boy, that was a tough conversation for him, I know, but he's my brother and I love him for trying.

I leave the food in the office then go to the bar. It seems I still need liquid courage to deal with our little situation, especially after talking with Jonathan. It's true, I was my happiest with Andrew. What if he changes *his* mind after thinking about me holding back what happened and doesn't want us to try again? My stomach is now in knots. I don't know why I'm still nervous about him.

I shouldn't expect anything else, but out of nowhere, he comes up behind me.

"Hello, lovely," he says. "I'm really happy to see you." Then he kisses me on the side of the head before I can turn around. He ordered a Coke and asked me how long I could stay tonight. He wants to talk more about some things and really doesn't want to wait another day.

That's good, because I don't think I can go through this much longer either. I want it sorted, too.

I stayed around until the Englishman was able to take his break. We ate together in the office like old times. We talked about things that were broken with us because of that night again. We both decide to work on our newly formed trust issues together and agree that neither of us was out to intentionally hurt the other. That was a huge first step. Talking with him like this, I realize that through everything, I never stopped being in love with him.

I wanted to talk to him more, but his time was short — he needed to return to the booth. He wished that he could stop by after work, he said, but he had a really early call time and needed to go straight home to catch up on his sleep. He told me that he had a few other recent gigs coming up, because he'd filled his sudden free time without me with work since that night. Or more correctly, since I stopped seeing him, he teased.

Since I stopped seeing him? Really? So he's feeling clever again, I see. I ignore that comment because it's kinda true.

I'm not sure if I'm disappointed or not about him not being able to stop by after work. It might be a little too soon for that still. I did mention to him that we would be at work together tomorrow night and could talk more then.

He reminded me that I was welcome to go to his place any time, if I'd like, using my key, of course, and that made me ask if he still had the key I had left him before.

"Of course I have it still, love. Why wouldn't I?"

Of course he does. That makes me smile.

When we worked together Friday night, it was almost as if nothing had changed between us. He was not holding on to what happened and was really working on trying to move forward.

Early in the night, he told me that he had an early appointment Saturday at 8:30 am so he wouldn't be able to spend time with me until after that, if I wanted. Him having an appointment was perfect because I needed to be somewhere at 8:30 am, too, I told him.

He took his supper break with me, played a song for us to dance to, and it was all I needed to be truly under his spell again; and since I had walked to work, Andrew drove me home, of course, then stayed.

CHAPTER 139

MY OWN REVENGE

Saturday morning. Spending the night with Andrew was much better than I remembered. The makeup is definitely better than the breakup. I'm such a sap. Gabe was right, I would have always had Andrew in the back of my mind if I hadn't given us a second chance. We owed it to ourselves to try again.

We woke up a bit early, so we ate breakfast and talked a little more. He told me that his appointment today was with an attorney. He simply cannot sit around and do *nothing* in reference to Nvette drugging him. He's having the hardest time facing her every day and needs to do this.

"Wow, I never considered it from that angle," I admitted. Getting a lawyer was the last thing I had thought about. It makes sense for him. Still, I have my own need to get back at her and it's revenge that I have in mind.

He asked what I had planned so early today, and I told him about meeting with Lizzie at the farmers' market, but of course I did not tell him why. That key piece of information I needed to keep to myself. I told him that I believed Brian was going, too, and asked if he wanted to meet us when he was finished with his appointment.

He would let me know when he was finished and wasn't sure he would be out before we left the market, but if he could meet up with us, then he definitely would.

    We said our goodbyes and headed off. As I drove, I thought how happy I was to offically have Andrew back in my life. I just have one small part to sort out so I can be at peace with this whole episode. Hopefully I can take care of that today before he meets us and be done with all of this once and for all.

CHAPTER 140

TO MARKET, TO MARKET

When I arrive at the market, I meet up with Lizzie and Brian right away. They look great together; being engaged agrees with them. They both look so happy. I'm glad for them.

Lizzie and I walk around doing the girlfriend thing of talking and laughing; Brian is in tow carrying a few of our bags as we go along. They know that Andrew and I are back together and he may meet up with us later.

I don't look for Nvette. I'm hoping to just run into her, but I am hopeful, too, that we didn't miss her already.

The market opens at 7:00 am. We arrive and start walking around 8:30 am; that's a long hour and a half in between when you're trying to catch up with someone. I didn't see Nvette as the waking up with the sun type of person, so I thought 8:30 am would be early enough to coincidentally 'run' into her without raising any red flags with Lizzie.

It's a large enough market and it's still pretty early; I need to just let this happen.

I am starting to get bored now. I have all of the goodies I could want for today. Lizzie is having a great time with Brian and some cute local farmer guy learning about cheese with milk from goats versus cheese with milk from cows. We are in the dairy area, just where we need to be, and there are a few cheesemakers set up around selling their goods. I wander slowly to the next couple of booths to give the hint that I am ready to go when it happens. Nvette runs into me.

"What are you doing here?" she says in a loud, demanding tone. "Why are you following me?"

I guess she is saying this louder than needs be because there is an audience to be had. Always on stage, I suppose. That's okay with me because she's behaving just like I had hoped she would.

I just look at her. I get a good look and I see that she's a pretty person, really, and she seems likable enough from her interviews that I've seen. I just don't get it. Why does she have to stoop to such tactics to get help for getting away from her man? Why doesn't she just ask someone? *Maybe it's that winning diva attitude she puts on that's getting in the way*, I answer to myself. That makes me chuckle, which seems to really piss her off. I think she's the only one who heard that, though.

"Well, I asked you a question! WHY. ARE. YOU. FOLLOWING. ME?" she asks, almost screaming at me now.

"I'm not following you. I'm here with friends. Me being here has nothing to do with you," I say. "This market is not exclusive to you, you know."

I look for Lizzie and I see her and Brian making their way to us. I also notice that people have their phones out again, taking pictures and videos because she's a star, no doubt.

"Look, just because your boyfriend slept with me and prefers me over you, doesn't mean it's okay to stalk me," she announced proudly.

"Oh no, she didn't just try to go there!" I hear Lizzie say from too far away still.

She takes a step towards me, so I quietly but firmly say, "I know for a fact he doesn't prefer you. You did not sleep with him at all. You faked the entire incident." She lets out a tiny gasp then takes a quick look around. "Who did you spend your evening hiding from the other night?" I ask. She tries to hide how that affected her, but I can tell she's shaken, so I continue. "Because Andrew was with me until this morning," I say in a low whisper, so really only she can hear. She takes another step closer. I give another little smirk and say, "You had to drug him to even get him to leave the club with you. Are you that much of a desperate bitch?"

SLAP!

Nvette back hands me hard in the face, with a hand full of rings on, and grabs my arm, shouting for me to just shut the fuck up. I can't help myself. I jerk my arm from her grip, drop my things, and begin to punch her in the face as many times as I can. I get in at least four good licks, I think, before someone pulls apart. It may have been Brian, I'm not sure.

The next think I know, the police are here, putting us both in the back of our own squad car. I feel a little satisfied, and that gives me the peace I need to not to worry about what's happening.

The crowd that's watching is huge now. I see Lizzie with Brian talking to a few police officers and when we make eye contact, she holds up my things to show that she has everything. Then she slowly shakes her head as if to say she knows this little get-together was no accident. I blow her a kiss and give her a little smile to let her know that I'm okay anyway. I mean, I *was* just assaulted.

I see that a couple of policemen are working the crowd, getting statements and checking phones.

My assigned officer finally took my statement and told me to sit tight. I look around and see that an ambulance has arrived and the police are escorting Ms. Nvette to get looked at. Give me a break. Fucking actresses.

Then I think I hear his voice in the back of the crowd. Christ, if that's really him, I can't imagine how in the hell he got here so fast. It's not even 10:00 am yet. I look up and see the Englishman talking with Lizzie and Brian. He has that damn angry face, and it scares me again a little. He's watching me while he listens to what happened. I have no idea what version of the story Lizzie could be telling him; the one where I plotted to come here or the one where that chick randomly slaps me out of nowhere. The wrong version and this could mean real trouble for me.

He walks over to one of the police officers and talks to him a bit, then they both turn in my direction and

Andrew points at me. The police officer lets him past. He is making a beeline for me, and I get nervous for the first time this morning.

"Hey, love, are you alright then?" he asks with more care in his voice than I expected. He kneels next to me.

"Yeah, I'm fine," I say.

"You're not fine, Samantha. Your face is red and bruised on this side," he says as he gently touches my cheek. "Is this where she hit you?"

"Yes."

"Bloody hell," he says as he turns and looks in Nvette's direction. He turns back to me and says, "I am so sorry for all of this, love. But I am going to put a stop to it right now." He caresses my cheek again, then stands up and goes towards Nvette with a look of hate on his face.

CHAPTER 141

THE ENGLISHMAN

I can't believe it when Brian calls me to tell me that Samantha and Nvette just had a cat fight at the market. He said it wasn't pretty. The police were called, and Samantha is sitting in the back of a police car. How does this shit always happen just before I am about to arrive?

When I do finally get there, I can't believe how many people are standing about watching. I find Lizzie and Brian; they begin to tell me that they aren't really sure what happened. They were there enjoying the morning and all of a sudden, Nvette walked up to Samantha, accusing her of following her and screaming. There was a little bit of arguing, more so on Nvette's part, and next thing they knew, Nvette slapped the mess out of Samantha. After that, there was no stopping Samantha from punching Nvette in the face over and over and over until she was pulled off.

Shit. Something tells me to ask if this was plotted or if this just happened. Lizzie says they had plans to come to the market since Thursday, so she's not really sure. She says that she doesn't put anything past Samantha, and that something was bound to happen between them.

Samantha would never let what happened that night go. But she doesn't understand how this could have been the plan for coming here today.

I don't know what to think. I told Samantha before that I would not let Nvette get to her again and I've failed. The guilt from that is all I can think about now. I speak to the first police officer I see to find out how much trouble my lady has gotten herself into. He explains that she's basically free to go. That no one is being arrested, but if we wanted to press charges against Nvette, then we would have to go to the station to do so.

The story is the same. The witnesses side with Samantha, stating that Samantha was minding her business when Nvette walked up to her, yelling and shouting. There was no provocation from what anyone could tell and so it looks as if Nvette assaulted Samantha and Samantha was just defending herself.

The officer told me that it appears Samantha hit Nvette three or four times (maybe more), but he understands that this is not the first time Nvette has become physical with Samantha, so the self-defense thing should stick.

I've been on the end of that punch, and I know there is a lot of power in that little arm of hers. If she got off a few licks, Nvette must be a ruddy mess. I can now understand why an ambulance was called.

The officer allows me to speak with Samantha and the only thing I can focus on is the huge red and blue mark there on her face.

"Hey, love, are you alright then?"

"Yeah, I'm fine."
"Your face here, is this where she hit you?"

I can't stand this. I've got to stop this little bitch once and for all. I am able to go to where they are holding Nvette. When I see her, her face is worse than I imagined. I'm proud of the beating my girl put on her. Nvette is a mess, but that's nothing compared to what I want to do. She's caused way too much trouble in our lives, and it takes everything I have not to beat her to death myself when I walk up; but I have been raised better than that. Instead, I give her the warning of a lifetime.

"If you go near Samantha again, please know...I will be the one to end all of this, I promise you."

CHAPTER 142

NVETTE

I can't believe they have me sitting here all alone. This bitch has been such a problem. She keeps getting me into trouble. How did she know what I really did? I have to get out of here. What the hell am I doing here like this? Oh my God. How am I going to explain to him why I got into this fight? *He's* definitely going to automatically assume it's over a guy. I'm done. He's going to kill me this time for sure.

I feel like a fool sitting in the back of this ambulance. I need to leave. Wait, that's Andrew coming over. Oh, thank God. I knew he cared for me. Maybe this isn't going to end so bad after all.

"Oh, Drew, I knew you would come," I say, as he gets nearer.

"No. You don't get to say anything," he says.

"What? Why? She hurt me, can't you see?" I say in my defense. "She did this because of us."

"There is no us!" His voice is strained with anger as he comes closer still.

The look on his face really scares me now. He comes and stands so close to me as he asks me what happened, watching me intently.

I'm not sure how to respond at first, but I know he's not leaving without an answer. "She hit me, Drew, she just kept hitting me," I explain.

"Why? Why would she do that?" he asks.

"She was following me and I couldn't take it anymore. She was stalking me because she was jealous of us. I was so afraid of what she would do to me. I just freaked out."

"Just shut it!" he says, just as I was getting good with my explanation. He puts his head next to mine, with his mouth next to my ear. He holds my right hand with his right hand and then puts his other hand around my throat then begins to squeeze my hand. Hard. I'm in shock. I begin to panic and can barely breathe. I start to hyperventilate as he says in a tone that sends a chill down my spine, "You really know nothing about me, so believe it when I tell you this. If you ever start with her, or go near her again, I will be the one to end it, full stop...I will do whatever it takes to protect her from you. Whatever I have to do, is this clear? There is no us. I do not fancy you in any way, and I am tired of you trying to bully my girl. I know you drugged me, and you will pay for that in another way, but if you go near Samantha again, I will be the storm you never see coming. I promise you that, yeah?"

He pulls his head back, looking at me eye to eye, to make sure I understand completely. I nod my head, letting him know that I do. He lets go of my throat first, looks at me again, then lets go of my hand and walks away.

I'm so defeated, I can't help but cry as I watch him leave.

One minute later, a police officer comes around to tell me that I am free to go.

CHAPTER 143

THE ENGLISHMAN

Talking to Nvette makes me angrier than I was prepared for. I take a step back and think about what I was about to do. I wanted to squeeze her throat instead of her hand so badly. I know that I've got to get out of here before I end up reacting in a way that I will regret later. It takes a lot of willpower to let her go, turn and walk away. I hear someone say that Samantha's free to leave as I walk back to where she's been waiting. I grab her by the hand and take her straight to my flat.

PART VI
AFTER

CHAPTER 144

WHAT NEXT?

"You're free to go ma'am. If you would like to press charges for assault, you may do so at the station. There are plenty of witness statements that show you were not the aggressor; that you struck back in self-defense. But otherwise, you're free to go," says the officer.

Just after I'm told that, I see Andrew returning, and he looks really disheveled. I don't dare ask what just happened to him. He takes me by the hand, and we leave.

The next day, it was reported that Nvette was in the hospital because of a domestic violence incident and her live-in boyfriend was arrested.

I still wasn't definite about wanting to press assault charges or not against her because of him, the boyfriend, so I decided to go see her at the hospital. Although I did get some satisfaction punching in her face, it's not what I planned. If she weren't with that biker dude, it would have been a done deal. No question.

I was shocked when I walked into her room. She looked like a truck hit her. I had no idea she was really in that type of situation at home. That would explain the angry phone calls I overheard on the set before, though.

"What the hell are you doing here?" she asked in a slight whisper.

"I wanted to see how you were doing."

"Why do you even give a fuck about me?"

"Honestly, I was planning on pressing charges against you, using the incidents at the club as back up to the farmers' market, but then I heard you were in here and I wanted to come talk to you first. Before I made my decision."

"Oh, so what now? You want me to beg you not to press charges?" she said half-heartedly.

"No, I'm not looking for begging. I'm looking for answers."

"Of course you are. Little Miss Perfect wants to know why."

"I'm not perfect. I've never claimed to be, but yeah, damn straight I want to know why."

She said nothing, so I continued, "I want to know why you did this. Why did you drug Andrew and pretend to be having sex with him when I showed up? What was the point to all of that?"

She shoots me a look, so I explain, "We have cameras at the club. They showed everything: the bar, the parking lot, and even the V.I.P." I pause, then remember the bear and tell her about that, too.

She frowned at me, but I made it clear that I was not going to leave. She waited a long time before she finally began to answer my questions. She said that she saw us together and wanted what we had. She thought that if she were to get Andrew, he could be her knight in shining armor. She hated her relationship; he was mean, he used her money, and he beat her. She tried, but she did not know how to really get away from him. She thought that if Andrew was in an impossible situation and no longer had a chance with me, then she could win him over and finally have a man who would treat her right. Then he would help her get rid of that bully she had at her house.

I believed that to be an honest answer. Okay, she wanted a good relationship, but getting another man wasn't going to solve her problems. Especially another woman's man. She just needed to get rid of the old one and move forward from there.

I told her that Andrew *was* a good man, but just because she saw the way things were between us, there would have been no guarantee that she would have that if she were to get together with him because of what she did. The way she went about it all, he did not love her.

She fell silent again. After a moment, she seemed to remember who she was speaking to because she tried to be that old diva-wannabe again, but I didn't fall for it. I sat down next to her bed and just watched her for a moment. She yelled at me to leave her alone, but when that didn't work, she just broke down and cried.

I don't know why I stayed with her as long as I did. I didn't feel sorry for her. It's funny how someone who seemed to have so much, in reality had nothing at all. I left after she had cried herself to sleep. I still wasn't sure if I was going to press charges or not. It would be a shame to waste all the setups of her publicly bullying me, but I don't really see the point. She's already miserable.

Andrew, on the other hand, is going full steam ahead. There is nothing to be said or done to stop him from filing his charges. He has nothing but hate for her now, which is horrible for me to think about, because I think that he's such a good guy at heart.

I don't fully know what really happened between the two of them, but *there's more to that story*, I keep thinking to myself. When I ask him, he plays all innocent, like he has no clue what I could mean. Okay, I get that. Then he tries to play as if he's more upset at the fact that she hit me and all of that other physical stuff at the club than he is over being drugged. That I don't get.

When it comes up between us, he has tried to make light of things by telling me how proud he is of that little hook of mine, as he begins to duck and weave. Not funny. He's changing the subject, taking the focus off of him, but her drugging him is the absolute worst thing in my eyes.

Gabe, Jonathan, Lizzie, and even Brian try to tell Andrew that I'm not the one he should feel sorry for. Really. I was going to take care of things on my own terms either way, regardless. Saying that Nvette never stood a chance against me when I decided that I wanted the revenge was an understatement. They try to convince him that after I found them together, then Nvette having the nerve to show up at the club and what they know about me, there was no way in hell that all of this was a coincidence.

They know he's heard the stories about me. Everything that happened after the night she drugged him was simply the set up for me to get her back. He acted as if he couldn't believe any of it. My man. He did casually question me about it once or twice, but I thought it best not to say anything. I played innocent too. I'm not sure if he really fell for it, though; I caught him laughing to himself a little the last time he asked, and that really made me smile.

I still hadn't made a decision about what I was going to do about pressing charges, so I went back to the hospital to visit Nvette again two days later, but she had already checked herself out. The next time I would see her would be in court for Andrew and she looked completely broken.

CHAPTER 145

THE ENGLISHMAN

I received notice from the studio that Nvette will not be returning to the show next season. Her contract has been released due to the improper conduct she showed against me and Samantha, which was a direct violation of the terms of integrity for the show. Good on them.

I hated that, because of me, Samantha was put in harm's way. I was able to convince her to go ahead with the assault charges. I told her after everything that happened, if she didn't follow through on her terms by filing the charges then I would have no choice but to follow through on doing absolutely whatever I needed to do to stop Nvette from being able to do anything else to her. I believe that scared her a little and that, of course, sorted things.

She filed charges the next day.

It hasn't been that easy of a go, getting back to the way we were, but I'm confident that we're almost there. There are so many other factors, like the media, that are making it hard to move forward. We are working things out, though. I love her completely. There is no one else I would want by my side.

CHAPTER 146

FINALLY SETTLED

The time to sort out the events with Nvette and the courts is taking forever, it seems. She will receive some amount of jail time because Andrew and I both filed charges against her. And, since *they* are considered high profile people, being actors in a show that's popular now, the trial will receive a lot of attention. The media hasn't stopped.

I tried to see her again before the trial, Nvette, but couldn't locate her. I went to the condo I saw her at when I followed her, but she was no longer there. She went into hiding because of the press. I then realized that there was only one way for me to send any communication to her and that was through her cousin, Kate.

I sent her a letter secretly through her cousin, who still comes to the club, and now is officially dating Gabe. I didn't let Andrew know about the letter; I don't think he would understand.

I wanted to explain to Nvette the reason why I went ahead and pressed charges, but the letter was returned unopened. Kate said that Nvette wanted no part of what I had to say and refused to take the letter. Who could blame her? I would've probably done the same.

As I understand it, Nvette basically lost everything. Her contract with the series was terminated, her live-in boyfriend got real jail time because his assault on her violated his parole, and the media crucified her as a manipulative, drugging, lying, bullying homewrecker (not that Andrew and I were married, but still). Not good for that girl-next-door image she had before all of this mess. Yep, the media attention was out of control.

Andrew and I are doing pretty well considering everything that has happened. He was right: this madness is making our relationship stronger in certain ways. We learned good lessons about each other: I know he can be trusted, without a doubt, and he knows that I really am as crazy as they say, and that's working for us.

He took a picture of himself the day after I punched him in the face, and he has a huge framed print of it at his place sporting that black eye I gave him. You see it as soon as you walk in through his front door.

He thinks he's funny, but I'm funnier.

I named it Winky after what I called him in my head when I saw my handy work that first night after. I crack myself up every time he asks where that name of the pic came from. It never gets old for me.

CHAPTER 147

MOVING FORWARD

The club has gotten even busier, if you can believe it, with all of the attention about the incidents in the media.

Even though Andrew is becoming quite the acting star in his own right, he still insists on DJing at the club when he can and makes certain he is always the DJ on my favorite night.

I overheard Andrew and the fellas talking about the possibility of him buying in as a real partner in the club. No way. They better not try and make that 'effing decision without me. I don't know what Andrew has up his sleeve, but a buy-in is not the solution.

This is my thing. I love that this is something that was built before him. It's part of who I am; it does not have to change into a part of who *we* are as a couple. Gabe will be on my side with this, certainly. Jonathan will just think about the dollar signs, I'm sure.

Besides, I know the fellas remember what happened the last time they plotted Andrew in without me. I'm really not playing around this time. There will be hell to pay, and I mean it.

THE END
♡

Song List
in order of appearance

1. *Floetry: Butterflies*
2. *Soul II Soul: Back to Life*
3. *Loose Ends: Hangin' on a String*
4. *The Sugar Hill Gang and Grandmaster Flash: Freedom*
5. *Beyonce ft. Andre 3000: Party*
6. *Usher: There Goes My Baby*
7. *Ne-Yo: Stay*
8. *Raheem DeVaughn: You*
9. *Musiq Soulchild: So Beautiful*
10. *Faith Evans: You Gets No Love*
11. *Miles Davis: Kinda Blue*
12. *Carl Thomas: Giving You All My Love*

About Atmosphere Press

Founded in 2015, Atmosphere Press was built on the principles of Honesty, Transparency, Professionalism, Kindness, and Making Your Book Awesome. As an ethical and author-friendly hybrid press, we stay true to that founding mission today.

If you're a reader, enter our giveaway for a free book here:

SCAN TO ENTER
BOOK GIVEAWAY

If you're a writer, submit your manuscript for consideration here:

SCAN TO SUBMIT
MANUSCRIPT

And always feel free to visit Atmosphere Press and our authors online at atmospherepress.com. See you there soon!

About the Author

Toni McBride was born into a delightful mix of British wit and Southern hospitality. Her unique perspective comes from her rich family heritage: a mother from Manchester, England, who was a passionate advocate in the Disarmament Protests, and a father from Birmingham, Alabama, who made his mark in the Civil Rights Movement. She now finds herself living in New Jersey, perfectly nestled between the vibrant cities of Philadelphia and New York City.

A loving wife and mother of two, her journey led her to Rutgers University and then to a career in education. When she's not busy inspiring her students, savoring family time, or enjoying the beautiful chaos of life, Toni loves escaping into the world of her characters. Toni's stories are a heartfelt blend of humor, romance, and the occasional twist. She draws from her diverse background and observations of daily life to weave stories that reflect her own belief in the power of true love and how both magical and wonderfully unpredictable it can be.

www.ingramcontent.com/pod-product-compliance
Ingram Content Group UK Ltd.
Pitfield, Milton Keynes, MK11 3LW, UK
UKHW042001010225
454478UK00012B/79/J